D0906067

WILLIAM F. MAAG LIBRARY
YOUNGSTOWN STATE UNIVERSITY

WITHDRAWN

Camel Xiangzi

Camel Xiangzi

LAO SHE

Translated by Shi Xiaoqing

Published in Association with Foreign Languages Press   Beijing

Indiana University Press   Bloomington

Copyright © 1981 by Indiana University Press and Foreign Languages Press.
Other translations have used the title *Rickshaw Boy*.

All rights reserved

No part of this book may be reproduced or utilized in any form or by
any means, electronic or mechanical, including photocopying and
recording, or by any information storage and retrieval system, without permission in writing from the publisher. The Association of
American University Presses' Resolution on Permissions constitutes
the only exception to this prohibition.

Manufactured in the United States of America

Library of Congress Cataloging in Publication Data
Lao, She, 1898-1966.
 Camel Xiangzi.
 Translation of: Lo t 'o Hsiang-tzu.
 I. Shi, Xiaoqing.   II. Title.
PL2804.C5L613   1981   895.1'35   81-47584
ISBN 0-253-31296-5   AACR2
ISBN 0-253-20275-2 (pbk.)
1 2 3 4 5 85 84 83 82 81

PL
2804
.C5 L613
1981

ABOUT THE AUTHOR

*L*AO She (1899-1966) is the pen-name of the writer Shu Sheyu, who was born in Beijing. In 1924 he went to England, where he was a lecturer in Chinese at the School of Oriental Studies, London University. It was in London that he wrote his first three novels. After his return to China in 1930 he taught at Qilu (Cheeloo) University in Jinan and Shandong University in Qingdao. He continued to write and during the war against Japan (1937-45), when he was in Chongqing, he took an active part in organizing the National Writers' and Artists' Resistance Association. Later he left China for the United States, where he gave lectures and continued to write until his return in 1949. He threw himself into the work of New China as a member of the Cultural and Educational Committee in the Government Administration Council, a deputy to the National People's Congress, a member of the Standing Committee of the Chinese People's Political Consultative Conference, Vice-Chairman of the All-China Federation of Literary and Art Circles, Vice-Chairman of the Union of Chinese Writers and Chairman of the Beijing Federation of Writers and Artists.

Before Liberation he wrote many works of literature, including his best novel *Camel Xiangzi* (or *Rickshaw Boy*) to expose and denounce the old society. After the founding of New China he wrote the plays *Dragon Beard Ditch, Spring Flowers and Autumn Fruit, Fang Zhenzhu, Teahouse* and many other works which are loved by the people. He enjoys great prestige in China and was named a "People's Artist" and a "Great Master of Language".

WILLIAM F. MAAG LIBRARY
YOUNGSTOWN STATE UNIVERSITY

PREFACE

*L*AO She came from a very poor family. His father, a member of the Imperial Manchu guards, was killed by imperialist troops of the Eight Allied Armies in 1900 when Lao She was just a year old. From then on, his mother and elder sister made a living washing and mending soldiers' clothes. Later, his mother became a charwoman in a primary school. The whole family was illiterate. Lao She studied in schools which did not charge for tuition, finally graduating from normal school, and so was the only one in his family who could read and write. While he was studying, he would often come home at lunchtime to find the cooking-pot empty. He would ask, "Is there anything to eat?" and when told there was not would go pluckily back to school to listen to the afternoon lessons on an empty stomach.

Lao She's neighbours were all poor people. He understood them and knew all about them. They worked at different jobs: some pulled rickshaws, others were coolies, scrap-collectors, artists, servants or peddlers. . . . Lao She himself was never a rickshaw puller, but he had friends who were and whom he had grown up with. In Chapter Sixteen of *Camel Xiangzi*, he describes at great length the tenement courtyard where Xiangzi and Tigress lived. He describes how the old people lay hungry on the cold brick-beds, how the women waited till old and young had gone to bed before washing, making and mending clothes for other people by the light of a small kerosene lamp, how the young girls had no trousers and stayed indoors, their natural prison, wrapped in torn pieces of cloth, helping their mothers. All these people were modelled on ones Lao She had known in his childhood. In a short essay, he men-

3

tioned how he never felt happy at the prospect of the New Year festivities because they reminded him of the many times in his childhood when, having nothing to eat, he had gone early to bed to the sound of other people's fire-crackers.

Lao She never went to university. His knowledge was acquired by diligent study after graduating from normal school. Very early he took on the heavy task of providing for the entire family. One of his close friends remembers seeing him thinly clad in the dead of winter, working hard in a draughty room. Lao She told him with a bitter smile that he had pawned his fur gown to get some extra money for his old mother. Undoubtedly, these experiences were the rich, substantial material upon which he drew for his *Camel Xiangzi*. But Lao She was not satisfied with this alone. While writing the book, he spent a great deal of time collecting other material, and also asked many friends to jot down regularly or from time to time what they knew of the customs and ways of Beijing. He collected all this carefully, regardless of whether it was useful or not.

In 1936, Lao She's last paragraph of *Camel Xiangzi* read like this, "Xiangzi, honorable, enterprising, dreamy, selfish, unconforming, strong, great Xiangzi had been a mourner at countless funerals, without knowing where or when he would end up burying himself, degenerate, self-centred, unfortunate victim that he was of that individualistic sick society." At that time, Lao She made Xiangzi's life end in tragedy. It was just as the lovable old man, Little Horse's grandfather said, "To try to make a go of it all by oneself is the hardest thing on earth. When a single grasshopper is caught and tied up by a child, it can do nothing. But wait until they swarm, then no one can stop them!" The only way out would have been for hundreds and thousands of Xiangzis to unite and struggle together, and this is precisely the social lesson of Xiangzi's tragedy.

After Liberation, Lao She very much wished to write a sequel to *Camel Xiangzi*. I remember he used to invite his old friends, the rickshaw men, the Xiangzis, to a meal with him, for he maintained close ties with his old neighbours. All these people were now liberated and very happy, and full of wonder at the great changes in their life. At their request, Lao She readily agreed to write a sequel which would describe Xiangzi's rebirth, his revolt, his happiness. This new *Camel Xiangzi* would have a happy ending. Unfortunately, due to Lin Biao and the Gang of Four, Lao She died too early and this wish can never be fulfilled. But *Camel Xiangzi* lives on to spur everyone, today just as yesterday, to strive for a brighter future. Surely this is the happiest ending of all!

Hu Jieqing (Lao She's widow)

February 2nd, 1979

CHAPTER 1

THIS story is about Xiangzi, not about Camel, because "Camel" was only his nickname. So let us start with Xiangzi, just mentioning in passing how he became linked with camels. The rickshaw pullers of Beiping fall into many different categories. There are strong, fleet-footed young men who rent smart rickshaws and work round the clock, starting work or knocking off whenever they please. They pull their rickshaws to a rickshaw-stand or the gate of some big house and wait for fares who want a fast runner. With luck, a single trip can net one or two silver dollars; but it may happen to that they spend the whole day idle, not even recouping their rickshaw rent. Still, they take this all in their stride. These fellows generally have two ambitions. One is to get a job on a monthly basis, the other is to buy their own rickshaw. For with their own vehicle, it doesn't matter whether they have a monthly job or take odd fares, the rickshaw is their own property anyway.

Then there is a category of slightly older men, and others who for health reasons run not quite as fast, or who for family reasons cannot afford to let a day go by without earning anything. Most of them pull fairly new rickshaws, and because both puller and rickshaw are quite smart-looking they can still demand a respectable price. Some of them work round the clock, some only half days. Of these latter, the more energetic take the night-shift* all the year round. At night more care and skill are needed, so naturally the fee is higher.

The pullers over forty and under twenty find it hard to join either of these categories. Their rickshaws are ramshackle and

---

* The night-shift starts at four in the afternoon and continues until daybreak.

7

WILLIAM F. MAAG LIBRARY
YOUNGSTOWN STATE UNIVERSITY

they dare not take on the night-shift. So they have to make a very early start in the hope that, by three or four in the afternoon, they will have earned enough for the richshaw rent as well as their daily needs. Their broken-down vehicles and lack of speed mean they must make longer trips for lower payment. They are the ones who haul merchandise to the melon, fruit or vegetable markets; for this they earn less, but at least they can take their time.

The under twenties — some of whom have been plying this trade since they were eleven or twelve — rarely become crack pullers later on, because as boys they over-taxed their strength. They may pull all their lives and never make the grade, not even in this trade. As for the over-forties, some have strained their muscles by pulling for eight or ten years and are content now to take second place, in the growing awareness that sooner or later they will topple over and die in the road. Their pulling posture, their adroit bargaining, their shrewd use of short-cuts or circuitous routes are enough to make them relive past glories and turn up their noses at the younger generation. But these shades of past glories can in no way diminish their dismal prospects, and so they often sigh as they mop their sweat.

However, compared to another group of over-forties, they seem not to have reached rock-bottom yet. This group is composed of men who had never associated themselves with rickshaws but were forced to take up the trade, having reached the end of their tether. When policemen, school janitors and cleaners are dismissed and bankrupt peddlers or unemployed artisans have nothing more to sell or pawn, they grit their teeth and with tears in their eyes take this last desperate step, knowing it to be a dead end. These men have already sold the best years of their lives, and now the maize muffins on which they subsist are transformed into blood and sweat which drip on to the road. Weak, inexperienced and friendless, they are eyed askance by even their fellow pullers. Their rickshaws are the most wretched of all and their tyres are always having punctures. Even as they run they beg their fares to excuse them and consider a mere fifteen coppers a very good fee indeed.

There is yet another category of pullers distinguished by their special beats and know-how. Those living in the western suburbs around Xiyuan and Haidian naturally prefer to take fares to the Western Hills or the universities of Yanjing and Qinghua; those from the northern suburbs outside Andingmen Gate ply the Qingho and Beiyuan route, while those in the south outside Yongdingmen Gate will go as far as Nanyuan.... These long-distance runners will only make trips which pay and scoff at the paltry three or five coppers which is all that one gets for short distances. But they still lose their wind sooner than the rickshawmen of Dongjiaominxiang, the "Legation Quarter".

These are real long-distance runners who cater solely for the foreign trade and pride themselves on being able to run non-stop from the diplomatic quarter all the way out to the Jade Fountain, the Summer Palace or the Western Hills. And, stamina apart, these men have a special skill which makes it impossible for rivals to snatch away their clientele: they all speak foreign languages. They can understand when English and French soldiers ask for the Summer Palace, the Yongho Lamasery or the "Eight Alleys" red-light district, and they will not teach their foreign lingoes to others. Their way of running is special too. Going at a fair speed, head lowered, looking neither to right nor left, they hug the side of the road, seemingly indifferent to the world yet supremely self-assured. Because they serve foreigners, they do not have to wear the numbered jacket compulsory for other rickshaw pullers. Instead they all wear long-sleeved white shirts, baggy black or white trousers bound at the ankles with tapes and black cloth-soled shoes with a rib sewn up the middle. They are clean, smart and alert. Other rickshaw men, seeing this outfit, will not compete with them for customers or race with them, and in fact they seem to belong to a completely different trade.

After this brief analysis, let us come back to Xiangzi's status so as to place him as accurately — we hope — as a specific screw in a machine. Before Xiangzi became linked with the nickname "Camel", he was a relatively independent rickshaw puller; in other words, he was young and strong and owned his own rickshaw. Belonging to the category of those who owned their vehicles, he was master of his own fate, a high-class puller.

But this was certainly not easy to come by. It had taken him at least three or four years and untold tens of thousands of drops of sweat to acquire that rickshaw of his. He had earned it by gritting his teeth in the wind and rain, by skimping his food and drink. That rickshaw represented the fruit and reward of all his struggles and hardships, like the single medal of a warrior who has fought a hundred battles. In the days when he rented a rickshaw, he was like a top sent spinning north, south, east and west from dawn to dusk, at the beck and call of others. But this spinning never made him so dizzy that he lost sight of his objective.

In his mind's eye he could picture that distant rickshaw which was going to bring him freedom and independence, becoming a part of him like his hands and feet. With his own rickshaw he would no longer be bullied by the rickshaw owners, would no longer have to humour anyone else. With his strength and his own vehicle, earning his living would be mere child's play.

Xiangzi was not afraid of hardships, nor did he have the excusable but deplorable bad habits of most other pullers. He was clever and hard-working enough to make his dream come true. If his situation had been a little better, or if he had had a bit more education he would certainly not have fallen among the "Tyre Brigade". And no matter what his trade, he would have made the most of every opportunity. Unluckily, he had no choice but to be a rickshaw puller. Very well then, even in this job he would prove his ability and intelligence. Had he been a spirit in hell, he would probably have made the best of his surroundings.

Xiangzi was country born and bred. At eighteen, having lost his parents and their few *mu* of poor land, he fled to the city. He brought with him his country boy's sturdiness and simplicity, and tried his hand at most jobs that called only for brawn. However, he soon realised that pulling a rickshaw was an easier way to earn money. The pay for other hard manual jobs was limited whereas pulling a rickshaw offered more variety and opportunities, as there was no telling when and where one might earn more than one had expected. Of course he also knew that this would not be entirely a matter of chance, that the rickshaw had to be smart and the puller brisk-looking to attract discriminating customers.

But after consideration, Xiangzi felt that he had the requisite qualities, for he was young and strong. Though his lack of experience meant that he could not begin with a new rickshaw, this was not an insurmountable difficulty; and with his fine physique he was sure that after ten days or two weeks he would be running quite presentably. Then he would rent a brand-new rickshaw, and might very soon land himself a monthly job; after which by skimping and saving for a few years he was bound to be able to buy himself a really beautiful rickshaw. Gazing at his young muscles, he felt sure it was just a matter of time. This goal he had set himself could definitely be reached — it was no pipe-dream.

Though hardly twenty, he was tall and robust. Time had not yet moulded his body into any set form but he already looked like a full-grown man — a man with an ingenuous face and a hint of mischief about him. Watching those high-class pullers, he planned how to tighten his belt to show off his sturdy chest and straight back to better advantage. He craned his neck to look at his shoulders: how impressively broad they were! His slender waist, baggy white trousers and ankles bound with thin black bands would set off his "outsize" feet. Yes, he was surely going to be the most outstanding rickshaw puller in town. In his simplicity, he chuckled to himself.

Xiangzi was not handsome. What made him engaging was the expression on his face. He had a small head, round eyes, a fleshy nose, and thick, short eyebrows. His scalp was always shaved clean. There was no spare flesh on his cheeks, yet his neck was virtually as thick as his head. In those days he had a ruddy complexion, and running from his cheekbone to his right ear was a large, bright, shiny scar — legacy of a donkey bite received while napping under a tree in his childhood. He did not pay much attention to his appearance, liking his face just as he liked his body because both were strong and sturdy; ·

in fact, to him, his face was another limb and its strength was all that mattered. Even after coming to the city, he could still do long hand-stands and, holding this position, he felt like a tree upright from top to toe.

Xiangzi was indeed rather like a tree, sturdy, silent yet full of life. He was canny and had his own plans, but did not like to disclose them. Among rickshaw pullers, personal wrongs and difficulties are food for common talk, and whether at rickshaw-stands, in little teahouses or in the large crowded courtyards, everyone reports, describes or bawls out his troubles. These then pass from mouth to mouth like folksongs, becoming public property. Xiangzi, being a country boy, was not as glib as city-dwellers. If volubility is a natural gift, then he was clearly not endowed with it, so he did not try to imitate the townsfolk's spiteful talk. He minded his own business and held his tongue, which gave him more time to think, as if his eyes were always directed inwards. His mind made up, he embarked upon the course he had mapped out; and if he made no headway, he would lapse into silence for a couple of days, gritting his teeth as if gnawing at his own heart.

Once he had decided to be a rickshaw puller he went straight into action. First he rented an old, broken-down rickshaw in order to get some practice. The first day he made practically nothing: the second, business was quite good. But then he was flat out on his back for two days because his ankles had swollen up so badly. He put up with the pain because he knew that this was inevitable, and unless he passed this test he would never be able to really let himself go.

His feet better, he could run freely and he gloated that now he had nothing else to fear. For he knew the city well, and even if he happened to take the long way round it did not matter, as he had strength and to spare. When it came to learning how to pull that was not too difficult either, with all his previous experience of pushing, pulling and carrying loads. Besides, he figured that by taking care and not competing for fares he could keep out of trouble.

When it came to bargaining over the price of a fare, he was too slow of speech and too easily flustered to compete with his slick colleagues. So he rarely went to the rickshaw-stands but waited around where there were no other rickshaws. In some quiet spot he could take his time over fixing the price, and sometimes he would just say, "Get on, and pay what you please!" His honest, simple, likeable face made it hard not to trust him, for it seemed impossible that such a country bumpkin could ever cheat anyone. People might suspect that he was a newcomer from the countryside who did not know the way and so had no idea of rates. But if asked "Do you know that address?" he would grin knowingly, as if playing the buffoon, leaving his fare quite perplexed.

After two or three weeks, he had really run his legs into condition and he knew his running was a pleasure to watch. The style of running is what indicates a rickshaw man's skill and status. Those who run with their toes turned out, slapping their feet down like palm-leaf fans, are sure to be greenhorns fresh from the countryside. Those who lower their heads and shuffle along, in what only looks like a run are men over fifty. Other old hands drained of strength have a different method: they strain forward, raise their legs high and thrust up their heads at each step, as if pulling with might and main; but in fact they are no faster than the others, and put on this act to retain their self-respect.

Xiangzi naturally did not adopt any of these styles. With his long stride, steady back and silent, springy step, his shafts did not rock about and his passenger was borne along smoothly and safely. No matter how fast he was running he could stop in a trice just by lightly scraping his large feet on the ground for a step or two. Back slightly bent, hands loosely holding the shafts, he was lithe, smooth and precise, and though he never looked hurried he ran fast and sure-footedly. All these were rare qualities, even among rickshawmen hired on a monthly basis.

He switched to a new rickshaw. The same day, after inquiry, he found out that a vehicle such as his — with soft springs, fine brass work, tarpaulin rain-hood and curtain in front, two lamps and long-throated brass horn — was worth something over one hundred silver dollars. If the paint and brass work were not in such good condition then one hundred would be enough to buy his own rickshaw. If every day he could put aside ten cents, one hundred dollars would take one thousand days. One thousand days! Why, he could hardly reckon how long that would be. But he was determined to buy his own rickshaw, if it took one thousand, even ten thousand days.

The first step, he decided, was to find a job on a monthly basis. If he could land himself a convivial employer with many friends, it would mean about ten banquets a month and an extra two or three dollars for him in tips. Plus the one dollar odd he could save from his monthly pay that would come to three to five dollars a month, and fifty to sixty dollars a year! This would bring him much, much closer to his goal. And since he did not smoke or drink or gamble and had no family, all he needed was to grit his teeth and everything was sure to work out. He swore to himself that in a year and a half, he, Xiangzi, was going to have his own rickshaw. And it had to be a brand-new one, not an old one overhauled.

He really did manage to get a monthly job. But reality does not completely accord with hopes, and though he gritted his teeth for a year and a half his wish was still unfulfilled. Though he landed monthly jobs and took great pains in his work, there are two sides to everything in this world and his cautiousness did not prevent his employers from sacking him. Sometimes after two or three months, sometimes after only a week or ten days, he had to look around for a new job. Naturally while doing so he had to return to pulling fares, which was like riding one horse while looking for another, for he couldn't afford to remain idle.

This was when things would go wrong. He drove himself hard, not just to earn his keep but to go on saving for his rickshaw too. However, forcing oneself is always risky and he found it difficult to concentrate when he ran. His mind kept wandering and the more he thought, the more panicky and upset he became. At this rate, when would he ever get his own rickshaw? Why were things like this? Wasn't he trying hard enough? While so preoccupied, he forgot his usual cautiousness. His tyres picked up bits of scrap metal and punctured, and there was nothing for it but to knock off for the day. Worse still, he sometimes ran into people and once he even lost a hub cap as he was squeezing hurriedly over a crossing. None of this would have happened if he had a monthly job, but now disappointment made him clumsy and awkward. Of course, he had to pay for the damages, increasing his desperation; so that, to avoid even greater calamities, he sometimes slept for a whole day at a stretch. Then, when he woke up he would hate himself for wasting so much time.

During such periods, too, the more worried he was the more he stinted himself, under the illusion that he was made of iron. But he discovered that he too could fall ill, yet begrudged spending money on medicine. As a result, he grew worse and not only had to buy medicine but also rest for several days in a row. These setbacks made him grit his teeth and try harder, but the money didn't come in any faster.

He finally managed to scrape together one hundred silver dollars. It had taken him three whole years.

He couldn't wait any longer. Originally he had set his heart on buying the newest, best equipped rickshaw, but now he would have to make do with one within the hundred dollar range. No, he definitely could not wait any more, for suppose something happened to make him lose a few dollars! By chance he heard of a custom-built rickshaw, practically like the one he had in mind, which its would-be purchaser had been unable to pay for. As he had forfeited his deposit on it, the rickshaw shop was willing to let it go for less than its original cost — more than a hundred.

Xiangzi, red in the face, his hands shaking, clapped down ninety-six dollars and said, "I want this rickshaw!"

The shop-owner, hoping to raise the price to a round figure, pulled the rickshaw in and out of the shed, folded and unfolded the hood and sounded the horn, singing the vehicle's praises all the time. Finally he kicked the steel spokes.

"Listen to that!" he said. "Clear as a bell! You can pull it till it falls to pieces, but if one of those spokes buckles, you come back and throw it in my face! Not a cent less than a hundred and it's yours!"

Xiangzi counted his money again. "I want this rickshaw. Ninety-six!"

The shop-owner knew he was up against someone with a one-track mind. He glanced from the money to Xiangzi and finally sighed, "All right, for friendship's sake, I'll let you have it. It's guaranteed for six months and, short of smashing the whole works, I'll do all the repairs free of charge. Here, take the guarantee!"

Xiangzi's hands were shaking even more violently as he tucked the guarantee away and pulled his rickshaw out, feeling ready to burst into tears. He made for a quiet out-of-the-way place and stopped to scrutinize this precious possession. He saw his own reflection in the shiny paint work, and the more he gazed at the rickshaw the more he loved it. Even those parts that hadn't quite come up to his expectations could be overlooked now that the vehicle was his very own. After gazing his fill, he sat down on the new carpeted foot-rest, his eyes fixed on the shiny brass horn attached to the shaft. Suddenly he remembered that he was now twenty-two. As his parents had died when he was very young, he had forgotten the actual date of his birthday and since coming to town he had never celebrated it. Well, today he had bought his own rickshaw, why not make it his birthday too? That would make it easier to remember; and anyway, since the rickshaw was the fruit of his sweat and blood why shouldn't they share the same birthday?

How to celebrate this "double birthday"? Xiangzi decided that his first fare must be a well-dressed gentleman, on no account a woman, and the destination should be Qianmen Gate or the Dongan Market. There he would have a meal at the best food-stall, hot sesame cakes with grilled mutton; then if he could pick up another good fare or two, so much the better; if not, he would knock off for the day. After all, this was his birthday!

Now that he had his own rickshaw, things began looking up for him. Whether hiring himself out on a monthly basis or taking odd fares, he need no longer worry about the rental, all he earned was his own. Contentment made him even more amiable, and his business thrived. After six months he was full of confidence that, at this rate, in another two years at most he would be able to buy another rickshaw, and then another. Why, he would be able to start his own rickshaw business!

But most hopes come to nothing, and Xiangzi's were no exception.

CHAPTER 2

*T*HIS new happiness brought greater courage and, with his own rickshaw, Xiangzi ran even faster. Of course he was extra careful with his own property, but looking at himself and at it he felt it would be a come-down not to do his very best.

Since coming to the city, he had grown another inch. And instinct told him that he would keep on growing, for though more robust than before and already sprouting a small moustache he wanted to grow still taller. Every time he had to duck through a low street-gate or door, his heart would swell with silent satisfaction at the knowledge that he was still growing. It tickled him to feel already an adult and yet still a child.

With his brawn and his beautiful rickshaw — springs so flexible that the shafts seemed to vibrate; bright chassis, clean, white cushion and loud horn — he owed it to them both to run really fast. This was not out of vanity but a sense of duty. For after six months this lovable rickshaw of his seemed alive to what he was doing: every time he swerved, bent a leg or straightened his back, its response was immediate and most satisfactory. They were never at cross-purposes in the least. Whenever they came to a flat open stretch, Xiangzi would run with only one hand steadying the shaft, the soft swish of rubber tyres behind spurring him on to run swiftly and steadily. On reaching their destination, his clothes would be wringing wet, as if just fished out of water, and he would feel tired but happy and proud, as if he had ridden a pedigree horse for many tens of *li*.

Daring is not the same as foolhardiness, and Xiangzi though daring was never foolhardy. If dawdling would be unfair to his passenger, speeding so that he damaged his rickshaw would

18

be unfair to himself. This rickshaw was his life, and he knew how to take good care of it. Combined daring and caution increased his confidence and convinced him that they were both indestructible.

And so, he not only ran with might and main but did not mind what hours he kept. To him, pulling a rickshaw for a living was the most manly thing in the world and, if he wanted to work, no one was going to stop him. He paid scant attention to the rumours flying about town — the appearance of soldiers at Xiyuan, renewed fighting at Changxindian, forced conscription again outside Xizhimen Gate, Qihuamen Gate already closed for half a day — none of this bothered him. Of course, when shopkeepers boarded up their shops and armed police and security forces filled the streets, he did not go looking for trouble and would hurriedly stop work like everyone else. But he didn't believe the rumours. He knew how to be careful, especially as the rickshaw was his own; however, coming from the country, he was not as alert to danger as city-folk. Besides, he had confidence in his own strength, and believed that even if landed in a tight corner he would be able to extricate himself. After all, a tall, broad-shouldered fellow like himself was not that easily bullied.

Nearly every year, rumours and news of war sprang up with the spring wheat. For Northerners, ears of wheat and bayonets could be said to symbolize their hopes and fears.

Xiangzi's rickshaw was just six months old when the wheat needed a fall of spring rain. Though rain does not always fall when it is most hoped for, war always comes, whether one wants it or not. But whether the news this time was false or true, Xiangzi seemed to have forgotten that he had once tilled the fields and did not much care if war devastated the crops or if there were no spring rain. His sole concern was his rickshaw. This could provide griddle cakes and all sorts of food; it was a horn of plenty which followed him meekly around. Xiangzi knew that lack of rain and news of war boosted the price of grain; but like all city people he could merely complain, he had no remedy. If grain was dear, what could anyone do about it? This attitude of his made him think only of his own livelihood.

He pushed all thought of calamities out of his mind.

City people may be powerless in other ways but they know how to spread rumours — some total fabrications, others with only a grain of truth in them — to prove that they are neither fools nor idlers. Like tiddlers when they have nothing else to do, they swim to the surface of the water and complacently blow completely useless bubbles. Their most interesting rumours are the ones about war. Others are often out-and-out fabrications, as in the case of tales of ghosts or fox-spirits which you can be sure will never materialize. But precisely because there is no reliable war news, war rumours prove most prophetic. On minor details they are often far out, but as to whether or not there will be fighting they are accurate eight or nine times out of ten. "There's going to be a show-down!" Once these words have been spoken fighting is sure to break out sooner or later. As for which armies will contend and how they will fight, each one has his own version.

Xiangzi was not unaware of this. But while those who sell their brawn — rickshaw pullers included — never welcome war, they need not be ruined by it either. The most panic-stricken are the rich. As soon as they get wind that the situation is deteriorating, they start thinking of flight. Money paves their way and hastens their departure. But they cannot run away themselves, being too weighted down by their wealth, so they must hire many other people's legs. There are cases to be carried, old and young to be carted off. It is then that those who sell their brawn find that it will fetch a good price.

"Qianmen Gate, the East Station!"

"Where?"

"The East — Station!"

"Right, just give me a dollar forty cents. No need to haggle, with troops on the rampage!"

It was in such circumstances that Xiangzi took his rickshaw outside the city gates. Rumours had been flying about for over ten days and prices had risen, but for the time being war still seemed remote from Beiping. Xiangzi plied his trade as usual, not considering the rumours an excuse for taking time off. One day, he went to the western city and noticed something unusual.

At the western end of Huguo Monastery Road and at Xinjiekou, there were no rickshaws offering to run to Xiyuan or Qinghua University. He strolled about the district a while and heard that no vehicle dared leave the city, for whether carts or rickshaws all were being seized just outside Xizhimen Gate. He decided to drink a bowl of tea then head south. The lack of activity around the rickshaw stand spelled real danger, and though no coward he saw no reason to put his head in a noose. Just at that moment, two rickshaws heading north appeared. The passengers looked like two students and the pullers were shouting as they ran, "Anyone going to Qinghua, to Qinghua?"

The few pullers at the rickshaw stand did not reply. Some of them looked on with indifferent grins, others sat there with small pipes between their lips and did not even bother to raise their heads.

"Are you all deaf? To Qinghua!" the two pullers kept on calling.

"I'd go for two dollars!" A short, shaven-headed youngster said jokingly into the silence.

"Come on then, find another one!" The two rickshaws stopped.

The young fellow was nonplussed. Still no one moved. Xiangzi could see that leaving the city was really dangerous; otherwise why did no one snap up the chance to make two dollars just by going to Qinghua, a trip which normally cost only twenty to thirty cents? He did not want to go either. But the shaven-headed youngster had apparently decided that if someone else went with him he was willing to take the risk. He eyed Xiangzi and said, "How about it, tall one?"

"Tall one." Xiangzi was tickled, this was praise. He considered the proposition. After receiving that kind of compliment he should back up this daring, shaven-headed shorty. And besides, two dollars was quite a sum, not to be picked up every day. As for danger, was he sure to run into it? Just two days ago he had heard that the gardens of the Temple of Heaven were crammed with soldiers, but he hadn't seen hide or hair of one himself. Reasoning this way, he pulled his rickshaw forward.

When they reached Xizhimen Gate, there was hardly any traffic on the road. Xiangzi's heart misgave him. Even the other puller was uneasy, but he said with a grin, "Let's go, buddy! If your luck is out it's out, this is it!" Xiangzi knew they were in for trouble, but after all these years knocking about in town he couldn't back out now like an old woman.

Beyond the city gate there was not a single cart in sight. Xiangzi lowered his head, not daring to look right or left, his heart thumping against his ribs. When they reached Gaoliang Bridge, he glanced about but to his relief there was not a soldier in sight. He thought to himself: After all, two dollars is two dollars and it takes guts to find a windfall like this. The road was alarmingly quiet and, though normally never one for speech, he suddenly felt like saying something to his companion.

"How about taking a short cut on the dirt track? The road. . . ."

"Of course." The other understood at once. "That way is safer."

But before they had branched off the main road, both pullers, their rickshaws and passengers all fell into the hands of about a dozen soldiers.

Although it was already the time of year for pilgrims to offer incense at the temple on Fantasy Peak, a single thin shirt was not enough to keep out the night chill. Xiangzi was unencumbered, being clad only in a grey army tunic and blue cloth trousers reeking of sweat — they had been like this before he put them on. He thought of his white cotton shirt and indigo blue lined suit. How smart and clean they had been! Of course in this world there are many things smarter than indigo blue cloth, but Xiangzi knew how difficult it had been for him to reach even that level of cleanliness and spruceness. Now the rancid smell of his clothes made his previous struggles and successes seem ten times more noble. The more he recalled the past, the more he hated those soldiers. Everything had been snatched from him, his clothes, shoes and hat, his rickshaw, even his cloth girdle, leaving him nothing but a body bruised black and blue and feet covered with blisters. However, his clothes were nothing, his bruises would heal, but his rickshaw, that precious rickshaw for which he had sweated years of blood and tears, had vanished! After pulling it to the barracks it had clean disappeared. All his other trials he could dismiss and forget, but how could he ever forget that rickshaw?

He wasn't afraid of hardships, but it would take him several years at least to buy another rickshaw. All his previous efforts had gone down the drain, he would have to start from scratch all over again. At the thought, Xiangzi wept. He hated those soldiers, hated the whole world. What right had they to bully and humiliate people like this? What right?

"What right?" he shouted.

The sound of his own voice — though it brought some relief — reminded him abruptly of his danger. Everything else could wait for the time being, the important thing was to flee for his life.

But where was he? He couldn't say for sure. These last days he had followed the retreating soldiers, bathed in sweat from head to foot. When on the move, he had to carry, push or pull their equipment; when they halted, he had to fetch water, light the cooking fires and feed the pack animals. From morning till night, he forced the last vestiges of his strength into his hands and feet, his mind an utter blank. When he lay down finally, he went out like a light the moment his head touched the ground, and he felt it wouldn't be such a bad thing if he never woke again.

He had a vague recollection of the troops retreating first towards Fantasy Peak; later, when they reached the north side of the mountain, his whole attention had been focussed on climbing, for he was obsessed by fear of falling to the bottom of the valley and having his bones picked clean by birds of prey. They had wound their way through the mountains for several days, till the terrain became less hilly, and one evening as the sun was setting behind them he made out a distant plain. When the bugle for supper sounded, several soldiers returned with rifles on their shoulders and leading some camels.

Camels! Xiangzi's heart missed a beat and suddenly his mind started working again, just as when a familiar landmark reorientates a man who has lost his way. Camels cannot climb, which meant that they had reached the plains. As far as he knew, camels were raised in villages west of Beiping. Could it be that all these detours had brought them to Moshi Pass? What strategy this was he did not know, if these soldiers able only to loot and retreat had any strategy at all. But of one thing he was certain, and that was that if they had really reached Moshi Pass, the troops had discovered there was no way out through the mountains and were heading for the plains to get away. Moshi Pass was a strategic link between the Western Hills to the northeast and Changxindian or Fengtai to the south, while due west lay another way out. As he considered the troops' possible movements he plotted his own route too, for now was the time to make his get-away. Should the soldiers retreat to the mountains once more, he might starve even if he managed to escape from them. So now was his chance if he was going to run for it. Once out of their clutches, he believed he could dash straight back to Haidian! For he knew all the places in between.

Why, he had only to close his eyes to see a map before him: here was Moshi Pass, — Merciful Heavens, make it Moshi Pass! If he headed northeast past Gold Peak Mountain and Prince Li's Grave he would get to Badachu; then turning due east at Sipingtai would take him to Apricot Pass and Nanxinzhuang. In order to have more cover, he had better hug the hills and head north from Beixinzhuang, through Weijiazhuang, north again to Nanhetan, still north again to Red Hilltop and Prince Jie's Palace and finally to Jingyi Gardens. Once there, he could find his way blindfolded back to Haidian. His heart was pounding in his chest. These last days, it had seemed as if all his blood had been drained into his four limbs, but now it was flowing back into his chest so that his heart was burning hot while his arms and legs were icy cold. Feverish hope made him tremble from head to foot.

At midnight, he was still wide-awake. Hope buoyed up his spirits, but fear made him nervous. He wanted to sleep but could not drop off as he lay sprawled out on some hay. Everything was still, only the stars throbbing in time to his heart. Suddenly a camel let out a plaintive cry, not far away. Like a cock's sudden crow in the night, it struck him as forlorn yet comforting.

Cannon rumbled in the distance, very far away but unmistakably cannon. He dared not move, but the camp was in an uproar immediately. He held his breath, now was his chance! The troops would surely start retreating again and most certainly head for the mountains. The experience of the last days had taught him that these soldiers behaved like bees trapped in a closed room, blundering wildly in every direction.

The troops would surely flee at the sound of cannon, so he had better look sharp. Holding his breath, he crawled slowly along in search of the camels. He knew very well that they would be of no help to him, but since they were all prisoners together he felt a certain affinity to them. Pandemonium reigned in the encampment now. He found the camels crouching like humps of earth in the darkness, absolutely quiet apart from their heavy breathing, as if nothing had disturbed them. This boosted his courage and he crouched down beside them, like a soldier taking cover behind sandbags. It struck him then in a flash that the cannon fire coming from the south might not mean a real battle, but it was at least a warning that that way out was closed. So the soldiers would have to retreat again to the mountains. If so, they could not possibly take the camels. So he and the camels were in the same boat. If the troops took the camels, then he was lost; but if they forgot them then he could get away. He pressed his ear close to the ground, listening for footsteps, his heart beating furiously.

He did not know how long he waited, but nobody came to lead the camels away. Finally he plucked up courage, sat up and peered out between their double humps. All was dark around, he could not see a thing. Now was the time to make a run for it, for better for worse!

CHAPTER 3

XIANGZI had run two dozen steps when he stopped short, unwilling to leave those camels behind him. All he had left in the world now was his life. He would gladly have picked up a useless hempen rope from the ground, for it would comfort him to feel that his hands were not entirely empty. Of course the main thing was to save his life, but what use was a life stripped bare of everything? He must take the camels with him, though he had no idea what to do with them, because at least they were something, and a quite sizable something at that.

He tugged the camels to make them get up. While not knowing how to handle them, he was not afraid of them for coming from the countryside he was used to animals. Very, very slowly the camels rose to their feet and, without stopping to make sure that they were roped together, as soon as they were all up he set off, regardless of whether he had the whole lot in tow.

Once on the move, he regretted his decision. Camels being accustomed to heavy loads walk slowly. Not only that, but they walk very carefully for fear of slipping. A puddle of water or a patch of mud may make them break a leg or sprain a knee. A camel's value lies entirely in its legs; once its legs are done for, it's finished. Yet here was Xiangzi flying for his life!

Still he could not leave them behind. He would trust to Providence and hold on to these camels which he had picked up for nothing.

After pulling rickshaws for so long Xiangzi had a good sense of direction. Even so, he felt lost. Preoccupied with finding the camels, by the time he had coaxed them to their feet he had no idea where he was, for it was so dark and he felt so frantic. Even had he known how to take his bearings from the stars, he would not have dared to do this for — to him — the stars seemed still more frantic, jostling each other in the black night sky. He dared not look twice at that sky and lowered his head, burning with impatience but afraid to move quickly. It occurred to him: With the camels in tow, he would have to take the main road instead of following the foothills. Between Moshi Pass — if it really was Moshi Pass — and Huangcun, the road was straight, so the camels negotiating it wouldn't take him out of the way. This last factor carried great weight with a rickshaw puller, but there was no cover on that road. What if he ran into another lot of soldiers? Even if he didn't, who would believe that he with his tattered army uniform, his muddy face and long hair was a cameldriver? No, he definitely didn't look like one. What he looked like was a deserter! Being picked up by troops wasn't so serious; but if some villagers caught him, at very least he would be buried alive! He began to tremble all over. The soft steps of the camels padding behind him made him suddenly jump for fright. If he wanted to get away, he had better leave these encumbrances behind. But still he could not bring himself to let go of their nose-string. Better press on, no matter where he ended up, and cross that bridge when he came to it. If he came out alive, he would have got a few animals for nothing; if not, too bad!

However, he did take off his army jacket and rip out the collar; after which the last two brass buttons still doing their duty were torn off and tossed into the darkness where they fell without a tinkle. He slung the new collarless, buttonless jacket over his shoulders and tied the two sleeves in a knot on his chest as if he were carrying a pack on his back. He felt that now he looked less like a defeated soldier and rolled his trousers up a bit further. Maybe he still did not seem an authentic camel-driver, but at least he was less like a deserter. All the mud and sweat on his face probably made him look more like a coal-miner than anything else.

Xiangzi's mind worked slowly but thoroughly, and once an idea occurred to him he immediately acted on it. As there was no one to see him in the pitch darkness, he didn't have to act right away; but he couldn't wait as he didn't know how soon the day would break. Since he wasn't going through the hills, there would be nowhere for him to hide, so if he was to travel during the day he would have to convince the passers-by that he was a coal-miner. After acting on this supposition he felt easier in his mind, as if now the danger was past and Beiping was just around the corner. He must move on steadily to the city and not waste any time, as he had neither money nor food on him. He thought of riding a camel to conserve his strength and stave off hunger; but he would have to make the camel kneel before mounting it and that would mean further delay which he couldn't afford. Time was money. What's more, perched up so high he wouldn't be able to see the ground. If the camel were to fall he would come tumbling down too. No, it was better to continue like this.

He had no idea where he was nor where he was heading, but sensed that he must be walking along a highway. He felt uncomfortable from head to foot and uneasy at heart, due to the late hour, the last few exhausting days and his hair-raising escape. After trudging for some distance, his slow steady steps acted as a soporific. The pitch darkness and the dank mist made him feel more lost. When he fixed his gaze on the ground it seemed hummocky but his feet encountered only a flat surface. Caution and the impression of being taken in increased his uneasiness and irritation. He decided not to look at the ground but just gaze straight ahead and shuffle along. He could see absolutely nothing around him. It was as if all the darkness in the world was waiting for him and that he was going from one black world to another. All the time, the silent camels followed him.

Gradually he became accustomed to the darkness and his mind seemed to stop working. His eyes closed of their own accord. Was he still walking or was he standing still? He was conscious only of a seesaw motion as if rocking on some black sea, and the darkness merged with his sensations, unsettled and confused. Suddenly he felt a jolt, as if he had heard some sound or been struck by some idea — he couldn't say for sure. His eyes opened. He was still moving forward, all was still and what had just occurred to him had slipped his mind. His heart thumped a while, then gradually calmed down. He told himself not to close his eyes again, nor give way to foolish fancies; the main thing was to get to the city as fast as possible. But with his mind a blank, his eyes were liable to close once more; he must concentrate on something to stay awake. If he dropped in his tracks, he knew that he would sleep for three whole days and nights.

What should he think about? He felt dizzy and uncomfortably damp; his head itched, his feet ached and there was a dry bitter taste in his mouth. All he could think of was his own sorry plight, but he couldn't even concentrate on that with his head so empty and dizzy. It was as if just as he remembered himself, he forgot himself again, like a guttering candle trying to illuminate itself. On top of that, the darkness all around made him feel as if he were floating in a black cloud. He knew he existed, that he was moving forward, but with nothing else to prove it he was as uncertain of himself as if he were drifting quite alone out at sea. Never had he suffered from such an agony of uncertainty and utter loneliness. Although in the normal way he was not much given to making friends, in the broad light of day, with the sun shining on him and everything around him, he did not feel afraid. He was not afraid now, but this uncertainty about everything was more than he could stand.

If camels were as hard to handle as horses or donkeys, he would have had to rouse himself to look after them; but they were annoyingly well-behaved, so well-behaved that they got on his nerves. At the height of his confusion, he had suddenly suspected that they were no longer behind him and this had given him a few bad moments: he almost convinced himself that those large beasts could quietly disappear down some dark side-road without his knowing it and gradually melt away, as if he had a piece of ice in tow.

At some point — he couldn't remember when — he sat down. If he had died then and recovered his memory after death, he would have been unable to say how or why he had sat down, or whether he remained seated for five minutes or one hour. Neither did he know whether he had first sat down and then fallen asleep or the other way round. Probably he had fallen asleep first and then sat down, because his exhaustion was such that he could have slept standing up.

He awoke suddenly. It was not a slow natural awakening but a sudden start, as if in the second it took him to open his eyes he had jumped from one world to another. Still all was dark, but he distinctly heard a cock crow. The sound was so distinct, it seemed to pierce his brain, making him wide-awake. Where were the camels? Nothing else mattered for the moment. The rope was still in his hand, the camels still beside him. He calmed down. He felt too lazy to get up and was aching all over, yet he dared not go to sleep again either. He must think carefully, that was the thing to do. At this point he remembered his rickshaw and cried out, "By what right?"

"By what right?" Yet shouting was going to get him nowhere. He went to check on how many camels he had. Feeling with his hands he counted three. To him that wasn't too many but too few and he concentrated on them now, for though he hadn't thought out the best thing to do with them he vaguely realized that his future depended entirely on them.

"Why not sell them and buy another rickshaw?" He almost leapt to his feet, but then didn't move, ashamed of not having thought of this most natural, obvious solution before. But joy was stronger than shame, and he made up his mind. Hadn't he heard a cock crow? Even if cocks sometimes crowed at one or two in the morning, it still meant that dawn was at hand. And where there were cocks there must be a village. Maybe it was even Beixinan where people bred camels. He must hurry to get there by daylight. Once the camels were off his hands, as soon as he reached the city he could buy another rickshaw. The price must be lower too in these troubled times, with fighting going on. All he could think of now was buying a rickshaw. He saw no difficulty in selling the camels.

His spirits rose at the prospect, and all his discomfort disappeared. Had he been able to buy one hundred *mu* of land for the price of these three camels, or trade them for a few pearls, he would not have been so happy. He jumped up hurriedly, pulled the camels to their feet, and started off. He didn't know the present price of camels but had heard that in the old days, before there were trains, one camel would fetch fifty ounces of silver, because camels are strong and eat less than horses or mules. He did not expect to get a hundred and fifty ounces for three camels, all he hoped for was eighty to a hundred dollars — just enough to buy a rickshaw.

As he walked on, the sky became brighter and brighter in front of him. Yes, he was definitely heading east. Even if he were on the wrong road his general direction was right. He knew that the mountains were to the west, the city to the east. His surroundings had been pitch black, but now he could make out light and dark though he couldn't yet distinguish any colours, and fields and distant trees took shape in the gloom. The stars grew fainter and the sky, shrouded by a murkiness that could have been clouds or mist, seemed much higher than before. Xiangzi dared lift his head again. Once more he could smell the grass by the road and hear a few birds twitter. Now that he had made out objects indistinctly, he regained the use of his other faculties too. He could see himself again and, though he was certainly in very poor shape, at least he was still alive — no doubt about it. Life seemed particularly sweet, as it does after awakening from a nightmare.

Having looked himself over he turned to look at the camels. They were just as scruffy as he was and just as dear to him. It was the moulting season and patches of their greyish red skin showed through the scattered tufts of limp, dangling long hair ready to drop from their sides at any moment. They were like huge beggars of the animal kingdom. Most pathetic were their hairless necks, so long, bent and clumsy, craning out like scraggy, disconcerted dragons. But no matter how scruffy they looked, Xiangzi did not find them disgusting because they were, after all, alive.

And he counted himself the luckiest man in the world, now that Heaven had given him these three precious creatures — enough to exchange for a rickshaw. Such luck was not to be met with every day. He couldn't help chuckling aloud.

The grey sky began to turn red, the fields and distant trees seemed darker than ever. Red and grey blended so that in places the sky was lilac, in others crimson, while most of it was the purple-grey of grapes. Presently, bright gold appeared through the red, and all the colours glowed. Suddenly everything became crystal clear. Then the morning clouds in the east turned deep red and the sky above showed blue. The red clouds were pierced by golden rays, interweaving to spin a majestic, glittering web in the southeastern sky with the clouds as warp, the rays as weft. Fields, trees and wild grass changed from dark green to bright emerald. The branches of ancient pines were dyed red-gold, the wings of flying birds sparkled: everything seemed to be smiling. Xiangzi felt like hailing that expanse of red light for it was as if he hadn't seen the sun ever since the soldiers seized him. His head bowed, his heart filled with curses, he had forgotten the sun, moon and sky. Now he was walking freely along a road that grew brighter the further he walked. The sun made the dewdrops on the grass sparkle, shone on his eyebrows and hair, and warmed his heart. He forgot all his trials, all the danger and pain. What did it matter that he was shabby and filthy? The heat and light of the sun had not excluded him, he was living in a world of light and warmth. He was so happy he wanted to shout for joy.

Laughing at his own tattered clothes and the three moulting camels behind him, he thought how strange it was that four such bedraggled creatures should have escaped from danger and be able now to walk down this sunny road. No need to wonder who was right and who wrong, to him it was all the will of Heaven. Reassured, he continued slowly on his way. As long as Heaven protected him, he need fear nothing. Where was he? He no longer felt like asking, although peasants were already working in the fields. Best to keep going, and even if he couldn't sell the camels right away it didn't matter much. It could wait till he got back to town. How he longed to see

Beiping again! Though he had neither family nor property there, it was after all his home. The whole city was his home, and once there he would find some way out.

There was a fairly large village in the distance. The willow trees outside it were like a row of tall guards and some wisps of cooking smoke drifted over the low dwellings. The distant barking of the dogs sounded beautiful to him. He headed straight for the village, not that he expected to meet with good luck there but rather to show that he was afraid of nothing. After all, he was an honest man, why should he fear the good village-folk? Weren't they all basking in the same peaceful sunlight? He hoped to get a drink of water there, but if he couldn't it didn't matter either. What was a little thirst to someone who had escaped death in the mountains?

The way the dogs barked at him didn't worry him, but the stares of the women and children made him uneasy. He must be a very strange-looking camel-driver for people to gape like that. This nettled him. First the soldiers had treated him like dirt, now all the villagers were looking at him as if he were a monster. What could he do about it? He had always taken pride in his size and strength, but these last days — without rhyme or reason — he had been shamefully treated. Over the roof of one cottage he glimpsed the bright sun again, but somehow it seemed less enchanting than just a moment ago.

The village had only one main street dotted with smelly puddles of slops and pig and horse urine. Afraid the camels would slip and fall, Xiangzi decided to rest a while. On the north side of the street stood a relatively well-to-do villager's house. It had a tiled building in the back, but just a lattice door in front, with no proper gate and no gatehouse. Xiangzi's heart leapt. A tiled roof meant a man of property, while a lattice door instead of a gatehouse meant a camel-owner. Very well, he would rest here a while and he might just get a good chance to dispose of the camels.

"Suh, suh, suh!" He urged the camels to kneel. That was the only camel-call he knew and he used it proudly to show the villagers that he really knew his business. The camels actually knelt down, and he seated himself with a swagger under a small willow tree. Everyone stared at him and he stared back, knowing this was the only way to allay suspicion.

Presently an old man came out of the yard. He was dressed in a blue cotton jacket open in front and his face shone. You could tell at a glance that he was a man of property. Xiangzi made a quick decision.

"Have you any water, sir? I'd like a bowl to drink."

"Ah!" The old man, rubbing mud off his chest, glanced appraisingly at Xiangzi then carefully looked over the three camels. "There's water. Where are you from?"

"From west of here." Xiangzi dared not be more specific for he still did not know where he was.

"Soldiers over there?" The old man's eyes were fixed on Xiangzi's army trousers.

"I was nabbed by them, but just managed to escape."

"Ah! No danger to camels outside the western pass?"

"The soldiers have all gone into the mountains. The road is very quiet now."

"Umm." The old man nodded slowly. "Wait a moment, I'll get you some water."

Xiangzi followed him into the courtyard where he saw four camels.

"Why don't you keep my three, sir, and make up a caravan?"

"Huh, a caravan! Thirty years ago I had three! But times have changed. Who can afford to keep camels!" He stood staring blankly at the four animals. After some time he continued, "A few days ago I was thinking of joining up with a neighbour and sending them outside the pass to graze. But with soldiers to the east and soldiers to the west, who dares go out? I hate to see them cooped up here in summer — it really gets me down. Just look at those flies! And when it gets hotter there'll be mosquitoes too. It's terrible to watch good animals suffer and that's a fact!" He nodded repeatedly as if carried away by wretchedness and frustration.

"Keep my three camels, sir, and take the whole lot outside the pass to graze." Xiangzi was nearly pleading. "The liveliest animals, if they spend the summer here, will be half killed by flies and mosquitoes."

"But who has the money to buy them? Who can afford to keep camels in times like these?"

"Keep them, any price will do. Once I've got them off my hands I can get back to the city and earn a living."

The old man sized Xiangzi up — he was no bandit. Then he looked back at the three camels outside and really seemed to take a liking to them, though he knew quite well he had no use for them. But just as a bibliophile wants to buy every book he sees and a stud owner hankers after new horses, a man who has had three caravans of camels is always eager for more. Besides, Xiangzi was willing to let them go cheap. When a connoisseur has a chance to get a bargain, he tends to forget whether it will serve any purpcse.

"Young fellow, if I had enough spare cash I really would keep them!" The old man spoke from his heart.

"Keep them anyway, any price will do!" Xiangzi was so much in earnest, the other became quite embarrassed.

"To tell you the truth, young fellow, thirty years ago these would have been three big treasures. But in times like these, what with all the confusion and fighting.... You'd better try somewhere else."

"Any price will do!" Xiangzi could think of nothing else to say. He knew the old man had been telling the truth, but he didn't feel like trying to sell camels all over the place. If he didn't get rid of them, he might get into some other trouble.

"Well, see here, I'm ashamed to offer you only twenty to thirty dollars, but it's honestly hard for me to fork even that out. In times like these — there's nothing to be done."

Xiangzi's heart sank. Twenty to thirty dollars? Why that was nowhere near the price of a rickshaw! But he was in a hurry to clinch the deal, and he couldn't count on having the luck to run into another customer for his camels.

"Give me whatever you can, sir!"

"What's your trade, young fellow? It's obvious you're not a camel-driver."

Xiangzi told him the truth.

"Aha, so you risked your life for those animals!" The old man sympathized with him and was relieved that the camels were not stolen goods. For though Xiangzi's taking them wasn't much different from stealing, there were after all the soldiers in between. In time of war, one could not judge things according to normal standards.

"Look here, friend, I'll give you thirty-five dollars. If I tell you that's not getting them cheap, I'm a dog. And if I could pay you one dollar more for them, I'd also be a dog. I'm over sixty, so what more can I say?"

Xiangzi was at a loss. He had always been tight-fisted. But the old man's frank and friendly way of talking, coming on top of his recent experiences with the soldiers, made him ashamed to bargain any more. Besides, thirty-five dollars in hand was more dependable than a hoped-for ten thousand, even though it was too little for risking his life. Three big camels, alive and kicking, were undoubtedly worth more than thirty-five dollars. But what could he do?

"The camels are yours, sir. Just do me another favour. Give me a shirt and something to eat."

"Done!"

Xiangzi had a deep drink of cold water. Then, clutching his thirty-five bright, shiny dollars and two maize cakes and wearing a tattered white jacket that barely covered his chest, he set off. How he longed to reach the city in one bound!

CHAPTER 4

F OR three days, Xiangzi rested in a small inn at Haidian, now burning with fever, now shivering with cold, his mind a blank. Purple blisters had appeared along his gums. He was racked by thirst but had no appetite. After fasting for three days, the fever abated and he felt as limp as taffy. It was probably during this time that people got to know about the three camels from his delirious raving, for when he finally came to his senses he was already "Camel Xiangzi".

Since coming to town he had been known only as "Xiangzi" as if he had no surname. Now with "Camel" tacked on, people cared even less about his family name. He had never worried about his name before, but now he felt he had got the worst of the bargain, getting so little for those animals yet landing himself with this nickname.

As soon as he could stand, he decided to go out and look around, but his legs were unbelievably weak and when he reached the door of the inn they suddenly gave way and he collapsed on the ground. He sat there in a daze for a long time, beads of cold sweat on his brow. He bore it stoically, then opened his eyes and heard his stomach rumbling. He felt a little hungry. Slowly he stood up and made his way to a peddler selling ravioli soup from a portable stove. He bought a bowl and sat down on the ground again. The first sip made him want to retch and he kept the liquid in his mouth for some time before finally forcing himself to swallow it. He didn't feel like drinking any more. However, a second later, the soup seemed to have threaded its way down to his stomach and he belched loudly twice. At that he knew he was going to survive.

With a little food in his stomach, he took stock of himself once more. He was much thinner and his tattered trousers were as filthy as could be. He didn't feel like moving yet was in a hurry to regain his old spruceness, not wanting to arrive in town looking so down and out. But that meant spending money. A shave, change of clothes, new shoes and socks all would cost money, yet he shouldn't touch a cent of the thirty-five dollars, already nowhere near enough to buy a rickshaw. However, he felt sorry for himself. Though he had not spent many days with the troops, it already seemed like a nightmare, a nightmare which had aged him considerably, as if overnight he had added years to his age. His big hands and feet were obviously his own yet it was as if he had suddenly found them somewhere. He felt very bad and dared not recall his past wrongs and dangers, though conscious of them all the time, just as one knows during a rainy period that it's a grey day without looking at the sky. His body seemed to him particularly precious, he really shouldn't be so hard on it. He stood up. Though he knew he was still very weak, he must lose no time in sprucing up, for once his head was shaved and he'd changed his clothes he was sure he would recover his strength right away.

All told it cost him two dollars twenty cents to make himself presentable once more. A jacket and trousers of undyed coarse-grained cloth cost one dollar, black cloth shoes eighty cents, coarse cotton socks fifteen cents and a straw hat twenty-five cents. His old rags he exchanged for two packages of matches.

Clutching his matches he set out along the main road towards Xizhimen Gate. He hadn't gone far when he began to feel tired and weak, but he gritted his teeth. He couldn't take a rickshaw, however he looked at it that was unthinkable. To a peasant, eight to ten *li* were no distance at all, and anyway he was a rickshaw puller himself. Apart from that, it was ridiculous for a strapping great fellow like himself to be beaten by a little sickness. Even if he fell down and couldn't get up again, he would roll all the way to Beiping sooner than give up! If he didn't reach town today then he was finished. The one thing he believed in was his own strength, no matter what illness he had.

He staggered unsteadily along. Not far from Haidian he started seeing stars. He caught hold of a willow tree to steady himself, but though earth and sky were spinning violently he refused to sit down. When the spinning slowed down, then stopped, his heart seemed to drop back from a great height into his chest and wiping the sweat from his brow he continued on his way. His head was shaved, his clothes and shoes were new; he considered he had done quite enough for himself, so now it was up to his legs to do their bit, to walk!

Without stopping again for breath he trudged to Guanxiang. The medley of horses and people there, the cacophony of sounds, the stench of dust so soft beneath his feet tempted him to stoop down and kiss the malodorous earth, the earth that he loved, that was his source of money. He had no parents or brothers, no relatives at all; the only friend he had was this ancient city. It had given him everything. So even if he starved here, he loved it better than the countryside. Here there were things to see and things to hear, light and sound everywhere. As long as he worked hard, there was money past counting here. Endless good things too, more than he could eat or wear. Here even a beggar could get soup with meat in it, whereas in the countryside there was nothing but maize flour. When he reached the west side of Gaoliang Bridge, he sat down on the bank and wept for joy.

The sun was sinking in the west. On the banks, old willows grew crookedly, their tops tipped with gold. There was little water in the river, but a profusion of water-weeds gave it the appearance of a long greasy green belt, narrow and dark, exuding a faint dank smell. The wheat on the north bank had already grown ears, and the leaves on their short dry stems were covered with dust. To the south, in the lily pool, floated small, limp green leaves, round which from time to time appeared little bubbles. On the bridge to the east, traffic moved back and forth. Seen in the slanting rays of the sun it seemed unusually hurried, as if the imminence of dusk had made everyone uneasy. But to Xiangzi it was all enchanting. To him, this was the only stream, these were the only trees, lilies, wheat and bridge worthy of the name — for they all belonged to Beiping.

He sat there quietly, in no hurry to leave. Everything about him was so familiar, so dear, he would gladly have sat feasting his eyes on it until he died. After a long rest there, he went to eat a bowl of beancurd at the head of the bridge. The vinegar, soya sauce, pepper oil and chopped chives mixed with the scalding white beancurd smelt so delicious it quite took his breath away. Holding the bowl, his eyes fixed on the dark green chives, his hands started to tremble. One mouthful, and the beancurd seemed to burn its way down his throat. He helped himself to another two small spoonfuls of paprika oil. When he had finished the bowl, his belt was soaked through. Half closing his eyes, he held out his bowl and ordered another portion.

When he stood up, he felt like a man again. The sun was at its lowest in the west, the sunset clouds had tinged the river with pink. He felt like shouting for joy. Fingering the smooth scar on his face and the money in his pocket, he squinted again at the sunlight on the watch-tower. He forgot his illness, forgot everything else. As if spurred on by some great longing, he decided to enter the city.

The gate-way through the city wall was crowded with vehicles and pedestrians of every kind, all in a hurry to get through although none dared move too fast. The cracking of whips, the cries, curses, the honking of horns, the tinkling of bells and the laughter all mingled to form one great din as if the tunnel were an amplifier with each individual in it clamouring. Xiangzi pushed through the crowd, finding place for his big feet now here, now there, like a long, thin fish following the leaping waves, till he squeezed his way into the city. Before him stretched the wide, straight boulevard of Xinjiekou. At the sight, his eyes shone as brightly as the reflected light on the eastern rooftops. He nodded to himself.

His bedding was still in Harmony Yard on Xi'anmen Road, so he naturally headed there. Having no family, he had always lived there though he didn't always pull their rickshaws.

The owner of this yard, Fourth Master Liu, was nearing seventy but was still a trickster. In his youth he had been a military depot guard, run gambling dens, dealt in the slave traffic and lent out money at the devil's own rates. He had all the qualifications for these occupations: strength, shrewdness, social connections and a certain reputation. Before the fall of the Qing Dynasty he had taken part in mob fighting, abducted women of good families and undergone torture. When tortured, he had neither batted an eyelid nor begged for mercy and had earned the reputation of standing firm at his trial.

As it happened, he came out of prison just after the republic had been set up, when the power of the police was increasing, Fourth Master Liu could see that no one could set himself up any more as a local hero, and that even if Tyrant Huang were to come to life again, he would find little scope. So he started a rickshaw business. Being a local slicker, he knew how to deal with poor people — when to be hard and when to ease the pressure a little. And he had a positive flair for organizing. None of his rickshaw pullers dared try any tricks on him. Laughing at them one minute and glaring the next, he had them completely flummoxed, as if they had one foot in heaven and one in hell. So they found it best to let him call the tune.

By now he already had sixty-odd rickshaws, even the oldest at least seven parts new, for he did not hire out broken-down vehicles. The rent he charged was higher than in other places, but at the three yearly festivals he allowed two more days rent-free than did the others. His Harmony Yard had quarters where bachelor pullers could live free of charge, on condition that they paid the rickshaw rent. Those who couldn't, yet tried to hang on, would have their bedding confiscated by him and find themselves thrown out like a broken teapot. However, if anyone had some pressing trouble or some sudden illness, they had only to tell the old man and he never hesitated to go through fire and water to help them out. That was another way he had won his reputation.

Fourth Master Liu was like a tiger. Though nearing seventy his back was straight and he thought nothing of walking ten to twenty *li*. With his large round eyes, big nose, square jaw and protruding teeth, he had only to open his mouth to look like a tiger. As tall as Xiangzi, he shaved his head till it shone and had no beard or moustache. He liked to think of himself as a tiger and only regretted having no son but only a "tiger" daughter of thirty-seven or eight. Anyone who knew Fourth Master Liu was sure to know his daughter, Tigress. Because she really looked like one she frightened men away, and though she was a good helpmate for her father no one had ever dared ask for her hand in marriage. All in all she resembled a man, even cursing with a man's forthrightness and sometimes a few extra flourishes of her own. With Fourth Master Liu managing outside affairs and Tigress the inside arrangements, Harmony Yard was most efficiently run. Its prestige was so high in rickshaw circles that the Liu family's methods were often cited by pullers and owners alike, just as scholars quote from the classics to prove a point.

Before buying his own rickshaw, Xiangzi had rented one from Harmony Yard. He had given his savings into Fourth Master Liu's keeping and, when he had made enough, had withdrawn them to buy his own rickshaw.

"Fourth Master, look at my rickshaw!" Xiangzi had pulled his new vehicle into the yard.

The old man eyed it and nodded. "Not bad."

"I shall be staying here until I find a job by the month, then I'll move out to where I'm hired," Xiangzi added proudly.

"All right." The old man nodded again.

So when Xiangzi was hired by the month, he moved to the house of his new employer; and when he lost the job and was pulling odd fares, he lived in Harmony Yard.

The other rickshaw men had rarely known cases of someone living in Harmony Yard without hiring one of its rickshaws. So some speculated that Xiangzi was a relative of Old Man Liu's, others that the old man had taken a fancy to him and was planning to marry him to Tigress, wanting a son-in-law humble enough to move into their house. There was some envy in this speculation, but if by any chance it came true then Harmony Yard would be Xiangzi's after the old man's death.

So they dared say nothing cutting to Xiangzi himself and only made wild guesses.

Actually Xiangzi's preferential treatment was on another account. He was the kind of person who stuck to his old ways in new surroundings. If he had joined the army, he would never have shammed stupid to bully people as soon as he put on a uniform. In the rickshaw yard he was never idle: as soon as he had stopped sweating, he would find something to do — cleaning the rickshaws, pumping tyres, sunning rain-hoods, oiling the machines. He needed no orders but did these things of his own free will, and cheerfully too, as if it were a real pleasure. The yard generally housed about twenty rickshaw men. When they knocked off, they would sit about chatting or go to bed and sleep. Xiangzi was the only one whose hands were never idle. At first, everybody thought he was sucking up to Fourth Master Liu to get into his good books; but after a few days they realized that he had no idea of ingratiating himself, he was so natural and sincere, and they had nothing to say.

Old Man Liu never gave Xiangzi a word of praise, never cast him so much as an extra glance, but in his heart everything was chalked up. Knowing Xiangzi to be a good worker, he was willing to let him live there though he didn't hire a rickshaw. Not to mention anything else, with Xiangzi there the yard and gateway were always swept clean as could be.

As for Tigress, she liked this tall bumpkin even more for, whatever she said, he listened carefully and never talked back. The other rickshaw men, soured by their sufferings, kept contradicting her. Though she wasn't afraid of them, neither did she pay them much attention, saving all she had to say for Xiangzi. Whenever he found a monthly job, father and daughter would feel as if they had lost a friend. Whenever he returned, even the old man's curses seemed less harsh.

Xiangzi came into Harmony Yard, his two packages of matches in his hands. It was not yet dark and Old Man Liu and his daughter were having supper. When she saw him come in, Tigress put down her chopsticks.

"Why Xiangzi!" she exclaimed. "Did a wolf run off with you or did you go to Africa to mine gold?"

"Huh!" Xiangzi volunteered no information.

Fourth Master Liu ran his eyes over him, but was silent.

Still wearing his new straw hat, Xiangzi sat down opposite them.

"If you haven't eaten yet, you might as well join us." Tigress acted as if welcoming a good friend.

Xiangzi sat still, his heart suddenly filled with indescribable warmth. He had always considered Harmony Yard his home. As a puller on a monthly basis he often changed masters, and when he picked up fares in the street they were never the same. This was the only place where he had always been allowed to stay, always had someone to chat with. He had just escaped with his life, coming back to the people he knew; they were even inviting him to eat with them. It nearly made him suspect that they were going to cheat him, yet at the same time he felt close to tears.

"I've just had two bowls of beancurd," he said politely.

"Where've you been?" Fourth Master Liu's large round eyes were fixed on him. "Where's your rickshaw?"

"Rickshaw?" Xiangzi spat in disgust.

"Come and have a bowl of rice. It won't poison you! Two bowls of beancurd, what kind of a meal is that?" Tigress pulled him over, rather like an affectionate elder sister-in-law.

Before picking up the bowl Xiangzi pulled out his money. "Fourth Master, first keep these thirty dollars for me." He slipped the loose change back into his pocket.

Fourth Master Liu's raised eyebrows asked more plainly than words, "Where's this money from?"

While Xiangzi ate he told them of his capture by the soldiers.

"Huh, you young fool!" Fourth Master Liu shook his head when he had heard him out. "If you had brought those camels into town and sold them to the knackers you could have got over a dozen dollars a head. In winter, when their coats have grown back, three camels could fetch sixty dollars!"

Xiangzi had already been having qualms, and this made him feel even worse. But on second thoughts he decided that it would have been wrong to sell three vigorous camels to the knackers. He and the camels had escaped together, they had an equal right to live. He said nothing, but felt easier in his mind.

While Tigress cleared the table, Fourth Master Liu tilted his head as if thinking something over. Suddenly he smiled, showing two fang-like teeth that seemed to grow firmer with age. "So you fell ill at Haidian, eh? Why didn't you come straight back by the Huangcun road, you fool?"

"I was afraid I might be caught on the main road, so I took the long way round by the Western Hills. Just suppose some villagers had taken me for an army deserter!"

Fourth Master chuckled and winked to himself. He had been afraid that Xiangzi was lying and that the thirty dollars were loot, in which case he did not want to take charge of it. In his own young days he had broken every law there was, but now that he claimed to have reformed he had to take precautions, he knew very well how to be careful too. That had been the only hole he could pick in Xiangzi's tale. Now that Xiangzi had explained it without turning a hair, the old man was reassured.

"What do you want done with it?" he asked, pointing to the money.

"Whatever you say."

"Buy another rickshaw?" The old man bared his fangs again as if to say, "Think you're still going to live here free with your own rickshaw?"

"It's not enough. If I buy one it's got to be a new one." Xiangzi was too taken up with his own thoughts to notice those fangs.

"Want a loan? Ten per cent interest. For others, it's twenty-five."

Xiangzi shook his head.

"Better to pay me ten per cent than pay the shop instalments."

"I shan't pay by instalments either," said Xiangzi as if in a trance. "I'm going to save up slowly. When I have enough I'll pay cash."

The old man stared at him as if at some strange cipher which might disgust you but couldn't make you angry. Presently he picked up the money. "Thirty dollars? You're not keeping anything back?"

"No mistake!" Xiangzi stood up. "I'm turning in now. Here's a package of matches for you." He placed a package on the table, then stood there blankly. "Don't tell the others about the camels," he said.

CHAPTER 5

*T*HOUGH Fourth Master Liu never breathed a word about Xiangzi's experiences, the camel story very quickly spread from Haidian into the city. Previously, people could find no fault with Xiangzi, but his doggedness made them feel he was different and rather strange. However, their attitude changed after his nickname "Camel" became known, though Xiangzi retained a grim silence and was far from sociable. The general opinion was that he had made a pile in a shady way. There were various versions of how he had done it: some said he had found a gold watch, others that he had picked up three hundred dollars for nothing; yet others, nodding knowingly, that he had led thirty camels back from the Western Hills.

However unpopular a man may be with his mates, if he comes in for easy money they invariably treat him with respect. Selling one's strength for a living is no easy thing, so everyone hopes for some ill-gotten gains; and these being so rare, a man with the good luck to get some must be a favourite of fortune, different from the common run. So Xiangzi's silence and stand-offishness suddenly became the seemly reticence of a great personage and it was only right for others to make up to him.

"Come on, Xiangzi, tell us! Tell us how you got rich!"

Xiangzi heard such talk every day, but held his peace. When pressed too hard, the scar on his forehead would turn deep red and he would burst out angrily:

"Rich? Me? Then where the devil is my rickshaw?"

True, where was his rickshaw? That set everyone thinking. But it's always better to rejoice than to worry for someone else, so everyone forgot about his rickshaw and thought about his good luck. After a while, when they saw that he still pulled a rickshaw, hadn't changed his trade or bought himself land and houses, their attitude towards him cooled. And when his name was mentioned, they no longer asked why he was called "Camel" of all animals, but seemed to consider it quite appropriate.

However, Xiangzi could not forget this business so easily. He was longing to buy a new rickshaw right away, and the more anxious he was to do this the more he thought of his first one. Day in and day out he worked uncomplainingly, but his past experiences kept preying on his mind till he felt suffocated. He could not help wondering: What use was it trying so hard? The world didn't give you a fairer deal because you went all out. By what right had they taken away his rickshaw for nothing? Even if he got another one, who knew when the same sort of thing might happen again?

The past was like a nightmare which made him lose faith in the future. He almost envied the others their drinking, smoking and whoring. If trying so hard was useless, why not enjoy the present? They were right. As for him, even if he stayed away from women, why not drink a glass or two and relax? Wine and tobacco seemed to have a special attraction for him, for he felt they were inexpensive yet from them he could surely draw comfort and the strength to struggle on, forgetting his past wretchedness.

Yet still he dared not touch them. He must save every cent he could, only then would he be able to buy his own rickshaw. Even if he bought it today only to lose it tomorrow, he must still buy it. It was his ambition, his hope, almost his religion. If he didn't succeed in pulling his own rickshaw, he would have lived in vain. He didn't aspire to become an official, get rich or go into business. All he was capable of was pulling a rickshaw, so his greatest hope was to buy one of his own. If he didn't, he would be disgraced in his own eyes. From morning till night he pondered the problem and reckoned up his money; forgetting it would have meant forgetting himself and becoming an animal only able to run through the streets, with no better prospects at all, nothing to live for.

48

No matter how smart the rickshaw, as long as it was rented he couldn't put his heart into pulling it — it was like carrying a rock on his back. Even with a rented one he never slacked, keeping it clean and well-polished and taking good care not to bump or damage it. But this was only from a sense of prudence: he took no pleasure in it.

Yes, cleaning up your own rickshaw was like counting your own money, a source of real satisfaction. So he still kept off tobacco and alcohol and couldn't even bring himself to drink better quality tea. Respectable rickshaw pullers like himself, after a good fast run, liked to repair to a teahouse to treat themselves to tea that cost ten cents a packet, and two packets of white sugar. That helped them to recover their breath and cool off. When Xiangzi had run till the sweat dripped from his ears and his chest seemed a ball of fire, he longed to do the same, not out of habit or to give himself airs, but because he really needed a good drink. Yet he only thought about it, and stuck to the tea-leaf sweepings which cost one cent a packet. At times he was tempted to curse himself for roughing it like this; but what else could a rickshaw puller do if he wanted to save a bit every month? Doggedly he gritted his teeth. Just wait until he had his own rickshaw! A rickshaw of his own would make up for everything.

Tight-fisted as he was about spending money, Xiangzi let slip no chance of earning it. When he wasn't hired by the month he worked round the clock, taking his rickshaw out early and bringing it back late, determined to earn a certain sum every day no matter what time it was or how tired his legs were. Sometimes he would not stop at all for a whole day and night in a row.

Previously, he had refrained from grabbing fares from others, particularly from down-and-out old, weak pullers. With his strength and superior rickshaw they were no match for him if he competed with them. But now he had no such scruples. All he thought about was money, the more the better, regardless of what the job was like or whom he snatched it from. If he could get a fare nothing else mattered — he was like a ravening beast. When he got a fare he raced off, relaxing somewhat, feeling that keeping on the move was his only hope of buying a rickshaw.

One way and another, Xiangzi's reputation now fell far short of what it had been before he became known as "Camel". He often ran off with somebody else's fare, followed by a volley of curses. Instead of shouting back he raced on with lowered head, thinking, "If I didn't have to buy a rickshaw I could never be so shameless!" This was, as it were, his unspoken apology to everyone.

At the rickshaw stands or in the teahouses, when he saw everybody glaring at him he wanted to explain things. But in view of their unfriendliness, plus the fact that normally he never drank, gambled, played chess or chatted with them, he could only swallow his words and lock them up in his chest. His frustration gradually turned to resentment and he fumed inwardly, so that when they scowled at him he would glare back. It made him feel even worse when he compared their present scorn with the respect they had shown him just after his escape from the mountains. Sitting alone in a teahouse with his pot of tea, or counting the coppers from a recent fare at a rickshaw stand, he tried with all his might to control his anger. Although he was not afraid of a fight, he didn't want one. The others never balked at a rough-and-tumble but they would have to think twice before taking Xiangzi on, for not one of them was his match while to gang up on him would be a poor show. Xiangzi managed to keep his temper, unable to think of any alternative to sticking it out until he had his own rickshaw, when things would work out all right. He would not have to worry then every day about the rental, but could afford to be generous and not offend others by taking their fares. That was the way to think, and he eyed everyone as if to say, "Just wait and see!"

He really should not have pushed himself so hard. After his return to the city, he hadn't waited to recover completely before starting work once more. Though he wouldn't admit it, he often felt exhausted, yet he did not dare to rest; and he believed that running and sweating more would overcome this inertia. As for food, he dared neither starve himself nor eat too well. He could see that he was much thinner, but since he was as tall as ever and his muscles were still hard that reassured him. He believed that because he was taller and bigger than others, he could certainly stand more hardships. It never occurred to him that being so big and working so hard he needed more nourishment. Tigress remonstrated with him several times, "Hey, you! If you go on this way, don't blame anyone else if you start spitting blood!"

He knew she meant well, but because things weren't going as he wanted and he was worn out, he was irascible. He would scowl at her and say, "If I don't go all out, when will I be able to buy a rickshaw?"

If anyone else had scowled at her like that, Tigress would have cursed him for hours; but with Xiangzi she was really extra polite and solicitous. She answered with no more than a curl of the lips, "Even so, you must take your time. Think you're made of steel? You ought to rest for three days." Seeing that he was unwilling, she would add, "All right, have your own way. Don't blame me if you drop dead!"

Fourth Master Liu was not pleased with Xiangzi either, because of course the way he went all out and the long hours he worked were hard on his rickshaw. Though rickshaws rented by the day could be taken out and returned at any hour, if everyone were to overtax them like Xiangzi they would be worn out at least six months before their time. Even the strongest couldn't stand such rough treatment. Also, Xiangzi was now so intent on hauling fares that he had little time to help clean rickshaws and do other odd jobs, and this was another loss. The old man felt a bit sore, but said nothing. Rickshaws were rented by the day with no restriction on their hours of use — that was the rule. Helping out was a question of friendship, not a duty, and a man of his reputation couldn't lower himself to take this up with Xiangzi. All he could do was to cast sidelong glances of disapproval and clamp his lips together.

At times he thought of throwing Xiangzi out, but when he looked at his daughter he didn't dare. He had never considered Xiangzi as a possible son-in-law, but since his daughter was fond of this pig-headed fellow, he had no business to meddle. She was his only child, and as there seemed no hope of marrying her off, he really couldn't chase her friend away.

If the truth were told, Tigress was such a good helper he didn't want her to marry at all and this selfish wish made him feel rather guilty and therefore a little bit afraid of her. All his life he had feared neither heaven nor earth, yet here he was in his old age afraid of his own daughter! He rationalized his mortification by thinking: As long as he was afraid of someone it proved that he was not entirely devoid of conscience. That being so, maybe his crimes would not catch up with him on his death-bed. Very well then, as his fear of his daughter was justified, he mustn't throw Xiangzi out. But this didn't mean that he need put up with any nonsense from her and marry her to him. No. He could see she wasn't averse to such a marriage, but Xiangzi hadn't presumed to make up to one so far above him.

So all he had to do was to watch his step. It definitely wasn't worth upsetting his daughter.

Xiangzi hadn't noticed the old man's expression. He had no time for such trivial. If he wanted to leave Harmony Yard, it was not because of any hard feelings but because he longed to get a monthly job. He was a little fed up with pulling odd fares, firstly because others despised him for stealing their customers, and secondly because he couldn't be sure what his daily income would be. Today he might earn more, tomorrow less; there was no way of reckoning when he would save up enough to buy his own rickshaw. So long as he could count on a set sum, however small, put by each month, he felt hopeful and reassured. He was one of those people who like things cut and dried.

He found a job by the month. But it turned out just as unsatisfactory as picking up fares in the streets. This time he was employed by the Yang family. Mr. Yang was from Shanghai, his principal wife from Tianjin and his second wife from Suzhou. Between them, with their medley of northern and southern accents, they had produced an amazing number of children.

The first day of work there nearly made Xiangzi pass out. Early in the morning, the No. 1 wife went to the market by rickshaw. On her return, the young masters and misses had to be sent to school. Some were in junior middle school, others in primary school, still others in nursery school. Their schools, ages and appearances were different, but they were all equally exasperating, especially in the rickshaw, when even the best-behaved seemed to have two more hands than a monkey. The children dispatched, Mr. Yang had to be taken to the yamen. Then Xiangzi had to hurry back to take the No. 2 wife to Dongan Market or to pay some calls. On their return, the children had to be fetched home for lunch. After lunch, off they went to school once more. At this point, Xiangzi thought he could have his own meal; but the No. 1 wife, the one with the Tianjin accent, now ordered him to fetch water. The household's drinking water was supplied by a water-carrier, but fetching brackish water for washing clothes was left to the rickshaw puller. Although this was outside the terms of his contract, in order to keep his job Xiangzi didn't argue but silently filled the water-barrel. He had put down the buckets and was on the point of picking up his bowl, when the No. 2 wife sent him out to buy something.

The two wives had always been on bad terms, but when it came to household affairs they were in complete accord. They agreed, for one thing, never to allow the servants a moment's respite, and both disliked seeing the servants eat. Xiangzi, not knowing this, thought this first day just happened to be a busy one. So again he said nothing and forked out his own money to buy some griddle cakes. Though it was like spending his life's blood, he gritted his teeth in order to keep the job.

When he got back from shopping, the No. 1 wife ordered him to sweep the courtyard. The master and two mistresses were always smartly dressed when they went out, but the yard and the house were like a huge garbage dump. The sight so revolted Xiangzi that he set about sweeping the yard, so intent on this that he forgot that a rickshaw puller shouldn't be given odd jobs. The yard swept, the No. 2 wife told him to sweep their rooms while he was at it. Still Xiangzi didn't protest, he was so amazed that the rooms where these smart, respectable ladies lived were too filthy to set foot in!

The rooms cleaned up, the No. 2 wife thrust a muddy brat barely one year old into his arms. Xiangzi felt utterly helpless. Any jobs that took strength he could cope with, but he had never held a baby before. He clasped this little master with both hands, afraid of dropping him if he relaxed his hold and scared of crushing him if he held too tight. He broke out in a sweat. He decided to give this treasure to Nanny Zhang, a woman with unbound feet from northern Jiangsu; but when he found her she let loose a torrent of abuse.

The Yang family seldom kept servants for more than three or four days because the master and two mistresses always treated them like slaves, as if only by working them to death could they get value for the pittance they paid them. This Nanny Zhang was an exception. She had been with the family five or six years simply because she dared bawl out anyone who annoyed her — whether master or mistresses. The combination of Mr. Yang's cutting Shanghai sarcasms, the No. 1 wife's Tianjin invectives and the No. 2 wife's fluent Suzhou abuse had been unbeatable until they came up against Nanny Zhang, a termagant who could give as good as she got. Like heroes encountering an amazon, they appreciated her worth and kept her on as their lieutenant.

Xiangzi had been brought up in a northern village where cursing was taboo. However, he dared not strike Nanny Zhang because no decent man will hit a woman. Not wanting to talk back either, he simply glared. Thereupon she fell silent too, as if sensing danger.

Just at this point, the first wife shouted to him to fetch the children from school. He hurriedly returned the muddy brat to the second wife, who took this as an insult and reviled him roundly. The first wife had been annoyed by his carrying the second wife's child and now, hearing these curses, also raised her unctuous voice to yell at him too. Xiangzi had become a butt of vituperation. He beat a hasty retreat with his rickshaw, forgetting even to feel angry; for nothing like this had ever happened to him before and he literally felt dizzy.

Batch after batch the children were brought back. The court-yard became noisier than a market-place. The curses of three women and the howls of a horde of children made a racket as loud and senseless as when the audiences pour out of the theatres of Dashala after a show. Fortunately Xiangzi still had to fetch Mr. Yang, so he hurried off once more. The cries of people and the neighing of horses in the street seemed more bearable than the pandemonium back in the yard.

It was midnight before Xiangzi, who had been on the go non-stop, could take a breather. Not only did he feel worn out, with a buzzing in his ears; but although the Yang family had gone to bed, he still seemed to hear the curses of the master and mistresses, as if three different gramophones were playing crazily in his brain to torment him. He had no time to think of anything but sleep. But as soon as he entered his little room, his heart sank and he stopped feeling sleepy.

It was a room in the gate-house, which had a door on either side and was divided by a partition in the middle. Nanny Zhang occupied one side, he the other. There was no lamp, the only light coming from a small two-foot window which happened to be under a street lamp just outside. The place was dank and fusty, with a layer of dust as thick as a copper coin on the floor; and apart from a wooden plank-bed against the wall, the room was empty. Xiangzi felt the bed and discovered that if he laid his head down he would have to prop his feet up on the wall, while if he stretched out his legs he'd have to sleep half-sitting. He couldn't sleep curled up like a figure eight. After some thought he pulled the bed out cross-wise. This way he could lay down his head and make do for the night with his legs dangling over the other end.

He brought in his bedding from the doorway, spread it out as best he could and lay down. But he was not used to lying with his legs dangling and he couldn't get to sleep. Forcing himself to close his eyes, he told himself consolingly: "Go to sleep; tomorrow you have to get up early. After everything you've put up with why shy at this? The food is lousy, the work too hard, but maybe they often have mahjong parties, invite guests and go out to dinner. After all, Xiangzi my boy, what did you come here for? For money, wasn't it? As long as you can rake more in, you can stand anything." These thoughts made him much easier in his mind, and now the room smelt less fusty. He began to drift off to sleep. Dimly aware that bed-bugs were biting him, he couldn't be bothered to catch them.

After two days, Xiangzi felt completely disheartened. But on the fourth day, some lady guests arrived and Nanny Zhang hurried to set up the mahjong table. His heart which had seemed like a frozen lake felt a sudden breath of spring.

When the two wives started playing mahjong, they handed all the children over to the servants. As Nanny Zhang had to pass round cigarettes, tea and hot towels, the troupe of little monkeys were naturally put in Xiangzi's charge. He couldn't stand the imps; but when he stole a glance inside, the first Mrs. Yang in charge of the tipping pool seemed to be taking her job very seriously. He told himself: For all she's such a tartar, she may have sense enough to take such a chance to let the servants make a bit more money. So he was particularly patient with the little monkeys — he owed it to the pool to treat them like young lords and ladies.

The game over, the mistresses ordered him to take the guests home. Both of them wished to leave at the same time, so Xiangzi had to call another rickshaw. The first Mrs. Yang made a great show of searching her person for money to pay the guest's fare, which the latter politely declined a couple of times.

"What, old girl?" bawled Mrs. Yang for all she was worth. "You come to my place and want to pay the rickshaw fare? Come on, old girl, get in!" It was only at this point that she managed to find ten cents.

When she handed it over, Xiangzi saw that her hand was trembling slightly.

After taking the guests home, he helped Nanny Zhang clear the table and tidy the room, then glanced at the first Mrs. Yang. She ordered Nanny Zhang to fetch boiling water, and when the servant had left the room she took out ten cents.

"Take this, and stop staring at me!"

Xiangzi suddenly went purple in the face. He drew himself up as if he wanted his head to touch the ceiling, grabbed the ten-cent note and threw it at her plump face.

"Give me my four days' wages!"

"What's that?" After another look at him, without saying any more she gave him his wages.

Xiangzi collected his bedding and had just walked out of the gate when a torrent of abuse broke out in the courtyard behind him.

CHAPTER 6

THAT early autumn evening, leaves ruffled by a fitful breeze cast their shadows in the starlight. Xiangzi looked up at the Milky Way so far above and sighed. Such a cool invigorating sky and he had such a broad chest, yet he felt suffocating. He wanted to sit down and weep bitterly. Why was it that, strong, tenacious and determined as he was, he got treated like a dog and was unable to keep a job? He not only blamed the entire Yang family but felt a vague sense of despair, a fear that his life would never amount to anything. Bedding in tow, he walked more and more slowly, as if he were no longer the Xiangzi who could up and run eight or ten *li* at a stretch.

The main street was already nearly deserted, its bright street lamps increasing his sense of desolation. Where to go? Naturally to Harmony Yard. But he felt unhappy about it. People in business or those who sell their strength don't worry about having no customers: what worries them is to have one yet fail to make a deal as when someone walks into a restaurant or barber's shop and after one glance around walks out again. Xiangzi knew that finding a job and quitting it was nothing so uncommon, that if one place didn't want him, another would. But for the sake of buying a rickshaw he had worked away so meekly and lost so much face, only to have the job peter out again after three days and a half. He was no different from those crafty fellows who make a habit of changing jobs frequently, and it was this that rankled. He was almost ashamed to go back to Harmony Yard and have everyone laughing, "Well, well! So Xiangzi is one of those three and a half day boys too!"

But if he didn't go to Harmony Yard, where else could he

go? To avoid worrying about it, he trudged in the direction of Xi'anmen Gate. The street-side of Harmony Yard was made up of three shop frontages, the middle one serving as the accountant's office. The pullers were only allowed in there to settle their accounts or discuss other business, but were forbidden to use it as an entrance to the yard behind, for the two rooms to the east and west were the bedrooms of the master and his daughter.

Next to the west room there was a rickshaw entrance with a big double gate painted green. Above this, hanging from a thick wire, was a very bright naked light bulb. Beneath this light hung a horizontal iron plaque inscribed with the gold characters "Harmony Rickshaw Yard". This was the gate the rickshaw men used whether they were working or not. The dark green gate and the golden characters shone in the bright glare of the electric bulb while the rickshaws going in and out were very smart-looking too — black or brown, they all glistened with paint and their white cushion covers gleamed like snow. Even their pullers felt a certain pride, as if they were the aristocrats among rickshaw pullers.

Once inside the gate, if you skirted the west room, you found yourself in a large courtyard with an old acacia tree growing in the middle. The buildings to the east and west which opened on to this yard sheltered the rickshaws. The building on the south side, and the small rooms in the little courtyard behind it, were the rickshaw men's sleeping quarters.

It must have been after eleven when Xiangzi sighted the brilliant solitary light outside Harmony Yard. The accountant's office and the east room were dark, but a light still shone in the west room and he knew then that Tigress was still up. He planned to tiptoe in so that she wouldn't see him; for he didn't want her to be the first to witness his defeat precisely because of her high regard for him. He had just pulled his rickshaw level with her window when she came out from the entrance.

"Why, Xiangzi? What . . . ?" She bit back the rest of her question at sight of his crestfallen look and the bedding in the rickshaw.

Now that what he dreaded had happened, Xiangzi's heart

swelled with shame and discomfiture and he stood still, stupidly, speechless, gazing at Tigress. There was something different about her. Whether because of the bright light or because she had powdered her face, it was much paler than usual, and this pallor masked much of her fierceness. There was actually rouge on her lips, which made her a bit more attractive too. All this seemed so strange to him that he felt even more bewildered. Because he had never thought of her as a woman, the sudden sight of her red lips made him feel rather embarrassed. She was wearing a short silk lined jacket of pale green and wide black crepe trousers.

The green jacket shimmered faintly and a little disconsolately in the lamplight; moreover it was so short that he could glimpse her white waist-band, which set off the delicacy of the green. Her wide black trousers were rustling in the breeze, as if some sinister spirit were trying to escape the glaring brightness and merge with the dark night.

Not daring to keep on staring, Xiangzi lowered his head abruptly, but he still had a mental picture of that small, shimmering green jacket. He knew that Tigress never dressed like this on ordinary occasions. The Liu family was rich enough for her to dress every day in silks and satins; but in her daily dealings with rickshaw pullers, she always wore cotton trousers and a cotton jacket, so that what designs there were looked inconspicuous. Xiangzi felt as if he were looking at something new and exciting, yet familiar. His bewilderment increased.

His unhappiness and this encounter with such a strange new apparition under the glaring lamplight robbed him of his initiative. He didn't feel like moving, but wished Tigress would hurry back inside, or else give him some orders. He simply couldn't stand this strain, which was unlike anything he had ever known, and quite unbearable.

"Hey!" She stepped forward and said in a low voice, "Don't stand there gawking! Go and put the rickshaw away and then come back quickly. I have something to say to you. See you inside."

Accustomed to helping her with her tasks, he complied. However, tonight she was so different from usual, he wanted to think it over; but just standing there was too awkward, so for want of anything better to do he pulled the rickshaw inside. The southern rooms were all dark, which meant that all the rickshaw men were asleep or hadn't knocked off yet. He parked the rickshaw and went back to her door. Suddenly his heart started to thump.

"Come on in, I've something to say to you," she said half laughingly, half impatiently, poking her head out of the doorway. Slowly he walked in.

On the table were some half-ripe still greenish pears, a pot of wine, three white porcelain wine-cups and a huge plate filled with half a jellied chicken cooked in soy sauce, smoked liver, tripe and other cold meats.

"Look." Tigress pointed to a chair and watched him sit down before continuing. "I'm having a treat tonight after all my hard work. You must have something too!" As she spoke she poured him a cup of wine. The sharp odour of the spirits, mixed with the smell of smoked and jellied meats, seemed extra pungent and heavy. "Drink up! Have some chicken. Don't stand on ceremony, I've already finished eating. Just now I told my own fortune with dominoes, so I knew you were coming back. Pretty good, eh?"

"I don't drink." Xiangzi stared fixedly at the wine-cup.

"If you're not going to drink, then get out! What's the matter with you? Don't you know when someone means well by you? You stupid camel! Wine won't kill you, even I can drink four ounces. If you don't believe me, just watch!" She picked up the wine-cup, drained it nearly dry, then shut her eyes, expelled her breath sharply and held out the cup. "Come on, drink! Otherwise I'll take you by the ear and force it down your throat!"

On top of all his bottled up resentment, this mockery made Xiangzi want to stare her down. But Tigress had always been good to him and he knew she was outspoken with everyone, so he really shouldn't provoke her. Instead, he might as well tell her about his troubles. Though normally not a man of many words, today it was as if he had thousands of them pent up inside him, choking him, and he just had to get them off his chest. Looked at this way, Tigress wasn't mocking him but was honestly showing her concern for him. He reached for the wine-cup and drained it. Slowly, surely and potently the fiery liquor went down. He stretched his neck, threw out his chest and belched a couple of times, rather awkwardly.

Tigress laughed. It had cost him an effort to get the spirits down, and her laughter at once made him glance in the direction of the eastern room.

"There's no one there." She stopped laughing but still smiled. "The old man has gone to celebrate Elder Aunt's birthday. He won't be back for two or three days as she lives out at Nanyuan." As she spoke she filled his cup again.

That set him thinking, and he sensed that there was something fishy in all this. At the same time he didn't want to leave, for her face so close to his, her clothes so clean and glossy, her lips so red, all stimulated him in a novel way. She was just as ugly as ever, but with a new animation which seemed to have changed her into a different person. She was still herself but with an additional something.

He dare not consider carefully what this new something was, and though for the moment he was afraid to accept it, he could not bring himself to refuse it either. He flushed and to give himself courage drank some more spirits.

A moment ago he had wanted to pour out his woes to her, but now he had forgotten them. Red in the face, he could not stop himself from looking at her. And the more he looked, the more bewildered he felt, for that something which he could not understand was growing more apparent, and the fiery force emanating so strongly from her was gradually transforming her into something abstract and immaterial.

He warned himself to be careful, but he wanted, too, to be bold. One after the other he drained three cups and forgot what caution was. In a daze he gazed at her, wondering why he felt so elated and brave, brave enough to grab immediately at some new experience, some new happiness. Ordinarily he was a little afraid of Tigress; now, there was nothing daunting about her at all. On the contrary, he himself had become so imposing, so strong, he could pick her up like a kitten. The light went out in the room.

The next day, Xiangzi got up very early and went out with his rickshaw. He had a slight hang-over from his first drinking bout, but this didn't bother him. Seating himself at the entrance to a small alley, he knew that the early morning breeze would soon blow his headache away. But other problems preyed on his mind, and he could think of no immediate solution. The events of the night had left him puzzled, ashamed and unhappy; moreover, he sensed danger.

He could not understand Tigress. That she was no virgin was something he had only discovered a few hours ago. He had always had great respect for her and had never heard any talk of her loose behaviour. Though outspoken and free and easy with everyone, no one ever gossiped about her behind her back. If the rickshaw men had any complaints, they were about her harshness, nothing else. Then why last night's performance?

Foolish as it may seem, Xiangzi began to have doubts about the previous night. Tigress knew he was out on a monthly job, so how could she have waited up just for him? Suppose anyone else would have done just as well. . . . Xiangzi lowered his head. He came from the countryside and though up till now he hadn't thought of marriage, he had his plans. If he managed to get his own rickshaw so that life became a bit easier, and if he felt like it, he could certainly go back to the countryside to pick himself a strong girl who could stand hardships, could wash clothes and do housework.

Practically all young fellows of his age, even those with someone to keep an eye on them, stealthily frequented brothels. Xiangzi had never been willing to follow suit. In the first place, he prided himself on his determination to make good and wasn't going to throw money away on women. In the second place, with his own eyes he had seen those fools who squandered their money — some of them only eighteen or nineteen — pressing their heads against the latrine wall, unable to urinate. Lastly, he must behave decently to be able to face his future wife. Because, if he did get married, the girl must be clean and spotless, and that meant he should be the same himself. But now, now. . . .

When he thought of Tigress as a friend, she was all right; but as a woman, she was ugly, old, sharp-tongued and shameless. Even those soldiers who had seized his rickshaw and nearly killed him now seemed less hateful and disgusting than her. She had destroyed the decency he had brought with him from the countryside, making him an abductor of women!

What's more, what if word of this spread and reached Fourth Master Liu's ears? Did he know that his daughter was a tart? If he didn't, then wouldn't he put the whole blame on Xiangzi? If he did, yet had never tried to keep her in hand, what sort of people were they? And what was he if he got mixed up with them? Even if father and daughter were both willing, he could never marry her, not if the old man had sixty, six hundred, or six thousand rickshaws!

He must leave Harmony Yard at once and break with them completely. After all, he had his own ability, and that would enable him to buy a rickshaw and find himself a wife. That was the only square and honest way of doing things. This decision reached, he held up his head again with a renewed sense of manhood. He had nothing to fear, nothing to worry about. As long as he worked really hard he was sure to succeed.

But after missing two fares, his discomfort returned. He wanted to banish this business from his mind, yet it obsessed him. For unlike other matters it could not be brushed aside, even though a solution had been found. He felt as if physically contaminated, as if even his heart had been blackened and he could never wash it clean again. No matter how much he hated her, how much she disgusted him, she still had a hold on him. The harder he tried to put her out of his mind, the more often she suddenly appeared before him in her nakedness, offering him all her ugliness and beauty.

It was like buying a pile of junk and finding, amongst the scrap-iron, a few little glittering baubles hard to resist. Never had he experienced such intimacy with anyone before, and though he had been taken by surprise and seduced, it was still not a relationship that could be easily forgotten. Even as he tried to brush it aside it might quite naturally twine itself round his heart, as if it had taken root there. Not only was this a new experience for him, it disturbed him in a way he could not describe and left him at a loss. He no longer knew how to cope with her, with himself, with the present or the future. He was like a little bug caught in a spider web; however much he struggled, it was too late.

Absent-minded he pulled a couple of fares, mulling over the whole business even while running. His thoughts followed no clear order, but would often focus on some observation, some odour or some feelings, all very vague yet close and real too. It was becoming so unbearable that he badly wanted to go off alone to drink, drink himself into a stupor which might give him some relief. But he didn't dare drink. He mustn't, because of this business, destroy himself. He tried to think of purchasing his own rickshaw, but could no longer concentrate on it — something always got in the way. Before he could picture the rickshaw, this other thing would stealthily slip out to occupy his mind like a black cloud, obscuring the sun.

That evening, when it was time to knock off, he felt even more miserable. He had to return to Harmony Yard yet he dreaded going back. What if he ran into her? He pulled his empty rickshaw round the streets and several times was quite close to the yard, yet each time he turned away again, like a child who has played truant for the first time and dares not go home.

Strangely, the more he wanted to avoid her, the more he longed to see her and the darker it got the stronger this longing grew.

In the grip of infatuation he felt bold enough to try again, although he knew it was wrong. Just as when, as a boy, he had taken a pole to poke a hornet's nest — he was scared but his heart was pounding as if some imp of mischief was egging him on. A force stronger than himself seemed to be kneading him into a small ball to cast into a blazing fire. He could no longer hold himself in check.

Once again he turned back to Xi'anmen Gate, this time with no thought of delay, meaning to go straight to the office to find her. She no longer had an identity, she was only a woman. He felt himself go hot all over. As he approached the gate, the lamplight showed a man of about forty walking by. Xiangzi thought he recognized his face and deportment, but hesitated to accost him. Instead, instinctively he asked him, "Rickshaw?"

The man stopped, stared at him and said, "Xiangzi?"

"Yes." Xiangzi grinned. "Mr. Cao?"

Mr. Cao smiled and nodded. "I say, Xiangzi, if you have no other monthly job, how about coming to my place? The fellow I've got is too lazy, he never cleans the rickshaw, though he does run very fast. How about it?"

"How could I refuse, sir?" Xiangzi seemed to have even forgotten how to smile. He kept wiping his face with a little towel. "When shall I start, sir?"

"Let me see." Mr. Cao thought for a second. "The day after tomorrow."

"Yes, sir." Xiangzi also thought a moment. "Shall I take you home now?"

"No need. Remember that I went to Shanghai for some time? After coming back I moved house. Now I live on Beichang Street and every evening I come out for a stroll. See you the day after tomorrow." Mr. Cao told Xiangzi the number of his house then added, "We'd better use my own rickshaw."

Xiangzi nearly jumped for joy. All the unhappiness of the last few days vanished in a trice, like paving stones washed clean and white by heavy rain. Mr. Cao was a former employer of his and, though they had not known each other long, they had got on well together. Mr. Cao himself was a very amiable person; moreover, he had a small family with only a wife and little son.

Xiangzi ran his rickshaw straight back to Harmony Yard. The light was still on in Tigress' room and at the sight he stopped dead.

He stood there for a while and then decided to go in, tell her that he had found another monthly job, hand in the rickshaw rent for the last two days, and ask her for his savings. That would make a clean break. Of course there was no need to say as much, but she would understand.

He first parked the rickshaw in the shed, then came back and boldly called her name.

"Come in!" He pushed open the door. She was sprawled out barefooted on the bed, wearing her everyday clothes. Still sprawling there she asked, "Well? Come for another treat, eh?"

Xiangzi flushed as crimson as the painted eggs which the parents of a new-born child distribute. He stood there for a while, then said slowly, "I've found another job, starting day after tomorrow. They have their own rickshaw. . . ."

Tigress cut in, "You don't know when you're well off, young fellow!" Half smiling, half provoked she sat up and pointed at him. "There's food and clothing for you here. Are you only happy when you're sweating your guts out? The old man can't boss me around and I'm not going to be a spinster all my life. Even if the old man gets mulish, I've got enough tucked away for the two of us to get two or three rickshaws and rent them out. We'd make about a dollar a day, wouldn't that be better than running your stinking legs off? What's wrong with me? I may be a little older than you, but not much. And I can take care of you and pamper you."

"I want to pull a rickshaw." Xiangzi could think of no other argument.

"You really are a block-head! Sit down, I shan't bite you!" She laughed, showing her canine teeth.

Xiangzi sat down jerkily, his muscles taut. "Where's my money?"

"With the old man. You won't lose it, so don't get jittery. You'd better not ask him for it, you know his temper. When you've got enough to buy a rickshaw you can get it back from him and it won't be one cent short. If you ask for it now, he'll curse you till you don't know whether you're on your head or your heels! He's good to you, you won't lose anything. If you're short one cent I'll give you two. You with your peasant mind — don't make me snap your head off."

Again Xiangzi could think of nothing to say. He lowered his head, dug around in his pocket and finally fished out the rickshaw rent which he put on the table. "That's for two days." He remembered to add, "I'm turning in the rickshaw today.

Tomorrow I'm taking a rest." Actually he had not the slightest desire to rest, but he felt that this way the break was cleaner. Once he had turned in the rickshaw, he didn't have to stay in the yard any more.

Tigress came over, picked up the money and stuffed it into his pocket. "For these last two days, you've had both me and the rickshaw free of charge! You're a lucky blighter, so don't be ungrateful!" With that she swung around and locked the door.

CHAPTER 7

XIANGZI went to work in the Cao household.

He felt a bit guilty towards Tigress. However, as she had started the whole thing by seducing him and he wasn't after her money, he saw nothing dishonorable in breaking with her. What did worry him was his small savings in Fourth Master Liu's keeping. The old man would probably smell a rat if he were to claim them now. If he steered clear of father and daughter, Tigress might get angry and run him down and then he'd never see that money again. If he went on trusting his savings to the old man, he would be bound to meet Tigress whenever he went to Harmony Yard, and that would be very awkward. Unable to think of any good way out, he grew more and more uneasy.

He thought of consulting Mr. Cao, but how to go about it? That bit about Tigress was something he couldn't tell anyone. Filled with remorse, he began to realize that this sort of relationship couldn't be broken off so easily. He would never be able to wash himself clean of it — it was like a freckle on the skin. For no rhyme or reason, he had got himself entangled. He felt done for: no matter how hard he tried he would never get anywhere. After thinking it over and over, one thing became clear to him: in the end, most likely, he'd have to pocket his pride and marry Tigress, not that he wanted to — or was it because he wanted those few rickshaws? He'd be a cuckold, eating left-overs. The idea was unbearable, but it might really come to that. He would just have to keep going and do his best, prepared for the worst. Gone was his previous self-confidence. Size, strength, determination all counted for nothing; for though his life was his own he had let someone else get control of it, and a most shameless creature she was too.

He should by rights have been happy, because of all the households he had worked for the Cao family was the most pleasant. The pay was no better than anywhere else, and apart from bonuses at the three festivals there was little extra money to be earned; but Mr. and Mrs. Cao were such agreeable people, they treated everybody decently. Though Xiangzi was so eager, so desperate to earn more, he liked having a proper room and enough to eat. The Caos' house was spick and span, even the servants' quarters; their food was good and they never gave the staff stale left-overs. With his roomy quarters, three leisurely meals a day, plus a most considerate employer, even Xiangzi could not think only of making money.

Besides, with board and lodging to his taste and the work fairly light, it was a golden opportunity to get himself back into shape. If he had had to buy his own food, he would certainly not have eaten so well. Now, with all his meals provided, and the chance to digest them in peace, why shouldn't he eat his fill? Food costs money and he knew just how much this was worth. It wasn't easy to find a job where he could eat well, sleep well, and keep clean and presentable.

Moreover, though the Caos didn't play mahjong and seldom invited guest, which meant no tipping, he could get ten or twenty cents extra for various chores. For example, if Mrs. Cao wanted him to buy pills for the little boy, she would be sure to give him ten cents extra and tell him to go by rickshaw, although she knew he ran faster than anyone else. Though the money was negligible, the consideration behind it warmed his heart.

Xiangzi had worked for a good many employers. Nine out of ten would delay paying wages if they could, to show that they would prefer not to pay at all and that servants were basically no better — perhaps even worse — than cats or dogs. The Caos were different, and so he liked it here. He would sweep the courtyard and water the flowers without waiting to be told, and each time they would say something pleasant, even taking the opportunity to hunt out some old things for him to exchange for matches, though the things were always usable and he would keep them for himself. At such times he sensed their genuine fellow-feeling.

In Xiangzi's eyes, Fourth Master Liu could be compared to Huang the Tyrant. He knew of only two great historical figures, one was Huang the Tyrant, the other was the Sage — Confucius. He had not the faintest idea what the Sage was like, but he had heard that Confucius had a great deal of book-learning and was very reasonable. Some of the masters for whom Xiangzi had worked had been literati, some military men. Not one of the military ones had measured up to Fourth Master Liu. As for the literary ones, although among them there had been university lecturers and officials with comfortable jobs in a yamen, all of whom naturally had considerable book-learning, he had never yet met one who was reasonable. If the master happened to be fairly reasonable, the mistress and daughters were sure to be hard to please.

Only Mr. Cao had book-learning and was reasonable too, while Mrs. Cao won all hearts by her modest behaviour. So for Xiangzi, Mr. Cao was the Sage Confucius and whenever he tried to picture that great man he would visualise him as resembling Mr. Cao, whether the Sage liked it or not.

Actually, Mr. Cao was not all that brilliant. He was simply a man of average ability who did some teaching at times and also took other jobs. He styled himself a "socialist", was something of an aesthete and had been considerably influenced by William Morris. Though having no profound views on politics or art, he had one strong point: the ability to put his few beliefs into practice in the trivialities of everyday life. He seemed to realize that he was no genius who would perform earth-shaking feats, so he organized his work and family in accordance with his ideals. This, though it did society no good, was at least honest and saved him from becoming a hypocrite. So he paid special attention to the small things of life, as if to say that as long as his household was happy the rest of society could do as it pleased. At times this attitude filled him with shame, at others with satisfaction, for it seemed clear to him that his home's sole significance was to serve as a small oasis in the desert, able only to supply those who came to it with food and water.

By luck, Xiangzi had come to this oasis, and after wandering so long in the desert he felt it was nothing short of a miracle. Never had he met anyone like Mr. Cao and so he identified him with the Sage — Confucius — either from inexperience or because such people are rarely seen in the world. When he took him out in the rickshaw dressed with such sober refinement and looking so animated yet dignified, Xiangzi, neatly turned out himself, stalwart and strong, took extra pleasure in running, as if he alone were worthy to pull such a master.

Their home, where everything was so clean and quiet, filled him with peace and contentment. In his village, he had often seen old men basking in the winter sun or sitting under the autumn moon, sucking bamboo pipes, silent and still. Though too young to imitate them, he had enjoyed watching them, certain that they must be savouring something very special. Now, although he was in the city, the peacefulness of the Cao household reminded him of his village and made him feel like smoking a pipe himself and ruminating.

Unfortunately, that woman and his scant savings preyed on his mind. His heart was like a green leaf entwined in silken threads by a caterpillar preparing its cocoon. He was so preoccupied that he often gave the wrong answers when questioned by others, even with Mr. Cao. This upset him badly. The Cao family went to bed early, he would be through with his work soon after nine. Sitting alone in his room or in the courtyard, he would mull over these two problems of his. At one point he nearly decided to get married right away, so as to put an end to Tigress' hopes. But how could he support a family by pulling a rickshaw? He knew what a wretched life his mates led in tenement compounds, the men pulling rickshaws, the women taking in mending, the children scrounging in the ash-heaps for cinders. In the summer they gnawed melon-rinds picked off garbage-piles, and in the winter the whole family went to relief kitchens for gruel. Xiangzi couldn't stand that. In any case, if he married, he'd never get back his savings from Old Man Liu. Tigress would certainly not let him off so lightly. He couldn't bear losing that money for which he had risked his life.

He had bought his own rickshaw early the previous autumn. Over a year had passed since and he had nothing now but thirty-odd dollars which he couldn't get back, plus an entanglement! The more he thought about it the worse he felt.

It was ten days after the Autumn Festival and the weather was getting cooler. He would need two extra pieces of clothing. Money again! If he spent it on clothes he wouldn't be able to save it, and how could he go on hoping to buy a rickshaw? Would he ever make anything of his life? And even if he managed to go on working on a monthly basis, what sort of life was that?

One evening, taking Mr. Cao back from the East City later than usual, Xiangzi took the main road in front of Tian An Men Gate as a precaution. There were few people on the wide, flat street, a cool wind blew gently, and the street lamps were still. He really got into his stride. For a while, the pad of his footsteps and the slight creaking of the rickshaw springs made him forget the depression which had weighed him down for so long. He unbuttoned his jacket and felt the cool wind on his chest. How invigorating! He could have run on and on to some unknown destination, run until he dropped dead and was done with everything.

He had speeded up now so that he overtook each rickshaw in front of him. In a trice, Tian An Men was left behind. His feet were like springs, barely touching the earth before bounding up again. The wheels of the rickshaw were turning so fast, the spokes were invisible and the tyres seemed to have left the ground, as if both rickshaw and puller were borne aloft by a strong wind. Mr. Cao was probably half-asleep, fanned by the chilly wind, otherwise he would certainly have forbidden Xiangzi to run so fast. Xiangzi was running for all he was worth, with the vague notion that if he could have a good sweat he would sleep soundly that night instead of brooding.

They were not far now from Beichang Street. The north side of the road lay in the dark shadow of the acacia trees outside the red walls. Xiangzi was on the point of slowing down when he bumped into an obstruction on the road. First his feet, then the rickshaw struck it. He was pitched headlong. One of the rickshaw shafts snapped.

"What's up?" exclaimed Mr. Cao as he was thrown to the ground.

Xiangzi didn't answer but scrambled to his feet. Mr. Cao also nimbly picked himself up and asked again, "What happened?"

Before them was a pile of newly unloaded stones for repairing the road, but no red lantern had been put there as a warning.

"Are you hurt?" Xiangzi asked.

"No. I'll walk back, you bring the rickshaw." Mr. Cao, still calm and collected, groped around the stones to see if he had dropped anything.

Xiangzi felt the broken shaft. "It's not badly broken. Get in, sir, I can pull it." He hauled the rickshaw off the stones. "Do get in, sir!"

Mr. Cao didn't want to ride back but he complied — he could hear that Xiangzi was very close to tears.

When they reached the lamp at one end of Beichang Street, Mr. Cao noticed a graze on his right hand. "Xiangzi, stop!"

Xiangzi turned his head. His face was covered with blood.

Shocked, Mr. Cao could think of nothing to say but, "Hurry, hurry . . . !"

Xiangzi misconstrued this to mean that he should run faster. He bent forward to put on a spurt. Very soon they were home.

When he put down the rickshaw, he noticed the blood on Mr. Cao's hand and rushed into the yard to get some medicine from the mistress.

"Don't worry about me," said Mr. Cao, running in. "See to yourself first!"

Xiangzi looked himself over and began to feel the pain. Both his knees and his right elbow were cut. What he had thought was sweat on his face was blood. Too dazed to do anything, even to think, he sat down on the stone steps of the gateway staring blankly at the broken shaft of the rickshaw. Against the fresh black paintwork, the bare white splintered shaft stood out jarring and ugly, like the millet stalks blatantly sticking out from under a fine paper figure which hasn't yet had its legs pasted on. He stared at the two white ends.

"Xiangzi!" Gao Ma, the Caos' maid-servant was calling him loudly. "Xiangzi, where are you?"

He sat motionless, his eyes riveted on the broken shaft as if it had pierced his heart.

"What's the matter with you, hiding here so quietly? You gave me quite a fright! The master wants you!"

Gao Ma always larded what she had to say with her own feeling about it. The result was both confusing and colourful. She was a widow in her early thirties, clean, straightforward, energetic and meticulous. Other households had found her too talkative and too opinionated, forever giving herself mysterious airs. But the Caos liked clean, forthright people and didn't pay much attention to minor quirks, so she had already been with them two or three years and they took her along whenever they moved house.

"The master's calling you!" she said again. When Xiangzi stood up, she saw the blood on his face. "Oh my, oh my, you're frightening me to death! What in the world happened? You'd better get a move on if you don't want to get lock-jaw. Hurry! The master has medicine!"

With Gao Ma behind him, scolding, they both entered the study where Mrs. Cao was dressing her husband's hand. When she saw Xiangzi, she too exclaimed in alarm.

"He really came a cropper this time, madam!" Gao Ma feared her mistress might overlook Xiangzi's injuries. She hurriedly poured water into a wash-basin and rattled away even faster. "I knew it all along! He always runs so recklessly, sooner or later I knew something would happen. Wasn't I right now? Come on, hurry up and wash, then put on some medicine. Really!"

Xiangzi, gripping his right elbow, stood stock-still. In that clean, refined study, this hulking fellow with blood all over his face was decidedly out of place. Everyone seemed conscious that there was something wrong, and even Gao Ma stopped talking.

"Master!" Xiangzi hung his head, his voice low but forceful. "You'd better find someone else. Keep this month's wages for the repairs. One shaft's broken and the glass of the left lamp is smashed. All the other parts are all right."

"First get washed and put on some medicine, then we can talk about it." Mr. Cao looked at his own hand which his wife was slowly bandaging.

"First get washed!" Gao Ma recovered her voice. "The master hasn't said anything yet, so don't be in such a hurry."

Still Xiangzi didn't move. "No need, I'll be all right in a moment. When a man hired by the month throws his master and smashes the rickshaw, he has no face left to. . . ." Words failed him, but his emotion was as fully disclosed as if he had burst out sobbing. In his eyes, giving up his job and forfeiting his wages amounted practically to suicide. Yet his duty and self-respect meant more to him at this point than life itself.

That was because it was Mr. Cao — not anybody else — that he had thrown. If he had spilled that Mrs. Yang, it would have served her right. With her he could be as rough as any brawler in the streets, because there was no need to be polite — she had never treated him like a human being. Money was everything, and self-respect didn't come into the picture — that was the general rule.

But Mr. Cao was a quite different case, so Xiangzi must give up the money to keep his self-respect. He didn't hate anyone, only his own fate and was seriously thinking of giving up pulling a rickshaw after he left the Caos. Since his own life was worth nothing, he could do what he liked with it, but what of other people's lives? If he really killed someone, what then? He had never thought of this before, but this accident to Mr. Cao had woken him up to this problem.

Very well then, he'd give up the money and change to a trade where he wasn't responsible for the lives of others. Rickshaw pulling was, to him, the ideal profession and quitting it meant giving up all hope. His life would be pointless and empty. It was no use thinking now even of becoming a good rickshaw man — he had grown so tall all for nothing!

When picking up fares in the street others had cursed him for snatching their business from them, but he could justify his shameless behaviour as he wanted to better himself and buy his own rickshaw. But after this accident what could he say for himself? If word got round that he'd thrown his master and smashed up his rickshaw, he'd become a laughing stock — a fellow who had bungled a steady job. There was no way out! He must quit himself before Mr. Cao dismissed him.

"Xiangzi." Mr. Cao's hand was bandaged now. "Wash yourself. There's no need to start talking about giving up the job. This wasn't your fault, the workman should have put a red light by those stones. Forget it, wash up and put on some medicine."

"Yes, sir." Gao Ma remembered to put in her bit. "Xiangzi's all upset and no wonder, with the master so badly hurt. But as the master says it's not your fault, you needn't feel so put out. Just look at him, a big, hefty fellow as worked up as a child! Do tell him, madam, to stop worrying!" Gao Ma's way of talking was like a gramophone record, going round and round and bringing in everyone without any apparent effort.

"Hurry up and wash, you're a fearful sight!" was all that Mrs. Cao said.

Xiangzi's brain was in a whirl, but when he realized that Mrs. Cao was afraid of blood he felt that here was a chance to reassure her. He took the wash-basin outside the study door and sluiced himself a couple of times. Gao Ma waited in the doorway with a bottle of medicine.

"What about your elbow and knees?" she asked, dabbing the disinfectant all over his face.

Xiangzi shook his head. "Never mind!"

Mr. Cao and Mrs. Cao went to bed. Gao Ma, still holding the medicine bottle, followed Xiangzi out of the study to his room. Putting the bottle down she said from the doorway, "Put some on yourself presently. And don't let this little accident upset you. Before, when my old man was alive, I was always quitting jobs too. Firstly, because it made me mad, the way he let things slide while I was wearing myself out outside. Secondly, because young people have short tempers, and if someone put my back up I would walk out. I'd say: 'I'm working for money, I'm not a slave. You may be stinking rich, but even a clay figure has earthy qualities. Nobody could wait on an old woman like you!' But I'm much better now. Ever since my old man died, I've had nothing to worry about and so my temper has improved a bit.

"As for this place, I've been here just short of three years — that's right, I started here on the ninth of the ninth month; there's not much tipping, but they treat you right. We sell our muscle for money and nice words don't do us a bit of good. On the other hand, it's better to take a long view. If you quit your job every two or three days, you're at a loose end six months a year, and that's certainly a dead loss. Much better to find a good-natured employer and stick it out longer. Though you don't get many tips, you can usually manage to put something by in the long run.

"The master hasn't said anything about that business today, so just forget it. Why not? I'm not trying to brag about my age, but you're still a young fellow and easily worked up. There's really no call for it. A quick temper isn't going to fill your belly. Decent and hard-working as you are, why not stick it out here quietly for a while? That would be much better than flying all over the place. It's not them I'm thinking of but you. We get on so well together!"

She stopped for breath, then added, "All right, see you tomorrow and don't be mulish. I'm blunt and direct and never mince words!"

Xiangzi's right elbow ached badly and kept him awake until past midnight. Reckoning up the pros and cons he came to the conclusion that Gao Ma was right. Everything else was bogus, only money was genuine. He must save up for his rickshaw, losing his temper would never fill his belly. This decision reached, he finally felt a placid drowsiness steal over him.

CHAPTER 8

*M*R. Cao had the rickshaw repaired and didn't deduct the cost from Xiangzi's wages. Mrs. Cao gave him two pills for trauma, which he didn't take. He said no more about leaving. For several days he felt sheepish, but finally Gao Ma's advice prevailed. Before long, life slipped back into its old groove, he gradually forgot the accident and hope sprang up anew in his heart.

When he sat alone in his room working out ways to save money and buy his rickshaw, his eyes would sparkle and he would mutter to himself like someone half crazy. His methods of reckoning were crude but he kept repeating to himself, silently as well as aloud, "Six sixes thirty-six". This had little connection with the sum of his money but its constant repetition increased his confidence, as if he really did have an account.

It was already early winter. In the alleys, to the cries of "Sweet roast chestnuts!" and "Peanuts for sale!" was now added the low plaintive call "Urinals-oh!" In his baskets, the vendor also had pottery money-boxes shaped like gourds, and Xiangzi chose one of the largest. He happened to be the first buyer and the vendor couldn't find change. Xiangzi, whose eye had been caught by an amusing little urinal, bright green with a pouting spout, said impulsively, "Never mind the change, I'll have one of those!"

After putting his money-box away he took the little green urinal over to the main apartments. "The young master isn't in bed yet, is he? Here's a little toy!"

Everyone was watching Xiao Wen, the Caos' little boy, have his bath. When they saw Xiangzi's gift, they couldn't help laughing. Mr. and Mrs. Cao made no comment. They probably felt that though the gift was crude, it was the kind thought that counted and so they smiled their thanks. Of course, Gao Ma had to add her bit:

"Just look at that! Really, Xiangzi! A hulking fellow like you, is that the best you could think of? What a disgusting thing!"

Xiao Wen was delighted with his toy and promptly scooped some bath-water into it. "This little teapot got big mouth!" he crowed.

Everybody laughed even harder. Xiangzi straightened his clothes, because he never knew what to do when self-satisfied. He left the room feeling jubilant, for it was the first time that everyone's laughing face had been turned towards him, as if he were a very important person. Still smiling, he took out his few silver dollars and gently dropped them one by one into his pottery gourd. He told himself, "This is still the surest way! When I've saved enough, just smash this gourd against the wall, and wham, there'll be more dollars than broken bits!"

He made up his mind never to ask for help from anyone. Trustworthy as Fourth Master Liu was, he still didn't like the set-up. Money in Old Man Liu's hands was safe enough, but he felt a bit uneasy. This thing called money was like a ring, it was always better to have it on one's own finger. Having reached this decision he felt relieved, just as if he had tightened his belt one notch and thrown out his chest to stand straighter and firmer than ever.

It was growing colder and colder, but Xiangzi seemed impervious. Now that he had a definite aim, everything was much clearer to him and cold could no longer affect him. The first ice appeared on the ground, even the dirt side-roads were frozen. Everything was dry and solid; the black earth appeared tinged with yellow as if drained of all moisture. Especially in the early hours, when the ruts made by carts were inlaid with frost, and piercing gusts of winds scattered the morning mist to reveal the exhilarating blue, blue sky high above. That was when Xiangzi liked taking the rickshaw out. The icy wind would funnel up his sleeves making him shiver as if having a cold bath. Sometimes there would be a raging wind which beat the breath out of him; but he would lower his head, grit his teeth and forge doggedly ahead, like a large fish swimming against the current. The stronger the wind the stiffer his resistance, as if it were a fight to the death. When a sudden blast would not let him breathe he would keep his mouth closed for some minutes, then let out a belch, as if he had taken a header into deep water. After letting out the belch on he would push, battling his way, every muscle taut and straining, a giant whom nothing could stop. He was like a green insect attacked by ants, its whole body quivering in its resistance.

What a sweat he would be in! When he put down the shafts and straightened up, he would let out a long breath and wipe the dust from around his mouth, feeling that he was truly invincible. He would nod as he watched the wind swirl dust and sand past him. The gale bent the trees lining the road, tore the cloth shop-signs to shreds, ripped the hand-bills clean off the walls. It shrouded the sun, it sang, shouted, howled, reverberated. Sometimes it careered ahead like a huge terrified spirit, tearing heaven and earth apart in its frenzied flight; then suddenly, as if in panic, it would swirl around in all directions like an evil demon which has run amok; then again it would sweep along diagonally, as if to take everything by surprise, breaking branches, carrying off roof-tiles and snapping electric wires. Yet Xiangzi stood there watching, for he had just come in out of the wind which had been powerless against him. Victory was his! As for times when the wind was with him, he need only take a firm hold on the rickshaw shafts and let himself glide along. The wind, like a good friend, would turn the wheels for him.

Xiangzi was not blind, so naturally he had noticed the old, weak rickshaw men. Their clothes were so tattered that a light wind blew right through them while a strong blast would tear them to shreds, and their feet were wrapped in heaven knows what rags. They waited, shivering, at the rickshaw stands, glancing furtively this way and that; and as soon as anyone appeared they would rush over and ask: "Rickshaw?!" Once they had a fare they would warm up and their tattered clothes would be soaked. When they stopped, the sweat would freeze on their backs. In a head-on wind, they could not lift their feet and barely managed to drag the rickshaw along; when the blast swooped down from above they ducked their heads, while upward gusts nearly swept them off the ground. When they met the wind head on, they dared not raise a hand for fear the rickshaw would be overturned, while if it came from behind they lost all control of the rickshaw and themselves. Yet they tried in every way, straining every muscle, to drag the rickshaw to its destination, nearly killing themselves for a few coppers.

After each trip, dust and sweat begrimed their faces, leaving only three frozen red circles — their eyes and mouth. Few people were about on the short, cold winter days, so even after a whole day of bitter toil they might still not have earned enough for a full meal; yet the older men had a wife and children at home, the young ones, parents and younger brothers and sisters. Winter was one long hell for them and it was only a breath of life that distinguished them from ghosts, whose leisure they certainly lacked — ghosts never wore themselves out the way they did! To die like a dog in the street was their sole hope of peace. A poor devil who froze to death always had a smile on his face, so it was said.

How could Xiangzi not see all this? But he had no time to worry about other people. They were all in the same boat but he, being young and strong, could stand hardships and feared neither cold nor wind. And with a clean room for the night and neat clothes for the day, he felt himself in a different category. Although they were putting up with hardships together, these differed in degree. He was suffering less than they did and later could escape their fate, for he was convinced that in his old age he would certainly not be pulling a dilapidated rickshaw and freezing and starving. He believed that his present superiority guaranteed his future victory.

Xiangzi's attitude towards his old, weak mates was similar to that of chauffeurs when they met rickshaw pullers outside restaurants or private residences. Never did they chat together because the chauffeurs felt it beneath their dignity to have any truck with rickshaw pullers. They were all in the same hell, but on different levels. It never occurred to them to stand together, and so each went his own way, blinded by his own hopes and efforts. Each believed that, empty-handed, he could set himself up in life and therefore went on groping alone in the dark. Xiangzi neither thought nor cared about anyone else, all that mattered to him were his money and future success.

The streets gradually took on a festive appearance as the New Year approached. On sunny, windless days, the air would be crisp and cold but both sides of the streets grew more colourful with displays of New Year posters, gauze lanterns, red and white candles, silk flowers for the hair, and sweetmeats of all sizes. It was a heartening sight but rather disturbing too, for though everyone hoped to spend a few days pleasantly over the New Year, each had his worries big or small.

Xiangzi's eyes brightened when he saw the New Year displays, knowing that the Cao family would be sending their friends gifts and for each trip he made he would get a tip. The New Year bonus set at two dollars wasn't much, but he would be taking home those who paid New Year calls and each time that could mean twenty or thirty cents extra. It all added up. No matter if the amounts were small, as long as they kept trickling in. His gourd money-box would not let him down. In the evenings when he was free, he would stare fixedly at this clay friend who could only swallow money but not disgorge it. In a low voice he would exhort it, "Eat more, old boy, eat more! When you've filled yourself up, I'll be satisfied too!"

The New Year was getting nearer and nearer and in no time at all it was the eighth day of the twelfth lunar month. Pleasure or worries forced people to plan and prepare. There were still twenty-four hours in the day, but they were different now and could not be spent just anyhow, but must be occupied in some way with an eye to New Year. It was as if time had suddenly developed consciousness and emotions which compelled people to think along with it and busy themselves according to its wishes.

Xiangzi belonged to the happy ones. The bustle in the streets, the calls of the vendors, the hope of bonus money and tips, the New Year holiday and the visions of good food filled him with thrilled anticipation like a child. He decided to spend eighty cents to one dollar on a gift for Fourth Master Liu. The gift might be small but would show his respect. He had to take something when he paid his visit, on the one hand as an apology because he had been too busy to call sooner; on the other, to enable him to collect those thirty-odd dollars of his. Spending one dollar to retrieve thirty was absolutely worthwhile.

Satisfied, he gently shook his money-box and imagined how lovely the heavy clinking would sound after he had added those thirty dollars. With the money back in his hands, he would have nothing more to worry about.

One evening, he was just going to shake his treasure-trove again when Gao Ma shouted to him, "Xiangzi! There's a young lady to see you at the gate. She asked me about you when I came in from the street." When Xiangzi came out, she added in a low voice, "She's like a great black pillar, a real fright!"

Xiangzi flushed red as if his face were on fire. He knew there was trouble ahead.

CHAPTER 9

XIANGZI barely had the strength to step across the threshold of the gate. Still standing inside the door he gazed out, dazed, and by the light of the street lamp saw Miss Liu. She seemed to have powdered her face again and the lamplight gave it a grey-green tinge, rather like a black withered leaf covered with frost. He dared not look her in the eye.

The expression on Tigress' face was mixed. Her eyes betrayed a certain longing to see him, yet her lips were parted in a faint sneer while the wrinkling of her nose suggested both disdain and anxiety. Her arched eyebrows and grotesquely powdered face were at once seductive and grimly overbearing.

When she saw Xiangzi come out, she pouted a few times and the mixed feelings on her face seemed not to know what expression to assume next. She gulped, as if to control her involved emotions. With a hint of her father's society manner, half teasing and half blustering, as if she couldn't care less, she cracked a joke.

"Well you certainly are a guy! A dog given a bone who doesn't come back for more!" Her voice was as loud as when she bawled out the rickshaw men in the yard. The faint smile had vanished from her face and suddenly she seemed to feel rather ashamed and cheap. She bit her lip.

"Don't shout!" All Xiangzi's strength went into blurting out these two words, which burst from his lips low-pitched but vehement.

"Hah, you think I'm afraid!" She gave a mean chuckle, but involuntarily lowered her voice slightly. "No wonder you're dodging me, now that you've found yourself a little bitch of an amah here. I've known all along you were a rotter. You big stupid dark lout, pretending to be dumb!" Her voice was rising again.

"Don't shout!" Xiangzi was afraid that Gao Ma might be listening behind the door. "Don't shout! Come over here!" As he spoke he started across the street.

"I'm not afraid, no matter where. My voice is just this loud!" Though she protested, she followed him.

Once across the street, they took an east side-road skirting the red walls of the park. Here, Xiangzi, who had not forgotten his country ways, squatted down on his haunches.

"What have you come for?" he asked.

"Me? Huh, for lots of reasons!" Her left hand was on her hip, her stomach stuck out. She looked down at him and thought a while, as if touched by compassion for him. "Xiangzi, I've looked you up for important reasons."

Some of his anger melted away at the sound of that low, soft "Xiangzi". He raised his head and looked at her. There was still nothing lovable about her, yet that "Xiangzi" echoed softly in his heart, tender and intimate, recalling past ties of affection impossible either to deny or break. In a low but gentler voice he asked, "What reasons?"

"Xiangzi." She came closer. "I'm in trouble!"

"What trouble?" He was startled.

"This!" She pointed to her belly. "What are you going to do about it?"

He gave a strangled cry as if struck on the head. In a flash everything was clear to him. Thousands of thoughts that had never occurred to him before flooded his brain, so many, so urgent, so confused that all of a sudden his mind became a blank, like a screen when the film snaps unexpectedly.

The street was very quiet, the moon veiled in grey clouds. Little gusts of wind stirred the bare branches and rustled the dry leaves. In the distance a cat was yowling. But as Xiangzi's confusion turned to utter blankness he did not hear these sounds. Chin in hand, he stared fixedly at the ground until it seemed to move before his eyes. He could think of nothing, nor did he wish to think. He felt as if he was shrinking, but wasn't yet small enough to disappear into the earth. His whole life seemed focused on this one painful moment, everything else was void. Only now did he feel the cold — even his lips were trembling.

"Don't just squat there! Say something, get up!" She too seemed to feel cold and wanted to move about.

Stiffly he stood up and followed her northward, still tongue-tied, his whole body numb, as if he had been frozen in his sleep.

"Any ideas?" She glanced at him, a loving expression in her eyes.

Still he had nothing to say.

"The twenty-seventh is the old man's birthday. You must come."

"It's the end of the year, too busy!" In spite of his confusion, Xiangzi had not forgotten his own affairs.

"You have to be handled roughly, I know that. Talking nicely to you is just a waste of time!" Her voice was rising again and in the quiet street sounded extra shrill, making him acutely embarrassed. "Who do you think I'm scared of? Go on, what are you going to do? If you don't listen to me, I've no time to waste breath on you! If we reach no agreement, I can stand outside your employer's gate and curse you three days and nights! I don't care who you are, wherever you go I can find you! So don't think you can get away!"

"Can't you stop screaming?" Xiangzi edged away.

"If you're afraid of my making a noise you shouldn't have put one over on me in the first place! You got what you wanted and now you expect me to take the consequences all on my own! Who the balls do you think I am anyway?"

"Slow down, take your time, I'm listening!" Xiangzi had been icy cold but now these curses made him hot all over, the heat breaking through his frozen pores so that his whole body itched. His scalp especially tingled.

"Now, that's better. Don't make things hard for yourself!" Her lips parted to show her canine teeth. "No fooling, I've really got a thing about you, so count yourself in luck! Believe me, it'll do you no good to get mulish with me!"

"Don't . . ." Xiangzi wanted to say 'don't slap me once to pat me three times', but he couldn't think of the whole saying. He knew quite a few humorous Beiping expressions but could not use them fluently though he understood when other people used them.

"Don't what?"

"Finish what you have to say!"

"I've got a good idea." Tigress stood still, confronting him. "See here. If you got a go-between to approach the old man, he would be sure to refuse. He owns rickshaws, you pull them, he wouldn't accept a son-in-law so far below him. As for me, I don't care about that. I like you and that's enough, to hell with the rest!

"No go-between can handle this because, at the first mention of the subject, the old man will think it's with an eye to his few dozens of rickshaws. He'd turn down even men better placed than you. This is something I have to fix myself. I've picked you and we've done what we've done without asking his opinion. And anyway, I'm pregnant so neither of us can run away!

"But we can't just march into the hall and announce it to him. The old man is getting more and more pigheaded. If he got wind of this, he'd take a young wife and run me out. I'm telling you, the old fellow is as strong as an ox for all he's nearing seventy. If he really married again, I bet you he could get himself at least two or three kids by her, believe it or not."

"Let's keep moving." Xiangzi noticed that the policeman on duty had walked past them twice, and he didn't like that one bit.

"We'll talk right here. Who's to stop us?" Following his gaze, Tigress also saw the policeman. "You haven't got your rickshaw, what are you afraid of? He can't bite anybody's balls off without rhyme or reason, can he? That would really be too much! Let him mind his own business and we'll mind ours!

"Look, here's my plan. On the twenty-seventh, the old man's birthday, you come and kowtow three times to him. Then, on New Year's Day, you come again to wish him a happy New Year. That'll put him in a good mood and I'll get some wine and tidbits and let him have a good drink. When he's nearly tight, you strike while the iron's hot and ask him to be your foster-father.

"Later on, I'll gradually let him know that I don't feel so well. He's sure to ask questions but I'll hold my tongue to begin with. When he gets really worked up, I'll say it was that Qiao Erh who died recently — the vice-manager of the undertaker's shop just east of our place. He had no family or relatives and is already buried in the paupers' cemetery outside Xizhimen, so where's the old man going to find out the truth? Once he's at a loss the two of us can hint that the best thing would be to give me to you. After all, you'd already be his foster-son, what's the difference between that and a son-in-law? That way, without any effort, we'd save ourselves a scandal. What do you think of my plan?"

Xiangzi was silent.

As if she felt she had said enough for the time being, Tigress started off in a northerly direction. Her head was bent, as if to savour her speech and also to give him a chance to think things over.

Just then, the wind blew a rift in the grey clouds, and in silver moonlight they reached the north end of the street. The moat, long since frozen over, stretched silent, silver-grey, flat and solid around the walls of the Forbidden City, as if to hold them up. There was not a sound within the Forbidden City. Its intricate watch-towers, magnificent archways, vermilion gates and the pavilions on Coal Hill seemed to be listening with bated breath for something they might never hear again. The light wind, like a mournful sigh, wove in and out of the pavilions and halls, as if to tell some tales of times gone by.

Tigress walked in a westerly direction and Xiangzi followed her to the archway at one end of Beihai Bridge. The bridge was practically deserted and faint moonlight shone, cold and desolate, on the wide stretches of ice on either side. The distant pavilions, half obscured by dark shadows, were immobile as if frozen on the lake, only their yellow tiles shimmering faintly. Trees stirred gently, the moonlight seemed hazier then ever. Above towered the white dagoba, its chalky whiteness casting a chilly gloom on all around so that the three lakes, despite their man-made adornments, revealed their full northern bleakness. When they reached the bridge, the icy breath from the frozen lake made Xiangzi shiver. He didn't want to go any further.

Normally, when he pulled his rickshaw over this bridge, he concentrated on his feet for fear of stumbling and had no time to look about him. Now, he was free to look around, but he found the scene somewhat frightening. That ashen-cold ice, those gently stirring trees and the deathly white dagoba were so desolate that he felt they might suddenly let out a shriek or leap up madly. Even this white stone bridge beneath his feet seemed abnormally deserted and so white that even the street lamps shed a mournful light. He didn't want to go any further or look any more, much less accompany Tigress. What he really wanted was to dive off the bridge, smashing through the ice and sinking down to the bottom to freeze there like a dead fish.

"See you tomorrow!" He wheeled around and started back.

"Xiangzi, we'll leave it like that then. See you on the twenty-seventh!" she called to his broad straight back. Then glancing at the white dagoba, she sighed and walked off to the west.

Without so much as a backward glance, as if the devil were after him, Xiangzi hurried on in such a dither that he nearly bumped into the wall enclosing the old palace grounds. He leaned one arm against it, on the point of bursting into tears. Motionless and dazed, he stood there awhile till he heard someone calling from the bridge.

"Xiangzi, Xiangzi! Come here, Xiangzi!" It was Tigress.

Very slowly he took two steps towards the bridge. Tigress was coming down towards him, inclining slightly backwards, her lips parted.

"I say, Xiangzi, come over here, I've something to give you!" Before he could move any further, she was standing in front of him. "Here, your thirty-odd dollars savings. There was some change but I've made it up to a round sum. Take it! This is just to show you how I feel. I really miss you, care for you and have your interests at heart. As long as you're not ungrateful, I don't care about the rest. Here, take it, look after it and don't blame me if you lose it!"

Xiangzi took the wad of notes and stood there blankly. He could think of nothing to say.

"All right, till the twenty-seventh! Mind you keep the date!" She smiled. "You're getting the best of the bargain, you know, just work it out yourself." With that she turned and went back.

He clutched the wad of notes, watching her in a daze till the arch of the bridge hid her from view. Clouds covered the moon again, the street lamps brightened, and the bridge seemed abnormally white, cold and empty. He turned and strode back at top speed, yet when he reached the gate of the Caos' house he still had a vision of that cold white forlorn bridge, as if it were but one blink away in time.

Back in his room, the first thing he did was to count the bills. He counted them two or three times and his sweaty palms made them sticky. Each time the total was different. Finally he stuffed them into his gourd money-box and sat down on the edge of the bed staring vacantly at the earthen receptacle, not wanting to think any more. There was always a way out when one had money and he had great faith that this money-box was going to solve all his problems. There was no need to think any more. The moat, Coal Hill, the white dagoba, the bridge, Tigress, her belly . . . all were a dream; yet when he woke up, there'd be thirty more dollars in his till! That was real.

When he had looked his fill, he hid the money-box away and decided to have a good sleep. No matter how great his troubles, he could sleep through them and shelve them till tomorrow.

He lay down but couldn't close his eyes. The events of the day were like a nest of wasps — barely had one flown in than another buzzed out, and each with a sting in its tail.

He was unwilling to think because really it was no use. Tigress had blocked every avenue of escape.

The best thing would be to clear out, but Xiangzi couldn't bring himself to do this. Rather than go back to the countryside, he would even be willing to stand guard over the white dagoba in Beihai. What about another city? There was nowhere better than Beiping. No, he couldn't leave, there was no point in cudgelling his brains. Tigress was quite capable of carrying out her threats. If he didn't toe the line, she would keep on pestering him. As long as he stayed in town, she could hunt him down. In fact, it was no use trying to give her the slip. Once angered, she could enlist the help of her father who might hire a man or two — it didn't need many — to do away with Xiangzi in some quiet, deserted spot.

As he thought over all she had said, he felt as if he had fallen into a trap and his whole body was pinned down — there was absolutely no escape for him. Unable to fault any of her reasoning, he could find no cracks in her armour. He felt she had cast a lethal net which not even a tiny inch-long fish could slip through. Failing to analyse the business in detail, he accepted it as one whole which weighed on him like a thousand-pound metal block. And this crushing weight convinced him that a rickshaw man's lot in life could be summed up in two words: rotten luck.

A rickshaw man, since he was a rickshaw man, should stick to his rickshaw and steer clear of women — any contact with one might land him in big trouble. Fourth Master Liu, because he owned several dozen rickshaws, and Tigress because of her smelly cunt, had swindled him and treated him like dirt. There was no point in thinking about it any more. If he accepted his fate, then he should kowtow, ask Fourth Master to be his "foster-father" and prepare to marry that hag. If he didn't accept this fate, then his life was in danger.

Having thought this far, he put Tigress and all she had said aside. This trouble wasn't because she was hard and cruel; it was a rickshaw puller's destiny, just as a dog is bound to be beaten and bullied even by children for no reason at all. Why hang on to a life like this? To hell with it!

Sleep deserted him and he kicked the quilt aside and sat up. He decided to buy some wine and get dead drunk. What the fucking hell did he care about his job or so-called rules of behaviour? Get drunk, sleep! The twenty-seventh? Not even on the twenty-eighth was he going to kowtow to anyone, and who dared touch him! He pulled his thick cotton quilted jacket over his shoulders, picked up the small bowl that he used for tea and ran out.

The wind was blowing harder and the grey clouds had dispersed. The moon, very small, was shedding a chilly light. The cold made Xiangzi — just out from his warm quilt — gasp. There were no pedestrians about, only a couple of rickshaws at the side of the road, their pullers standing by them, their hands cupped over their ears and stamping their feet to keep warm.

In one breath Xiangzi ran to the little shop on the south side. To preserve some warmth, it had already put up its shutters, but money could be paid in and purchases handed out through a small window. Xiangzi bought four ounces of spirits and three coppers worth of peanuts. Holding the bowl steady and not daring to run, he strode off with the speed of a sedan-chair carrier. Back in his room, he hurriedly slipped into his quilt, his teeth chattering violently, reluctant to sit up again. The spirits on the table gave off a sharp, pungent odour which he rather disliked, and even the peanuts didn't interest him. The icy air like a basin of cold water had woken him up completely, yet he felt too lazy to stretch out his arm while his heart was no longer burning.

After lying there for some time, he peeked over the edge of the quilt at the bowl of spirits on the table. No, he couldn't destroy himself over such a paltry affair, he couldn't break his resolution never to touch alcohol. He was in a mess, no doubt about it, but somewhere there must be some crack through which he could wriggle out. Even if there was no escape, he shouldn't first wallow in the mud himself. He must keep his wits about him to see just how other people shoved him down.

He put out the light and burrowed inside the quilt, hoping to fall asleep. Still it was no good. He pushed the covers back and looked around.

The moonlight in the courtyard had given his window paper a bluish sheen, as if it were nearing day-break. The tip of his nose felt how icy it was in his room, and a faint smell of spirits pervaded the freezing air. He sat up abruptly, reached for the bowl and gulped down a big mouthful.

CHAPTER 10

X IANGZI wasn't smart enough to solve his problems one by one neither was he forceful enough to make a clean sweep. So he was utterly helpless, resentment gnawing all the time at his heart. All living creatures, when they have been injured, seek desperately to make the best of a bad business. A fighting cricket that has lost its powerful legs still tries to crawl with its small, weak ones. And so it was with Xiangzi. Having no definite plan, he could only hope to get by from day to day, taking things as they came, content to crawl as far as he could with no further thought of leaping.

There were still about a dozen days till the twenty-seventh, the day on which all his attention was focused. It was always in his thoughts and dreams, and he kept muttering "the twenty-seventh" as if, once that day was past, all his problems would be solved — though he knew very well that this was wishful thinking.

At times his thoughts ranged a bit further. Suppose he took the few dozen dollars he had and went to Tianjin? Once there he might be lucky enough to land some other job and stop pulling a rickshaw. Could Tigress follow him to Tianjin? For him, any place you needed to take a train to was necessarily very far away; so she certainly wouldn't be able to follow him there! This seemed a good idea, but deep down he knew it was a last resort, because if he could stay in Beiping he would. And so, back he came to the twenty-seventh. Better to think of things closer to hand. If he could get over that hurdle he might get by without drastically changing the whole situation. And even if he couldn't make a clean break, every hurdle crossed was one hurdle the less,

But how to get over the first one? There were two ways: one, to ignore the whole business and not pay any birthday call; the other, to follow Tigress' advice. Either way, the result was the same. If he didn't turn up, she certainly would not let the matter drop; if he did, she would not let him off lightly either. He recalled, when he first started pulling a rickshaw, how he had tried to imitate the others by taking short cuts down alleys. Once, by mistake, he got into Luojuan Alley and went round in a big circle only to end up just where he had started. Now it was as if he were once more in just such an alley: whichever way he turned, the result was the same.

In his helplessness, he tried to look on the bright side. What was wrong with marrying Tigress anyway? Yet however he looked at it, the idea sickened him. The mere thought of her appearance made him shake his head. So forget her appearance, think of her behaviour, ugh! How could a decent fellow, so anxious to better himself, accept such shop-soiled goods? He would never be able to face anyone again, not even his parents' spirits after death!

Anyway, who could guarantee that the child was his? Or that she would bring him some rickshaws? Fourth Master Liu was no easy customer! And even supposing everything went smoothly, he couldn't stand it anyway, for when could he ever get the better of Tigress? She only had to point her little finger to keep him running until he was dizzy, all sense of direction lost. He knew what a terror she was! Even if he wanted to set up a family, he couldn't marry her. It was out of the question. If he took her that would be the end of him, and yet he had his own self-respect! There was really no way out.

Unable to deal with her, he turned to hating himself and was tempted to give himself a few hard slaps. Yet the fact was he had really done nothing wrong. She had planned it all and waited for him to fall into the trap. The trouble with him, it seemed, was being too decent — decent people always get worsted and put in the wrong.

What made him unhappiest of all was that he had nowhere to unburden himself. He had no parents, no brothers or sisters, no friends. Usually he felt proud of being a stout fellow with his feet on the ground, able to hold up the sky, free as the wind with no ties to anyone. Only now did he realize with dismay that nobody can live in isolation.

For other rickshaw men, especially, he now felt an affection. Had he made friends with a few before, he thought that a big fellow like himself need not fear any number of Tigresses, for his friends would have given him advice and taken his side. But he had always kept to himself, and you couldn't make friends on the spur of the moment! He felt a fear he had never known before. At this rate, anyone could cheat and bully him. One man alone could not hold up the sky!

This fear caused him to start doubting himself. In the winter, when his employer had dinner engagements or went to the theatre, Xiangzi was in the habit of taking the water can from under the carbide lamp and holding it to his chest, because if left on the rickshaw it would freeze. He would be in a sweat from running, and the icy little can against his flesh instantly set him shivering, and it would take some time for the can to warm up. But he had never felt this an imposition and had actually sometimes had a sense of superiority, because the pullers of ramshackle rickshaws could not afford carbide lamps. Now it occurred to him that he was earning a monthly pittance, putting up with all sorts of hardship and even hugging a water can to prevent it freezing. Apparently his broad chest was worth less than a small can. Whereas before he had believed that pulling a rickshaw was the ideal job for him and that he would be able to set himself up in this way, he now began to have silent doubts. No wonder Tigress bullied him — he wasn't even up to a tin can!

Three days after Tigress had tracked him down. Mr. Cao and some friends went to see the evening show of a film. Xiangzi waited in a small teahouse, nursing the ice-cold can. It was freezing and the doors and windows of the teahouse were tightly closed. The place reeked with coal fumes, sweat and the smoke of cheap cigarettes. Even so, the windows were frosted over.

The customers were mostly rickshaw pullers who worked by the month. Some sat with their heads against the wall, dozing in the warmth of the room. Others had a bowl of spirits and, after inviting those around to join in, would drink slowly, smacking their lips after each sip and breaking wind noisily. There were others eating large rolled up griddle cakes, biting off half in one mouthful so that their necks became distended and red.

One man was glumly relating his woes to the company at a large, telling how he hadn't stopped running since early that morning and how he'd lost count of the number of times he'd been soaked and dried out again. The others had mostly been chatting among themselves, but these last words brought about a sudden silence. Then, as vociferous as birds whose nests have been destroyed, they all burst out airing their own grievances. Even the fellow eating griddle cakes found room in his mouth to wag his tongue, talking and swallowing at the same time, the veins standing out on his head.

"You think a mother-fucking monthly puller doesn't have a rough time? Even since two o'clock — urp! — till now, I haven't had a bite to eat or a drop to drink! Three times I've pulled the mother-fucker — urp! — back and forth from Qianmen to Pingzimen! This cold has frozen my arse-hole till it's cracked and all I can do is fart!"

He looked around at the others, nodding to them, and took another bite of griddle cake.

This switched the conversation to the weather and gave everybody a chance to talk of the hardships brought on by the cold.

Xiangzi was silent throughout, but he listened intently. Though the tales the others told, their tones of voice and their accents were all different, each cursed his lot and complained of its injustice. And the resentment in Xiangzi's heart made him lap up such talk as the parched earth laps up rain. He had no way, did not know how, to tell them his own story from beginning to end. He could only take in something of the bitterness of life from what they said. Everyone was wretched and he was no exception; he could see himself and so wanted to sympathize with them all. At the sad parts of their stories he knit his brows, at the funny ones he grinned. His silence and his not knowing them did not prevent him from being at one with them and feeling that they were all fellow-sufferers. Before, he would have thought this pointless jabber — if they kept it up all day they would never get rich. Now, for the first time he felt it wasn't empty talk, they were speaking for him too and expressing the common suffering of all rickshaw pullers.

When the conversation was at its noisiest, the door suddenly swung wide open, letting in a blast of cold air. Everyone glared angrily round to see who was being so inconsiderate. The more impatient they were, the slower the newcomer moved, as if he were deliberately taking his time. One of the waiters called out, half jokingly, half urgently, "Hey there, uncle, hurry up! Don't let all the warm air out!"

Before he had finished speaking, the man outside had come in. He was a rickshaw puller too, who looked over fifty. His cotton padded jacket, neither long nor short, was as full of holes as a reed basket, tufts of padding sticking out of the front and the elbows. His face seemed to have been unwashed for days, so that no one could see the colour of his flesh except on his ears which were frozen bright red, like ripe fruit ready to drop. His white hair stuck out untidily from under a small ragged cap, and on his eyebrows and short beard there were drops of frozen moisture. As soon as he got in, he groped for a bench and sat down.

"A pot of tea!" he gasped.

This teahouse was frequented only by pullers with monthly jobs. Ordinarily this old puller would certainly not have come here.

Everybody looked at him, more deeply moved than by what they had been saying a moment before. No one spoke. Usually one or two green youngsters would have cracked some joke to make fun of such a customer, but today none of them said a word.

Before the tea was ready, the old man's head sank slowly lower and lower until he slid to the ground.

At once everyone leapt up. "What's happened? What's wrong?" All wanted to rush forward.

"Don't move!" The teahouse manager, an experienced man, stopped the crowd. Going over alone, he loosened the old man's collar, propped him up against a chair and held his two shoulders. "Bring some sugar water, quick." Then he put his ear to the old man's throat and listened, muttering, "There's no inflammation."

Nobody moved, but neither did they sit down again. They stood there blinking their eyes in the smoke-filled room and looking at the two figures by the door. All seemed to be thinking the same thought, "That's what we'll come to! When our hair is white there'll come a day when we'll fall and die in the street!"

As the bowl of sugared water was held to his lips, the old man moaned a couple of times. His eyes still closed, he raised his right hand — it was black and shone as if lacquered — and wiped his mouth with the back of it.

"Drink some of this!" the manager said in his ear.

"Eh?" The old man opened his eyes. When he saw that he was sitting on the floor, he drew up his legs, intending to get up.

"Drink first! There's no hurry!" The manager took his hands away from the old man's shoulders.

Everybody hurried over.

"Ai, ai!" The old puller looked around, then holding the bowl in both hands sipped the sugared water.

He drank slowly, and when he had finished he looked around at everyone once more. "Ai, excuse me for putting you out!" His voice was so gentle and kindly, it was difficult to believe it came from the mouth under that scruffy beard. Again he tried to rise and three or four men made haste to help him up. He smiled faintly and said, still gently, "It's all right, I can manage. What with cold and hunger, I came over faint. It doesn't matter." Though his face was so caked with dirt, the faint smile seemed to make it clean and kindly.

Everyone was moved. The middle-aged man who had been drinking spirits had finished his bowl. His bloodshot eyes filled with tears. "Here," he called, "bring me two more ounces!" By the time this arrived, the old puller was seated in a chair by the wall. The drinker was tipsy but he politely placed the spirits before the old man.

"This drink is on me, please take it!" he said. "I'm over forty myself and, if the truth be told, I can barely manage a monthly job. As the years go by, my legs tell me I'm no longer so strong. In two or three more years I'll be like you. You must be nearly sixty!"

"Not yet, fifty-five!" The old man took a sip. "In this cold there are no fares around. And I, well, my stomach is empty. My few coppers went to buying some wine to warm up on. By the time I got here, I was dead-beat so I came in to warm up a bit. The room was so hot, and I'd had nothing to eat, so I blacked out. It really doesn't matter. I'm sorry to have given you all so much trouble!"

By now, the old man's grey hair like withered grass, his muddy face, coal-black hands, shabby cap and padded jacket all seemed to be radiating a faint pure light, rather like the aura of dignity that still surrounds a crumbling idol in a tumble-down temple.

Everyone looked at him as if loath to let him leave. Xiangzi had remained silent all along, standing there woodenly. When he heard the old man say that his stomach was empty, he rushed out and came back at top speed with a large cabbage leaf. In it were wrapped ten steamed minced-mutton patties. He put them down in front of the old man and said, "Eat these!" Then he returned to his seat and lowered his head as if he were worn out.

"Ai!" The old man seemed happy but close to tears too. He nodded to everyone. "We really are mates, aren't we? You can pull a fare with all your might, yet how hard it is to get one single copper extra out of him!" He stood up and moved towards the door.

"Eat!" Everyone seemed to be calling out at once.

"I must fetch Little Horse, my grandson. He's outside watching the rickshaw."

"I'll go, you sit down!" said the middle-aged rickshaw man. "You can be sure you won't lose your rickshaw here, there's a police sentry-box just across the street." He opened the door a crack and yelled, "Little Horse, Little Horse, your grandfather's calling you! Bring the rickshaw over here!"

The old man fingered the patties several times but did not pick any up. As soon as Little Horse came in, he took one and said, "Little Horse, this is for you, laddy!"

Little Horse was not more than twelve or thirteen. His face was very thin, but his clothes were bulky. His nose, red with cold, was running. On his ears he wore a pair of tattered earmuffs. He stood in front of the old man, took the proffered patty in his right hand and automatically reached out his left for another. He took a rapid bite out of each.

"Hey, slowly!" The old man placed a hand on his grandson's head, with the other he picked up a patty and lifted it slowly to his mouth. "Two will be enough for grandad, the rest are yours. When you've finished we'll pack up for today and go home. If it's not too cold tomorrow, we'll start a bit earlier. What do you say, Little Horse?"

The boy nodded his head at the patties and sniffed some of the snot back into his nose. "Grandpa, you have three and the rest are mine. Presently I'll pull you back home."

"No need." The old man looked at everyone with a proud smile. "We'll walk back, it's too cold to ride in the rickshaw."

The old man finished his share and waited for Little Horse to eat up the rest. He fished out a rag, wiped his lips and nodded to the company again. "My son went to be a soldier and has never come back. His wife. . . ."

"Don't talk about that!" cut in Little Horse, his mouth so full that his cheeks were bulging like peaches.

"It doesn't matter, we're not strangers!" In a lowered voice he continued, "The lad takes things very seriously, he's so set on making good. His mother left too. For the two of us, grandad and grandson, that rickshaw is our living. It's very run-down but it's our own so we don't have to worry about paying rent every day. Whether we earn more or less, it's a hard life. But what other way out do we have?"

"Grandpa." Little Horse, still eating away, tugged at the old man's sleeve. "We've got to pull another fare. We have no money for coal tomorrow morning. It's all your fault. Just now we could have made twenty coppers by pulling that fellow to Houmen. I wanted to, but you wouldn't. How will you manage tomorrow with no coal?"

"There's always a way. Grandpa will get five catties of coalballs on credit."

"What about kindling?"

"Why of course! Eat up, there's a good lad, we must be moving along." As he spoke the old man stood up and, glancing around him, said, "Thanks, mates, for going to so much trouble." He took Little Horse's hand and the boy stuffed the last patty into his mouth.

Some of the men in the teahouse sat where they were, while others followed them out. Xiangzi was the first to do so. He wanted to see that rickshaw.

It was a most ramshackle rickshaw. The paint was peeling off, so that the grain of the wooden shafts showed through. The broken lamp rattled in the wind, and the spokes of the hood had been tied on with twine. Little Horse took out a match from one of his ear-muffs, lit it by striking it on the sole of his shoe, then cupped the flame in his small black hands to light the lamp. The old man spat on his palms, let out a deep breath, picked up the shafts and said, "See you tomorrow, mates!"

Xiangzi stood stock-still in the doorway watching the old man and the boy with that dilapidated rickshaw of theirs. The old man was speaking as they left, his voice rising and falling, while the street lamps and the shadows beneath them flickered. As Xiangzi listened and watched, his heart ached as never before. In Little Horse he seemed to see his own past, in the old man, his future. Never one to part lightly with money, he none the less felt very glad that he had bought the two of them those ten patties. He followed them with his eyes until they were out of sight before going back to the teahouse, where everyone was talking and laughing once more. He felt so confused that he paid for his tea and left, pulling his rickshaw to the cinema to wait for Mr. Cao.

It was bitterly cold. The air was full of fine sand, and the wind seemed to be high above. The only stars to be seen were a few of the larger ones, trembling in the void. There was no wind on the ground yet everywhere struck chill, with long cracks in the frozen cart-ruts and the earth, ashen white, cold and hard as ice.

After standing outside the cinema for a while Xiangzi began to feel cold, but he didn't want to go back to the teahouse. He preferred to stand here quietly all by himself and think. That encounter with the old man and his grandson had destroyed his fondest hope, for that rickshaw of the old man's was his own! From the very first day that Xiangzi pulled a rickshaw, he had made up his mind to buy one of his own and he was still going all out to reach this goal. He had believed that once he owned a rickshaw he would have everything. Well, just look at that old man!

Wasn't it for this same reason that he didn't want to marry Tigress? He had thought that with a rickshaw of his own he could put money by and take a wife with a clear conscience. Well, just look at Little Horse! If he had a son, the child might end up like that too!

Looking at it in this light, he saw no reason to resist Tigress' threats. Since he was caught anyway in this vicious circle, what difference did it make what kind of wife he married? Besides, she might bring a few rickshaws with her, so why not take it easy at her expense for a change? Once you've seen through yourself there's no need to despise other people. Tigress was Tigress, and that was that.

The film show had finished now. Hurriedly he fixed the little can of water on the lamp and lit it. He stripped off even his inner padded jacket and stood there in his shirt. He wanted to run as fast as he could so as to forget everything. If he fell and killed himself what did it matter?

CHAPTER 11

*W*HEN he thought of the old man and Little Horse, Xiangzi gave up hope and decided to enjoy himself while he could. Why grit his teeth all day and drive himself so hard? It seemed to him that the fate of the poor was like a jujube kernel, pointed at both ends and round in the middle: if you were lucky enough not to die of hunger as a child, you could hardly escape starving to death in your old age. Only during the middle period, when you were young and strong, able to put up with hunger and hard work, could you live like a human being. You'd be a real fool not to make the most of this time and enjoy yourself, for this was like the last hostel in the last village; you wouldn't get another chance! Seen this way, even Tigress and her affairs weren't worth worrying about.

Yet when he saw his pottery money-box he would change his mind again. No, he couldn't let himself go; only a couple of dozen dollars more and he would have enough for a rickshaw. He mustn't let his previous efforts be wasted; mustn't carelessly throw away those hard-earned savings of his! He must keep to the straight and narrow path, no doubt about it. But Tigress? That hateful twenty-seventh still preyed on his mind.

When he felt completely hopeless, he would hug his money-box to his chest and mumble, "Come what may, at any rate this money is mine! No one can take it away! With money, I'm not afraid of anything. If you push me too far, I'll up and away. With money you can get around."

The streets were growing livelier all the time, with displays everywhere of candy made into the shape of melons to honour the Kitchen God, and cries of "Malt candy!" resounding on every side. Xiangzi had been looking forward to the New

Year, but now it left him quite cold. The busier the streets the more tense he became. That fateful twenty-seventh was just round the corner! His eyes became sunken and even the scar on his face darkened.

When he took out the rickshaw, he had to be extra careful on the crowded slippery streets. At the same time, his own problem preoccupied him so that he felt unable to cope with both at once. The thought of one made him forgot the other, and then with a start he would tingle like a child coming out with prickly heat in summer.

On the afternoon of the day to make offerings to the Kitchen God, a gusty east wind blew dark clouds over the sky and it suddenly turned warmer. Nearing lamp-lighting time, the wind dropped and it began to snow sparsely. The vendors of candy melons became very worried, for fear that the warmth and the snow would make their wares stick together. They frantically sprinkled white powder over them. Not many snowflakes fell; soon they turned into tiny granules which swished softly down till the ground was covered with white.

After seven o'clock they began, in shops and homes, to make their offerings to the Kitchen God. The fine snow went on falling amid the glow of incense and the intermittent flashes of fire-crackers, adding a sombre note to the festive atmosphere.

The people walking or riding through the streets all had an anxious look, for they were in a hurry to get home to make their offerings yet dared not go fast on the slippery roads. The candy vendors, hoping to dispose of their stock before this feast day was over, were shouting and touting their wares at the top of their voices, with hardly a pause for breath. It was all very lively.

At about nine o'clock, Xiangzi was pulling Mr. Cao back from the West City. Having passed the busiest section around Xidan Arch, they turned east into Changan Street and the road gradually became less crowded. The wide, flat, tarmac surface was covered with a thin layer of snow, a dazzling white under the street lamps. Now and then a car would go by, its headlights probing far ahead and turning the small granules of snow yellow, like a shower of golden sand. Near Xinhua Gate, the

wide street thinly covered with snow seemed to stretch away
to infinity, and everything around took on a more solemn air.
Changan Arch, the gate tower of Xinhua Gate and the red
walls of Nanhai were all wearing white caps which contrasted
with their ruby pillars and red walls. Still and quiet, under
the glow of the street lamps, they displayed all the stateliness
of this ancient capital. The time and place made it seem as if
Beiping were uninhabited, composed solely of sumptuous halls
and palaces with a few ancient pines silently receiving the falling snow.

Xiangzi had no eyes for the lovely scenery, for gazing down the
imperial highway all he could think of was getting home as fast
as possible. In his mind's eye he could see the Caos' gate at the
other end of the straight, white, quiet street. But he couldn't
put on speed because the snow, though not deep, stuck to his
shoes and soon formed a thick layer on his soles. He stamped
it off but it quickly accumulated again. The heavy snow par-
ticles also blinded him, preventing him from running fast. His
shoulders were white with unmelted snow and, though it was
nothing, the dampness irked him. Although there were no shops
in the area, fire-crackers were still being let off in the distance,
and every now and then the darkness would be lit up by a
double-explosion rocket or one of those known as "Five Dev-
ils Resisting Judgement". As the sparks died away, the sky
seemed darker than ever, even frighteningly black. Xiangzi
heard the crackers, saw the sparks and the darkness and longed
to get home right away. But he could not lengthen his stride
and put on speed. It was exasperating.

What annoyed him most was that, all the way from the West
City, he was conscious that a cyclist was following him. On
West Changan Street, where it was quieter, he could even hear
its tyres crunching softly over the snow. Like all rickshaw
pullers, Xiangzi loathed bicycles. Cars were bad enough, but
were so noisy that you could get out of their way while still
a long distance off. But bicycles veered now east now west,
weaving through the traffic in a way that made you dizzy to
watch. And you had better not collide with one, because any
trouble was always the rickshaw man's fault, as the police in-

variably laid the blame on him, feeling that rickshaw men were easier to push around than cyclists.

Several times tonight, Xiangzi had felt like stopping suddenly and throwing the fellow behind him, but he did not dare. Rickshaw pullers had to put up with all kinds of treatment. So each time he stopped to stamp the snow off his feet he called out, "Stopping!" The street in front of Nanhai Gate was very wide yet the bicycle still tagged behind him. In mounting irritation, Xiangzi deliberately pulled up to brush the snow off his shoulders. As he stood there, the bicycle brushed past the rickshaw and its rider even turned to look at them. Xiangzi purposely took his time, waiting until the cyclist was a good distance away before picking up the shafts again.

"Confound him!" he swore.

Mr. Cao's "humanitarianism" made him unwilling to put up a cotton-padded hood and wind-breaker over the seat of his rickshaw and he only allowed the canvas hood to be put up if it was raining hard, to save his puller's energy. In this light snowfall he saw no need to unfold the hood, wanting, moreover, to feast his eyes on the snowy night scene. He, too, had noticed the bicycle and after Xiangzi swore at the cyclist he said in a low voice, "If he continues to tail us, don't stop at home but go to Mr. Zuo's place by Huanghua Gate. Don't get flustered!"

Xiangzi really was a bit flustered. He had always hated cyclists but had never thought them anything to be afraid of. If Mr. Cao daren't go home, there must be something sinister about this one! He hadn't run more than several dozen paces when he caught up with the cyclist who was waiting for them. As he passed him, Xiangzi saw at a glance that he was a member of the secret police. He had often run into them in teahouses and, though he had never spoken with any of them, he knew them by their bearing and style of dress. This fellow's get-up was familiar: a black padded gown and a felt hat, its brim pulled very low.

When they reached the cross-road at Nanchang Street and turned the corner, Xiangzi glanced quickly behind. The man was still following. He forgot the snow on the ground and put more strength into his stride. The long, straight road stretched white before him, lit here and there by cold street lamps and behind was a detective tailing him! This was something he had never experienced before and he broke out in a sweat. At the back gate of the park, he looked around, still there!

When they reached home he dared not stop, much as he wanted to, as Mr. Cao remained silent. He had to go on running north. In one breath he reached the northern end of the street, the bicycle still following! He turned down an alley, still there! Out of the alley, following still! As he reached the north end of the alley, he realized that this was not the way to Huanghua Gate and had to admit that he had lost his head which made him even angrier.

When they reached the back of Coal Hill, the bicycle turned north towards Houmen Gate. Xiangzi mopped his brow. The snow was falling less thickly and there were a few flakes amongst the granules. He loved snowflakes which fluttered gaily in the air, unlike those irritating little granules. He looked back and asked, "Where to, master?"

"Still to the Zuo house. If anyone asks you about me, say you don't know me."

"Yes, sir." Xiangzi's heart started thumping but he asked no further questions.

When they reached the Zuo house, Mr. Cao told Xiangzi to pull the rickshaw into the courtyard and quickly close the gate. He was very calm still but his face had lost colour. After giving these instructions he strode into the house. Xiangzi had just parked the rickshaw in the covered entrance-way when Mr. Cao came out with Mr. Zuo, a good friend of the Cao family.

"Xiangzi," Mr. Cao's lips were moving rapidly, "you're to go home by cab. Tell the mistress I'm here and tell them to come too, by cab. But call a different one; don't make the one you've taken wait for them. Got it? Fine! Tell the mistress to bring whatever she needs and those few scroll paintings from my study. Have you got that straight? I'm going to ring her right away, but I'm telling you too in case she gets excited and forgets. If she does, you can remind her."

"How about my going?" Mr. Zuo asked.

"There's no need. It's not certain that that fellow was a detective, but with this other business on my mind I have to take precautions. Would you ring for a taxi?"

Mr. Zuo went inside to telephone, while Mr. Cao gave Xiangzi some further instructions. "When the taxi comes I'll pay the driver. Tell the mistress to pack up quickly. The rest doesn't matter, but she must be sure to bring the child's things and those paintings in the study, those scroll paintings! When she's ready, let Gao Ma ring for a cab and come straight here. Have you got all that straight? When they've left, you lock the main gate and move into the study where the telephone is. Can you use a telephone?"

"Not to make calls, only to take them." In fact, Xiangzi disliked taking calls too, but he didn't want to add to Mr. Cao's worries.

"That's fine!" Mr. Cao was still speaking very fast. "If anything should happen, don't open the gate. With the rest of us gone and only you there they're sure to hang on to you. If things take an ugly turn, put out the light and jump over the back wall into the Wangs' yard. You know the Wang family, don't you? Right! Hide there a while before you leave. Never mind about my things or about your own, just jump over the wall and go before they nab you! If you lose anything I'll make it good to you later. Here's five dollars to be going on with. All right, I'm going to ring the mistress now, and when you get there you can repeat what I've said — but leave out the nabbing bit. That man just now may or may not be a detective. So don't lose your head."

Xiangzi's thoughts were in a whirl. There were many questions he wanted to ask but he didn't venture to, so anxious was he to remember all Mr. Cao's instructions.

The taxi came and Xiangzi got awkwardly in. The snow was still falling, neither heavy nor light, and everything outside the cab seemed unreal. He sat stiff and straight, his head nearly touching its top. He wanted to think but his eyes were drawn to the red arrow on the dash-board, so bright and attractive. Those windscreen wipers too before the driver, swinging back and forth of their own accord and wiping away the moisture on the glass were also very intriguing. Just as he was beginning to tire of watching them, the taxi stopped at the Caos' gate. Reluctantly he climbed out.

He was on the point of ringing the bell when a man appeared from nowhere, as if he had materialized out of the wall, and caught hold of Xiangzi's wrist. His first instinct was to wrench free, but he didn't move for he had already recognized the man. It was the detective on the bicycle.

"Xiangzi, don't you recognize me?" With a grin the man released him.

Xiangzi gulped, not knowing what to say.

"You've forgotten how we took you out to the Western Hills? I'm Lieutenant Sun, remember?"

"Ah, Lieutenant Sun!" Xiangzi didn't remember him. When the soldiers had dragged him off to the hills, he hadn't paid any attention to who was a lieutenant, who a captain.

"You don't remember me, but I remember you. That scar on your face is a good identification mark. Just now when I was tailing you all that way I couldn't be sure at first, but looked at from all sides there was no mistaking that scar!"

"Have you any business with me?" Again Xiangzi made a move to press the bell.

"Of course I have, and important business too! Why don't we go in and talk?" Lieutenant Sun, now a detective, raised his hand and pressed the bell.

"I'm busy!" Sweat broke out on Xiangzi's brow. Inwardly he was fuming, "Isn't it enough that I can't get away from him, do I have to ask him in too?"

"Don't get worked up. I'm here to do you a favour!" There was a faint smile on his face, a foxy smile. When Gao Ma opened the door, he strode in past her with a muttered "Excuse me!" And without giving Xiangzi a chance to say anything to her, he pulled him in and pointed to the gate-house. "Is this where you live?" He went in and glanced around. "Quite clean and cozy! Not a bad job you have!"

"What's your business? I'm in a hurry!" Xiangzi couldn't bear to listen to this drivel.

"Didn't I tell you it's important?" Detective Sun was still smiling but his voice was grim. "I'll give it to you straight. This Cao fellow is a member of the rebel party. When he's caught he'll be shot, and he can't get away! Now, we've had dealings with each other before, when you waited on me in the barracks. What's more, we both knock about the streets, so at the risk of heavy punishment I've come to tip you off. If you're one step too slow you'll be caught, because we're going to block all escapes and smoke them out, no one will get away! Why should fellows like us who sell our strength for a living get involved in such a compromising case? Don't you think I'm talking sense?"

"I'll never be able to face them again!" Xiangzi remembered Mr. Cao's instructions.

"Face who?" Detective Sun's mouth curved in a smile, but his eyes narrowed. "They've brought this on themselves, you haven't let them down. They've stuck out their necks and must take the consequences; it wouldn't be fair if we were dragged in too! To mention nothing else, could you stand three months in the lock-up in a black cell, accustomed as you are to living like a wild bird?

"Another thing, if they go to prison they have the money for bribes and won't do so badly. But you, mate, you have no dough so they're sure to rough you up. And this is nothing compared to the fact that, if they happen to have money and pull some strings, they'll get off with a few years in clink while you will be made the scapegoat when the officials can't wind up the case. You and me, we don't harm or offend anyone, how unfair to end up at the Tian Qiao execution ground with lead jujubes in our chests! Now you're smart and a smart fellow doesn't do something he knows he'll suffer for. Face them, ha! Let me tell you, mate, they've never done anything for us down-and-outs entitling them to look us in the face!"

Xiangzi was frightened. Remembering what he had suffered at the hands of those soldiers he could well picture what prison would be like. "Then I must clear off and not mind about them?"

"You mind about them, who's going to mind about you?"

Xiangzi could think of no reply. He remained stock-still until even his conscience felt clear. "All right, I'll go."

"Just like that?" Detective Sun laughed caustically.

Xiangzi was thrown into confusion once more.

"Xiangzi, old partner, how stupid can you get! I'm a detective, do you think I'd let you go?"

"Then . . ." Xiangzi was so frantic he didn't know what to say.

"Don't act dumb!" Detective Sun's eyes bored into him. "You probably have some savings, bring them out and buy your way out! I don't earn as much as you every month and I have to eat and dress and support a family, depending on the little I can make outside my regular pay. I'm talking to you frankly. Do you really expect to get out of my clutches like that? Friendship is friendship, and if I weren't your friend I wouldn't have come. But business is business. You expect me to come out of this empty-handed and let my family eat the northwest wind? We're both men of the world and don't have to waste words. Now what about it?"

"How much?" Xiangzi sat on his bed.

"As much as you have, there's no fixed price."

"I'd sooner go to prison!"

"Now *you* said that, don't be regretting it!" Detective Sun reached inside his padded gown. "Look at this, Xiangzi! I can arrest you right away and, if you resist, I'll shoot! If I nab you right away, you'll be stripped even of your clothes, not to mention money, when you get to prison. You're a smart fellow, figure it out yourself."

"If you have the time to squeeze me, why don't you squeeze Mr. Cao?" Xiangzi struggled for words.

"He's the principal offender. If I get him I receive a small reward, if I don't, it's my mistake. As for you, my stupid friend, letting you go would be like farting, shooting you like killing a bed-bug. Hand over the money and go your way; if not, see you at the execution ground! Come on, stop dithering and look smart — you're old enough! Besides, this bit of money won't be all mine, my mates each have to get their little cut and I don't know how many coppers will fall to me. Such a cheap price to pay for your life and you won't go along! Really you are the limit! How much money do you have?"

Xiangzi stood up, his brain bursting, his fists clenched.

"I'm warning you, raise a fist and that's the end of you. I've a whole gang of men outside. Come on, cough up the dough! I'm giving you face, so know when you're well off!" There was an ugly glint in Detective Sun's eyes.

"What wrong have I ever done to anyone?" There was a sob in Xiangzi's voice as he sat down again on the edge of the bed.

"You haven't wronged anyone, you just happen to be the one around! A man's fate is decided in his mother's womb, we're at the very bottom and that's that." Detective Sun shook his head as if deeply moved. "All right, take it that I'm wronging you and stop dithering!"

Xiangzi thought a while but could see no way out. With a shaking hand he reached inside his quilt and brought out his pottery gourd.

"Let me see!" Detective Sun grinned and, pouncing on the gourd, smashed it against the wall.

Xiangzi watched the coins scatter over the floor and felt his heart was bursting.

"Is that all?"

Xiangzi said nothing. All he could do was shiver.

"All right then! I don't want to drive a man too hard, a friend is a friend! And make no mistake, you've had a real bargain, buying your life with this little sum!"

Still Xiangzi said nothing. Shivering, he started to roll up his bedding.

"Don't touch that!"

"It's so cold. . . ." Xiangzi glared at him with flaming eyes.

"I told you not to touch, so hands off! Now get out!"

Xiangzi gulped, bit his lips, then pushed open the door and went out.

There was already more than an inch of snow on the ground. Xiangzi walked with his head bowed. Everything was clean and white, except for the big black footprints he left behind him.

CHAPTER 12

*X*IANGZI wanted to find a place to sit down and mull things over. Even if he only ended up by crying, at least he would know why. Events had moved too fast for his mind to keep up. But there was nowhere to sit, everything was covered with snow. All the little teahouses were boarded up as it was after ten, and had one been open he wouldn't have gone in anyway. He wanted to find somewhere quiet, because he knew that his tear-filled eyes would brim over any minute.

With no place to sit, he had best walk slowly on; but where should he go? In all this silver world there was no place for him to sit, nowhere for him to go. In this expanse of whiteness, there were only starving little birds and a man at a dead end sighing in despair.

Where to go? This was the problem on which to concentrate first. To a small inn? That wouldn't do. Dressed as he was, he might be robbed during the night, and anyway he shrank from all the lice there. A bigger inn then? He couldn't afford it. All he had in the world was five dollars. A bath-house? They closed at midnight, one couldn't spend the night there. There was nowhere to go.

This fact brought home to him the straits he was in. After so many years in town, here he was with just the clothes on his back and five dollars in his pocket. He had even lost his bedding! From this his thoughts turned to tomorrow: what should he do then? Still pull a rickshaw? Huh, that would land him up homeless again, robbed of his meagre savings.

Suppose he became a hawker? With only five dollars capital, out of which he'd have to buy a carrying-pole, how could he be sure of earning his keep this way? A rickshaw man, starting

114

with nothing, could make thirty to forty cents a day; but a peddler needed capital, and there was no guarantee that he could earn enough for three meals a day. If he sank his capital in this only to end up pulling a rickshaw again, it would be like stripping off his pants to fart — a complete waste of five dollars. No, he couldn't lightly let go of a single cent of these five dollars for they were his last hope.

A job as a servant, then? That wasn't in his line. Waiting on people? He just couldn't do it. Washing and cooking? He didn't know how to either. He had no training, no skills, he was just a big, bungling, useless lout!

Quite unawares, he had reached the bridge over the Zhonghai Lake. It stretched away on either side with nothing to be seen but a flurry of snowflakes. Only now did he realize that it was still snowing and, feeling his head, he found his woollen cap wet. The bridge was deserted, even the policeman on duty had disappeared somewhere. The falling snow made the few street lamps appear to be blinking. Xiangzi looked around, his mind blank.

For a long time he stood there, and the world seemed dead. There was not a sound; nothing stirred. The grey-white snow seemed to be taking this chance to flurry lightly and persistently down, to bury the whole world surreptitiously.

In the stillness, Xiangzi heard his conscience whisper: "Never mind about yourself, go back first to see how the Cao family is." Mrs. Cao and Gao Ma were alone there, without a man in the house. Wasn't it Mr. Cao who had given him these last five dollars? Not daring to stop to debate it with himself, he started back, striding swiftly.

Outside the gate there were footprints and on the road two fresh tracks made by a car. Had Mrs. Cao left? Why hadn't that Sun fellow arrested them?

He was afraid to open the gate in case he got caught. But there was no one about. His heart thumping, he decided to try it and see. Anyway, he had nowhere to go; if they arrested him it was just too bad. Gently he pushed the door, which unexpectedly opened. Hugging the wall, he advanced a few steps and saw a light in his room. His own room! A sob welled up in his throat. Stooping, he crept over and listened outside the window. There was a cough inside — it sounded like Gao Ma! He pulled open the door.

"Who's there? Heavens, it's you! You frightened me to death!" Gao Ma pressed her hands to her heart, then composed herself and sat down on the bed. "Xiangzi, what happened to you?"

Xiangzi could not reply. He felt as if years had passed since last he saw her, and there was a ball of fire blocking his chest.

"What's happened?" There were tears in Gao Ma's voice. "Before you got back, the master phoned and told us to go to the Zuo house. He also said you were coming back right away. You came back all right, didn't I open the door for you? When I saw you had a stranger with you, I didn't say a word but hurried back to help the mistress pack. You didn't come in once.

"There we were, the mistress and I, groping around in the dark. The young master was already sound asleep and we had to pull him out of his warm covers. The bags were ready, the paintings taken from the study and still no sign of you. Where were you? When we'd packed up as best we could, I came out to find you and, well, you'd vanished! The mistress was so angry — so upset too — that she kept trembling. So I called for a taxi. But we couldn't all go, leaving no one to keep an eye on things. So I swore to the mistress I'd stay and told her to go first. I said that when you came back I'd join them right away at the Zuo house. If you didn't come back, well, that was my bad luck. What have you to say for yourself? What happened to you? Speak up!"

Xiangzi had nothing to say.

"Say something! What are you staring at? What really did happen?"

"You'd better go!" Xiangzi finally found his voice. "Go!"

"You're staying on to watch the house?" Gao Ma had cooled down a bit.

"When you see the master, tell him that the detective nabbed me, but then — but then he didn't after all!"

"What does that mean?" Gao Ma almost laughed in her exasperation.

"Listen!" Xiangzi himself was getting heated now. "You tell the master to get away as quickly as possible. The detective said he was going to arrest him for sure. The Zuo house is no safe place either. Get away as quickly as possible! After you've gone, I'll jump over into the Wangs' yard and spend the night there. I'll lock the front gate here. Tomorrow, I'll go and look for a job. I've let the master down."

"The more you say the more muddled I get!" Gao Ma sighed. "All right, I'm going. The young master may have caught cold; I must go and see. When I see the master I'll tell him Xiangzi says he must get away as fast as he can. Tonight Xiangzi will lock the front door, jump over the wall into the Wangs' yard and spend the night there. Tomorrow he'll find another job. Did I get that right?"

In great shame, Xiangzi nodded.

When Gao Ma had left, he locked the front gate and returned to his room. The shattered pottery gourd lay on the ground. He picked up a few pieces and looked at them, then threw them down again. On the bed, his bedding was untouched. Strange, what did this mean? Could Detective Sun be a fake? Impossible! If Mr. Cao hadn't smelt danger, would he have abandoned his home and fled like this? He didn't understand this business at all.

Not knowing what he did, he sat down on the edge of the bed, yet barely had he touched the boards when he started up again. He mustn't stay here long! What if that fellow Sun came back again! His thoughts were in a whirl. He had let Mr. Cao down, but it wasn't so bad now that Gao Ma was taking the message telling him to get away as fast as he could. His conscience was clear. He had never deliberately done for anyone, but he'd had a raw deal himself. With his own money gone, he couldn't worry about Mr. Cao's any more. Muttering all this to himself, he gathered his bedding together.

Hoisting his bedding-roll on to his shoulders, he put out the light and hurried to the backyard. He put down his bedding, then pulled himself up to look over the top of the wall.

"Old Cheng!" he called softly. "Old Cheng!" Old Cheng was the Wangs' rickshaw man.

When there was no answer, he decided to jump over the wall and see what happened. He threw his bedding over and it landed soundlessly on the snow. His heart thumping, he quickly climbed up on to the wall and jumped down on the other side. Having picked up his bedding, he quietly headed for Old Cheng's room which he knew. Everyone seemed to be asleep, there was not a sound in the courtyard. It suddenly occurred to him how easy it was to be a thief. He plucked up courage and stepped more confidently across the firm snow, which crunched beneath his feet. Standing outside Old Cheng's room, he coughed. Old Cheng had evidently just gone to bed.

"Who's there?" he asked.

"It's me, Xiangzi. Open the door!"

Xiangzi spoke as naturally and cordially as if, in Old Cheng's voice, he had heard reassurance from someone dear to him.

Old Cheng turned on the light, threw a tattered fur-lined jacket over his shoulders, and opened the door. "What brings you here, Xiangzi, at this hour of the night?"

Xiangzi went in, put his bedding on the floor and plumped himself down on it, all without a word.

Old Cheng was in his early thirties and his muscles were so strong they bulged in knots all over his body and even on his face. Normally, Xiangzi had little to do with him, but when they met they would greet each other and chat. Sometimes, Mrs. Wang would go shopping with Mrs. Cao, giving the two men a chance to drink tea and rest together.

Xiangzi did not particularly admire Old Cheng because, though he ran very fast, he jolted the rickshaw instead of keeping his hands steady on the shafts. Although as a person he was fine, this failing of his made it out of the question for Xiangzi to respect him whole-heartedly.

But tonight, Xiangzi felt Old Cheng thoroughly admirable. Though he sat there speechless, his heart was full of warmth and gratitude. A while ago, he had stood on the bridge at Zhonghai, now here he was in this room with his mate. The speed of this change made him feel blank and somewhat feverish.

Old Cheng crawled back under his quilt, pointed to his tattered leather jacket and said, "Have a smoke, Xiangzi. There are some in the pocket."

Xiangzi didn't smoke, but this time he felt he couldn't refuse. He took a cigarette and started to puff.

"What's happened?" Old Cheng asked. "Left your job?"

"No." Xiangzi still sat on his bedding. "There's been trouble. The whole Cao family has run away and I don't dare to watch the house all alone."

"What trouble?" Old Cheng sat up again.

"Can't say for sure, but it's pretty bad. Even Gao Ma has gone!"

"All the doors wide open, and no one in charge?"

"I've locked the main gate."

"Hum." Old Cheng thought for a moment. "What do you say to my telling Mr. Wang?" He made as if to get dressed.

"Wait till tomorrow — I simply can't explain!" Xiangzi was afraid Mr. Wang would question him.

What Xiangzi had no means of explaining was this: Mr. Cao gave a few lectures each week in a certain university. He had offended the educational authorities who, to teach him a lesson, had accused him of being a radical.

Now Mr. Cao had got wind of this but thought it ridiculous. He knew he was not a thoroughgoing progressive and that his hobby — collecting traditional paintings — prevented him from taking any strong action. How ridiculous, to be labelled as one of the revolutionary party! So he did not take the business seriously, though his students and colleagues all warned him to be careful. However, in troubled times, keeping calm is no guarantee of security.

The winter vacation provided an excellent opportunity for cleaning up the university. Detectives set about making investigations and arrests. Several times, Mr. Cao had sensed that he was being tailed and this shadow behind him turned his amusement to fear. He went to see Mr. Zuo.

Mr. Zuo proposed, "If need arise, you can move in with me. They wouldn't go so far yet as to search *my* place!" Mr. Zuo had important connections, which counted for more than the law. "You come here for a few days and lie low, to show we're afraid of them. Then we can start smoothing things out. You may have to grease a few palms. Show them enough respect and buy them off, then you can go home and they should leave you in peace."

Detective Sun knew that Mr. Cao often visited the Zuo house and that he was sure to go there if hard pressed. The secret police dared not molest Mr. Zuo, they were just out to frighten Mr. Cao. Only by chasing him into the Zuo house could they hope to milk him and feel that they had face. Fleecing Xiangzi had not been part of their plans, but as they had run into him and it was no extra trouble, why not first shake him down for eight or ten dollars?

That was life, everyone had a way out, could find a loophole somewhere except for Xiangzi — he could not escape, because he was a rickshaw puller. A rickshaw puller swallows husks but spits out his life's blood, he strains his utmost for the lowest pittance. He stands on the lowest rung of society, the butt of all men, all laws, all adversities.

By the time he finished his cigarette, Xiangzi still had not figured things out. He was like a chicken grasped by a cook, unable to think of anything, thankful only for each extra minute of life. He longed to talk things over with Old Cheng, but there was nothing he could say for words were inadequate to express his feelings. So in spite of all his bitter experiences, he remained mute. He had bought a rickshaw and lost it, saved money and lost it, all his efforts ending up in his being bullied and humiliated. He dared not provoke anyone, even had to make way for wild dogs. And yet here he was so browbeaten that he could hardly breathe.

There was no point in dwelling on the past, but what about tomorrow? He couldn't go back to the Caos' house, so where should he go? "Can I spend the night here?" he asked, like a stray dog that has found a corner out of the wind and hopes to make do with it for the time being. But even in a little thing like that, he must be sure not to get in anyone's way.

"Sure, stay here, where else is there to go in this snow? Will you be all right on the floor? We can squeeze up together on the bed if you'd like."

Xiangzi didn't want to crowd him. He said the floor would be fine.

Old Cheng fell asleep, but Xiangzi tossed and turned in wakefulness. The cold draught on the floor quickly froze his mattress into a sheet of iron, and in the calves of his curled up legs he felt cramp coming on. The cold wind blowing through the cracks of the door pierced his head like countless needles. In desperation he closed his eyes and covered his head, yet still he couldn't sleep. The sound of Old Cheng's breathing filled him with irritation, and he felt the only way to relieve his feelings would be to jump up and to pummel him. As it grew colder and colder his throat itched, yet he was afraid to waken Old Cheng by coughing.

Unable to drop off, he thought of getting up surreptitiously and going back to the Cao house to have a look round. His job was gone, the place was empty; why shouldn't he go and take some things? Because of them, he'd been robbed of his hard-earned savings; it was only right, surely, for them to reimburse him? His eyes gleamed; he forgot the cold, he must get cracking! Such an easy way to get back his hard-earned money, what was keeping him?

He had already sat up, but then he hurriedly lay down again as if Old Cheng had seen him. His heart thumped. No, how could he become a thief? It was bad enough not following Mr. Cao's instructions and washing his hands of the whole business, how could he steal from his master too? No, no, he'd starve to death rather than steal!

But how could he be sure that others wouldn't rob the place? If that Sun fellow had taken something, who was to know? Again he sat up. In the distance, a dog barked a few times. He lay down once more. No, he still couldn't go. If others stole, well, let them, *his* conscience was clear. Poor as he was, he mustn't dirty his hands by theft.

Besides, Gao Ma knew he had come to the Wangs' house. If anything got lost during the night, he would be blamed whether he had stolen or not. Now, not only was he unwilling to steal himself, he was afraid that someone else might break in. Should anything be lost, he would never succeed in clearing himself, not if he jumped into the Yellow River!

No longer did he feel cold, in fact his palms were sweating slightly. What should he do? Jump over the wall and take a look? He daren't. He had given money for his life, he couldn't throw himself into another trap. But what if something got lost?

In a dilemma, he sat up again, his legs drawn up, his face nearly touching his knees. His head kept nodding and his eyes kept closing, but now he dared not sleep. Long as the night was, for him there was no time to rest.

How long he sat there he didn't know, considering one plan after another. Suddenly he had a brain-wave and reached out to shake Old Cheng. "Old Cheng! Old Cheng! Wake up!"

"What's the matter?" Old Cheng was loath to open his eyes. "Want to piss? The urinal's under the bed."

"Wake up, put on the light!"

"Thieves?" Old Cheng sat up in a daze.

"Are you wide-awake?"

"Hmm!"

"Old Cheng, look! This is my bedding, these are my clothes and here are the five dollars Mr. Cao gave me. Nothing else is there?"

"No. What's up?" Old Cheng yawned.

"Are you wide-awake? This is all I've got. I haven't taken a needle from the Caos!"

"Of course you haven't. How can we fellows who've always worked on a monthly basis for good families filch from them? If we can work, we work; if not, we quit. How can we steal their things? Is that what you're talking about?"

"Did you get a good look?"

Old Cheng smiled. "No mistake! I say, aren't you cold?"

"I'm all right."

CHAPTER 13

BECAUSE of the gleaming snow, the sky seemed to lighten earlier than usual. And as many families had bought poultry to keep for the New Year, more cocks were crowing than usual. The cackling of fowls everywhere and the new fall of snow seemed to promise abundance in the year to come.

Xiangzi, however, had hardly slept all night. In the early hours of the morning, he managed to doze off a couple of times, but it was an uneasy half-sleep as if he were floating up and down on some waves. He grew colder and colder until, by the time the cocks started crowing, he simply couldn't stand it any longer. Not wanting to disturb Old Cheng, he curled up his legs and covered his mouth with his quilt to muffle his coughing, but still he dared not get up. He stuck it out, waiting impatiently. Finally dawn broke and from the streets came the sound of carts and the cries of the drivers. He sat up.

As he still felt cold, he got up, buttoned his jacket and opened the door a crack to peep out. The snow wasn't very thick — it had probably stopped falling in the middle of the night. The weather seemed to have cleared but the sky was greyish and indistinct, there even appeared to be a faint grey shadow over the snow. His eye was caught by the large footprints he had made the night before. Although covered by snow the hollows still showed clearly.

Partly in order to find something to do and partly to wipe out his tracks, he quietly picked up a small broom from one corner of the room and went out to sweep away the snow. It was heavy and not easy to sweep, for he didn't know where the large bamboo broom was kept and therefore had to bend very low and sweep hard. He cleared away the top layer but there remained some which seemed to cling to the ground. He straightened up twice in the course of sweeping the whole outer courtyard, and finally piled the snow at the base of two small willow trees. By now he was perspiring and felt warmer and more limber. He stamped his feet and exhaled a long, white breath.

Returning indoors, he replaced the broom and decided to roll up his bedding. Old Cheng who had woken was yawning. His mouth still agape he mumbled, "Is it late?" Then he rubbed the sleep from his eyes and fished out a cigarette from the pocket of his fur-lined jacket. A puff or two and he was wide-awake. "Don't go yet, Xiangzi. Wait till I fetch some boiling water and we'll have a nice hot pot of tea. That must have been some night!"

"Let me go for the water," Xiangzi offered amiably. But hardly had he spoken when the terror of the previous night came back to him and his heart suddenly contracted.

"No, I'll go, after all you're my guest!" As he spoke, Old Cheng threw on his clothes without fastening the buttons, then slinging his tattered jacket over one shoulder he ran out, his cigarette between his lips. "Why, you've swept the courtyard! Good for you! You really must stay for a drink!"

Xiangzi began to feel a bit easier.

After a while, Old Cheng returned with two large bowls of sweet gruel and a whole lot of little "horse-hoof" buns and crispy fritters. "I haven't made tea, let's have some congee first. Come on, tuck in. If it's not enough, I'll buy more or get some on credit. Those who do heavy work mustn't stint themselves of food. Tuck in!"

By now it was completely light and the room was clear and bright. Holding their bowls in both hands, they smacked their lips as they lapped up the congee. Neither said a word and, in no time at all, the buns and fritters were gone.

"Well?" Old Cheng picked a sesame seed from between his teeth.

"I must be going." Xiangzi looked at his bedding on the floor.

"Tell me what's up. After all, I still don't understand." Old Cheng offered him a cigarette but Xiangzi shook his head.

On second thoughts, he felt ashamed to keep anything back from Old Cheng. So, haltingly, he stammered out the whole story of the previous night. It cost him a great effort, but he virtually left nothing out.

For some time Old Cheng digested his story in silence, his lips pursed. "The way I see it, you still have to find Mr. Cao. You can't let it go at that, and you can't lose your money just like that! Didn't you say that Mr. Cao's instructions were to make a break if things looked bad? Well, it's not your fault that the detective nabbed you the moment that you got out of the cab. It's not that you sold out, but that devil pounced so fast, of course you had to save your own skin first. I don't see that you let him down in any way. Go and find Mr. Cao and tell him all about it from start to finish. I don't think he can blame you, and with luck he may even refund you your money. Go on, leave your bedding here and look him up bright and early. The days are short, the sun comes up at eight, hurry up and get a move on!"

Xiangzi's thoughts were in a whirl. Though he still felt he had let Mr. Cao down, what Old Cheng said sounded very reasonable — when a detective threatened him with a gun, how could he worry about the Caos' affairs?

"Off you go," Old Cheng urged him again. "Last night I could see you were a bit befuddled. No one can guarantee to keep his head in a tight spot. I'm sure this way of mine will work; after all, I'm older than you and have seen more of life. Off you go, look, the sun's come out!"

The morning sunlight, reflected by the snow, bathed the whole city in light. Between the bright blue sky above the gleaming white snow below, everything was a golden shimmer so dazzling that one could scarcely open one's eyes. Xiangzi was on the point of leaving when someone knocked at the gate.

Old Cheng went out to see who it was, and called from the gateway, "Xiangzi, someone looking for you."

It was Wang Er from the Zuo household. He was stamping the snow from his feet and his nose, red with cold, was running.

When Xiangzi came out Old Cheng urged them both, "Let's all go inside and sit down." All three went into his room.

"Well, it's like this," Wang Er rubbed his hands. "I've come to look after the house. How do I get in? The gate's locked. Um, it sure is cold after the snow! Well, Mr. and Mrs. Cao left first thing this morning for Tianjin, or maybe Shanghai, can't say for sure. Mr. Zuo sent me to look after the house. Um, beastly cold!"

Xiangzi suddenly felt like bursting into tears. Just as he was on the point of following Old Cheng's advice, Mr. Cao left. At first he was dumbfounded, then he asked, "Didn't Mr. Cao say anything about me?"

"Uh, no. Up before daybreak they were, in too much of a rush to say anything. The train, well, it left at seven forty. Um, how am I to get into the next compound?" Wang Er was in a hurry.

"Jump over the wall!" Xiangzi glanced at Old Cheng as if he were handing Wang Er over to him. He picked up his bedding-roll.

"Where're you going?" Old Cheng asked.

"Harmony Yard, I've nowhere else to go!" All Xiangzi's bitterness, shame and hopelessness were packed into this one sentence. There was no other way out — he had to throw in the sponge. All roads were closed to him, he could only head through the white snow towards that black tower — Tigress. His self-respect and urge to better himself, his loyalty and integrity — all were quite useless. He was fated to lead a dog's life.

Old Cheng followed up with, "You go your way. Here's Wang Er to bear witness, you haven't touched a single thing belonging to the Caos. Go along then, and whenever you pass this way drop in for a chat. I may have heard of some good job I could recommend you for. After you've left, I'll help Wang Er get over next door. Is there coal there?"

"Coal and kindling all in the shed in the backyard." Xiangzi hoisted his bedding-roll on to his shoulder.

The snow on the streets was no longer so white. Tamped down on the tarmac by the wheels of cars it looked more like ice. On the dirt roads, the pity was that horse hooves had splodged black marks over the white. Xiangzi, his mind a blank, trudged on with his bedding-roll. Without pausing for breath he walked straight to Harmony Yard. He dared not stop at the gate, for if he did he knew he would never have the courage to enter. So he strode directly in, his face burning hot.

He had already thought up what to say to Tigress, "Here I am. Do as you see fit, it's all the same to me — I'm stumped!" When he saw her, however, although he repeated this several times to himself he couldn't somehow bring himself to say it.

Tigress had just got up, her hair was tousled, her eyelids were slightly swollen. And her dark face was all over goose-flesh, just like a frozen plucked chicken.

"Ha! You've come back!" she cried fondly, her eyes brightening.

"Rent me a rickshaw!" Xiangzi kept his head down, his eyes fixed on the unmelted snow on the tips of his shoes.

"Speak to the old man," she replied in a low voice and pouted in the direction of the east room.

Fourth Master Liu was drinking tea in his room. Before him was a large white stove from which flames six inches high were leaping. When he saw Xiangzi come in, he said half-crossly, half-jokingly, "Still alive and kicking, eh? Forgotten me I suppose! Let's see, how long is it since last you were here? How's the job? Bought your rickshaw yet?"

Xiangzi shook his head. A pang shot through his heart. "I still need a rickshaw, Fourth Master."

"Hum, lost your job again? All right, go and pick yourself one." He poured a cup of tea. "Come and have a drink first."

Xiangzi lifted the bowl and gulped down the contents. He was standing in front of the stove and its fierce heat on top of the scalding tea made him feel a little sleepy. He had put down the bowl and was going out when the old man called him back.

"Wait a bit, what's the hurry? You've come at just the right time. The twenty-seventh is my birthday, I plan to put up a marquee and throw a party. You may as well help out for a few days, so don't start pulling yet. "Those fellows," Fourth

Master Liu pointed towards the yard, "are none of them trustworthy. I don't want them messing about, so you help out. Don't wait to be told, just do what needs to be done. First go and sweep up the snow. For lunch, I'll treat you to a meat dip."

"Right away, Fourth Master!" Xiangzi didn't care any more. Since he had come back here it was all up to father and daughter. Let them do what they liked with him, he was resigned to his fate.

"Didn't I tell you?" Tigress, judging it the right moment, came into the room. "I said Xiangzi was the best, that the others weren't quite up to it."

Fourth Master Liu smiled, and Xiangzi bent his head even lower.

"Come here, Xiangzi!" Tigress called him out of the room. "Here's money to buy brooms with first. Get bamboo ones, easier to sweep snow with. You'll have to hurry, the men will be coming today to put up the marquee." She led him into her room where she counted out some money, at the same time whispering, "Come on, look spry! Try and butter the old man up! Then our business will have a chance."

Xiangzi said nothing nor did he get angry. He felt dead to the world, his mind no longer working. Just drag on from day to day. If there was food and drink he would eat and drink, if there was work he would do it. If he kept himself busy, in no time the day would have passed. Better still, he should learn from the donkey pulling the grindstone, plodding round and round, ignorant of everything else. He realized that, no matter what, he could never be really happy. Though he refused to think, speak or lose his temper, his heart was always heavy. While working he could forget this for a while, but whenever he had a spare moment he was conscious of something, soft yet very bulky, something tasteless yet choking as sponge blocking up his heart. With this suffocating him, he forced himself to work, hoping to wear himself out so that he could fall into an exhausted sleep. His nights he made over to dreams, his days to work — as if he were a zombie. He swept snow, went shopping, ordered kerosene lamps, washed rickshaws, moved tables and chairs, ate the food provided by Fourth Master Liu and slept, all without knowing what he did, without saying a word, without a thought in his head, but always dimly aware of the pressure of that sponge.

The snow on the ground was swept up, that on the roofs had gradually melted away. With cries of "Up we go!" the man putting up the marquee climbed on to the roof to erect the framework. They had orders to make a marquee the size of the whole courtyard with eaves, balustrades and glass windows on three sides so that it could be heated. Inside there would be glass partitions and hanging painted screens, while the poles were to be covered with red cloth. The main gate and side gates were to be hung with bright streamers; the kitchen would be set up in the backyard. Fourth Master Liu was determined, as this was his sixty-ninth birthday, to have a really lively celebration. The first step was, of course, to have a handsome marquee. Because winter days are short, the builders only had time to put up the framework, the balustrades and the cloth hangings. The interior decorations and the coloured streamers over the gates had to be left till the next morning. This infuriated Old Liu, who bawled at the builders until he was red in the face and dispatched Xiangzi to make sure that the kerosene lamps and the cook would be there on time. Actually, there was no possibility of anything going wrong, but the old man was anxious.

No sooner was Xiangzi back from this errand than Fourth Master Liu ordered him to go and borrow three or four sets of mahjong, for on the great day they were going to have a good gamble. Then he was sent to borrow a gramophone, for a birthday party called for a cheerful racket. Xiangzi was on the go until eleven that night. Accustomed as he was to pulling a rickshaw, he found running about with empty hands even more tiring. On the way back from his last errand, even he could hardly lift his feet.

"You're quite a guy! Really good! If I had a son like you, I'd be willing to live a few years less. Turn in now. Tomorrow will be a busy day."

Tigress who was standing by winked at Xiangzi.

The next morning, the builders arrived to finish the job. The painted screens were hung up. They depicted the three battles against Lü Bu, the Changban Slope, the burning of the united forces' camp and other scenes from the *Romance of the Three Kingdoms*.* The figures were made up as if on the stage and were all on horseback and wielding swords and lances. Old Man Liu craned his neck to look them over, and was very satisfied.

Shortly after, the furnishers arrived and installed eight tables and sets of chairs and stools in the marquee. The chair covers and the cushions for the stools were embroidered with bright red flowers. An altar to the God of Longevity was set up in the hall with cloisonné incense-burners and candle-sticks. Four red rugs were placed before it. Then Old Man Liu sent Xiangzi off to get apples, and Tigress slipped him two dollars to buy longevity peaches made of dough as well as longevity noodles. She told him that each peach must have one of the Eight Immortals shown on it. These were to be his own gift.

Xiangzi bought the apples and set them out on the altar. When, presently, the longevity peaches and noodles arrived he placed them behind the apples. The peaches, painted red, each had one of the Eight Immortals stuck on top and really looked most distinguished.

"These are from Xiangzi — see how thoughtful he is!" Tigress sang his praise to her father, and the old man smiled at him.

The big character "Longevity" which should hang in the middle of the back wall was still missing. According to custom, this should be presented by friends, not provided by the host. However, as yet no one had sent one and Fourth Master Liu, being testy, was ready to blow his top again. "I've always been the first to chip in towards other people's parties and funerals," he fumed. "Now when it's my turn they leave me in the lurch, the mother-fuckers!"

"Tomorrow's the twenty-sixth and the guests won't be coming till then, so what's the hurry?" Tigress called over to placate him.

---

* A famous Chinese historical novel by Luo Guanzhong (late 14th and early 15th century).

"I'd like to make everything ready in one go. This doing things bit by bit gets on my nerves! Hey, Xiangzi, the kerosene lamps must be set out today. If they haven't sent them by four, I'll skin them alive!"

"Xiangzi, you go and hurry them up!" Tigress made a point of showing her reliance on him, and kept assigning him jobs when her father was around. Xiangzi said nothing but went off to carry out his instructions.

"Maybe I shouldn't say this, Dad," remarked Tigress, pursing her lips. "If you'd had a son he'd have been like me or like Xiangzi. It's too bad I wasn't born a boy, but there's no help for that now. Actually, it would be a good idea to adopt Xiangzi as your son. Look at him, all day he doesn't so much as fart, but everything gets done!"

Fourth Master Liu did not answer — he was thinking. "Where's the gramophone?" he asked presently. "Let's have a song!"

Every sound from that broken-down gramophone, borrowed from goodness knows where, was as ear-splitting as a cat's yowl when you tread on its tail. But Fourth Master Liu didn't mind — he just wanted some noise.

By the afternoon all was ready and they were just waiting for the cook who would come the next day. Fourth Master Liu made a tour of inspection and nodded with satisfaction at the bright reds and vivid greens everywhere.

That evening, he invited the owner of Tian Shun Coal Shop to keep the accounts for him. This gentleman from Shanxi, whose name was Feng, kept very careful accounts. Mr. Feng immediately came over to have a look and told Xiangzi to buy two red account books and a roll of red paper. He cut the paper into strips and wrote some "Longevity" characters which he pasted up here and there. Fourth Master Liu, impressed by this attention to detail, promptly offered to invite two other people over for a game of mahjong. But Mr. Feng, knowing what a redoubtable player the old man was, said nothing.

Balked of his game and rather peeved, Fourth Master Liu called in a few rickshaw men, "Have you the guts for a round of gambling?" he asked.

They would all have liked to play but none had the courage to take on Fourth Master Liu, all knowing that he had once run a gambling-den.

"You lousy lot, how do you keep alive?" he fumed. "When I was your age, I dared play without a copper in my pocket. Wouldn't worry about losing till I lost. Come on!"

"Can we play for coppers?" one rickshaw man asked tentatively.

"Keep your coppers, Fourth Master Liu doesn't mess around with children!" The old man drained his teacup in one gulp and rubbed his bald head. "Forget it, I won't play even if you invite me. Go and tell the others that tomorrow afternoon guests will be coming, so all rickshaws must be in by four — I can't have you squeezing in and out after that. Tomorrow, no rickshaw rent, but all rickshaws back by four. You have a day's free pulling so try and be decent, and wish me good luck, will you?"

"The day after, my birthday, no one's to take out a rickshaw. At eight-thirty in the morning, you'll get your meal. Six big dishes, two seven-inch platters, four small dishes and a dip. Nobody can say I'm not treating you right. You're all to wear long gowns, anyone who shows up in a short jacket gets kicked out. When you've finished eating, scram, so that I can entertain relatives and friends. They'll be having three king-size bowls, six plates of cold meats, six cooked dishes, four large dishes and a dip. I'm telling you this in advance so that you won't look on greedily.

"Friends and relatives are friends and relatives, I'm not asking *you* for anything. Those with a heart can give me ten coppers as a present and I won't think it too little. If some of you just kowtow to me three times without giving a single cent, I'll accept that too. But you must behave yourselves, is that clear? Those who want to eat here in the evening must come back after six. All the left-overs will be yours. But you're not to come back early, is that clear?"

"Tomorrow some of us pull the night-shift, Fourth Master," said a middle-aged rickshaw man. "How can they bring back their rickshaws at four o'clock?"

"Those on night shift can come back after eleven. The thing is not to be squeezing back and forth while my guests are in the marquee. You're rickshaw pullers; Fourth Liu is in a different line, get it?"

Nobody had anything to say, yet unable to think of a way to make a dignified exit they stood there awkwardly. Fourth Master Liu's harangue rankled in each heart. Although a rent-free day was letting them off cheaply, they wouldn't be getting a free meal because each would have to fork out at least forty coppers for a present. What's more, the old man had spoken so offensively, as if on his birthday they all had to hide away like rats.

Apart from that, he had forbidden them to take out rickshaws on the twenty-seventh, just when there was plenty of business before the New Year. Fourth Liu might be willing to sacrifice a day's income, but they didn't want to sit around and stew with him — that was too much! They stood there, not daring to express the anger in their hearts, certainly not wishing Fourth Master Liu good luck.

Tigress tugged at Xiangzi, and he followed her out.

At this everyone's resentment seemed to have found an outlet and they all glared at his retreating back. These last two days they had felt that Xiangzi had become the Liu family's running-dog, that he was toadying to them as hard as he could by serving as their handy-man.

Xiangzi had no inkling of this. Helping the Liu family out lessened his sense of frustration. In the evenings he said nothing because there was nothing to say. But the others, having no idea of his misfortunes, thought he was keeping aloof from them to curry favour with Fourth Master Liu.

What embittered them most was Tigress' concern for Xiangzi. The old man wouldn't let them into his birthday marquee, yet Xiangzi would be able to feast the whole day through. They were all rickshaw pullers, why this division into high and low? Look! Miss Liu had called Xiangzi out again. The eyes of all followed him and, eager to be moving, they shambled out. Miss Liu was talking to Xiangzi under the kerosene lamp. They all nodded to each other.

CHAPTER 14

*T*HE Liu family celebrations were very lively. Fourth Master Liu was gratified by the number of people who came to kowtow and congratulate him, and his elation increased with the arrival of many old friends to wish him a happy birthday. Their coming convinced him not only that the party was a success but that he had "risen" in status, for they were shabbily dressed while his fur-lined gown and jacket were brand-new. Several of these friends had once been better off than him, but in the course of twenty or thirty years they had sunk lower and lower, and some even had difficulty now in filling their stomachs. He looked at them and then at his birthday marquee, longevity altar, the painting of Changban Slope on the hanging screen, the three king-size bowls of his feast, and felt that he really was a notch above them, had risen in the world. Even for gambling, he had prepared mahjong sets, so much more refined than common betting games.

Yet in the midst of all the jollity, he felt a little forlorn. Accustomed as he was to a bachelor life, he had imagined his guests would be confined to the managers and owners of nearby shops and some bachelor friends he had known in the old days. He hadn't expected any women to come. And though Tigress was now entertaining them for him, he suddenly felt very much alone, with no wife and only a daughter who looked like a man. Had Tigress been a son, by now he'd have had grandchildren; so even as an old widower he wouldn't have been so lonely. Yes, the one thing missing in his life was a son. And the older he got, the less likely he was to have one. A birthday should be a happy occasion, but now it seemed he should weep; for no matter how he had risen in the world he had no son to carry on his business, so what was the use of it?

The first half of the day he was in high spirits, grandly receiving everyone's birthday greetings, like a hero who had accomplished some great feat. By the afternoon, however, he was dispirited. The sight of the children the women guests had brought with them filled him with admiring envy. He would have liked to play with them yet dared not, which upset him; but he didn't want to fly into a temper in front of all these friends and relatives. He was a man of the world and couldn't disgrace himself like that. So he wished the day would end quickly to end his discomfort.

Another fly in the ointment was that Xiangzi had nearly got into a fight that morning when the rickshaw pullers were having their feast.

The meal had begun at eight and all the pullers had felt resentful. Though the day before had been rent-free, today none had arrived empty-handed. Some brought only ten cents, others forty, but big or small each had a gift of money. Ordinarily, they were the poor labourers and Fourth Master Liu was the boss. Today they were guests, why should they be treated like this? What's more, they had to clear out after the meal but couldn't take out their rickshaws, just at the end of the year when business was good!

Xiangzi knew he would not be told to leave after the meal, but he chose to eat with the others. He'd be free sooner that way to set to work, and besides it seemed more matey. But as soon as he sat down the others transferred their resentment against Fourth Master Liu to him. Someone said, "Hey, you're an honoured guest, what are you doing here with us?"

Xiangzi grinned vacantly, not catching his hidden meaning. Not having talked with anyone these last few days, his mind seemed to be working slowly.

As no one dared provoke Fourth Master Liu, the only thing to do was eat an extra mouthful of his food. There was only so much of it, but the wine was unlimited because this was a birthday. By tacit agreement they turned to the wine to dispel their discontent. Some drank in glum silence, others began playing guessing games. Old Man Liu couldn't stop them doing that. Xiangzi saw everyone drinking and, in order not to be left out, drank two cups too. The drink inflamed their eyes and loosed their tongues.

One of them said, "Hey Xiangzi, Camel, you've got a cushy job! A whole day's guzzling just for waiting on the old man and young lady! You won't have to pull a rickshaw after this. Better dance attendance on them!" Xiangzi sensed something wrong, but still didn't take it to heart. Since returning to Harmony Yard, he had decided to let things take their course and leave everything to fate. Let them say what they liked. He kept his temper.

Another said, "Xiangzi is different from the likes of us: we sweat outside for a living, he's an insider!"

They all roared with laughter. Xiangzi knew they were baiting him, but after all he'd put up with, why get excited about this? He still held his peace.

Someone at the next table decided to poke fun at him too, and called across, "Xiangzi, when you become master of the yard, don't forget your old mates!"

Still Xiangzi kept quiet.

Someone at his table challenged, "Come on, say something, Camel!"

Xiangzi's face flushed and he said gruffly, "How could I become master?"

"Huh, why not? Soon the cymbals will clash and the drums beat!"

Xiangzi didn't understand this reference to cymbals and drums, but guessed that it was connected with his relationship with Tigress. The colour drained from his face. His bottled up resentment nearly choked him. He couldn't hold back any more, like dammed-up water waiting to burst out of the first opening.

Just then, another puller pointed at him and said, "I tell you, Xiangzi, you're like the mute eating dumplings, you know how many you've downed! Aren't you now, Xiangzi? Speak up! Hey, Xiangzi!"

Xiangzi sprang to his feet, his face deathly pale, and challenged his taunter, "I dare you to come outside and say that!"

The others were taken aback. They had been baiting him for fun, but nobody wanted to fight.

The sudden silence was like that in a forest when twittering birds see an eagle. Xiangzi stood there alone, head and shoulders above the rest. He sensed his isolation, but his temper was up and he seemed confident that he could take on the whole lot of them.

He persisted, "Well, does anyone have the guts?"

The others at once recovered their aplomb and chorused, "Come on, Xiangzi, we were only joking!"

Fourth Master Liu had seen the whole business and said, "Sit down, Xiangzi!" He told the others, "Don't pick on someone because he keeps to himself. If you make trouble, I'll kick you all out! Eat up!"

Xiangzi left the table. The rest eyed Fourth Master Liu and picked up their bowls. Soon they were chattering away again, like birds twittering in the forest after the danger has passed.

Xiangzi squatted a long time outside the door, waiting for them. If anyone made any more snide remarks he would beat him up. He had lost everything anyway, what did he care?

But the others, coming out in small groups, ignored him. Though there had been no fight, he had at least vented some of his pent-up feeling. But on second thought, he realized he had offended many people. Already he had no intimate friends to listen to his grievances; how could he afford to go on offending people? He began to regret his actions. The little he had eaten seemed to lie uncomfortably cross-wise in his stomach. He stood up. What the hell, who cared? Those fellows who got into fights every other day and were loaded with debts seemed to get a kick out of life just the same. Was decency such a fine thing after all?

It dawned on him that he could take a completely different course from his earlier one. He'd be very sociable, take advantage of everyone, drink other people's tea, smoke their cigarettes, borrow money and not pay it back, never make way for cars, piss wherever he pleased, quarrel with policemen all the time and think nothing of going to clink for a couple of days. Certainly this kind of puller survived and enjoyed life more than Xiangzi had ever done.

Very well then, if decency and ambition got one nowhere, why not become one of those shameless rogues? Not only was it the right thing to do, he decided, it was almost heroic to fear neither Heaven nor earth, never to bow one's head or suffer in silence. That's right, that's what he would do. A good fellow could go to the bad.

He was actually beginning to regret not having got into that fight. Luckily, there was plenty of time, for from this day on he would bow to no man.

No one could throw sand in Fourth Master Liu's eyes. When he put together all he had heard and seen, he had a pretty good notion of what was going on. These last few days, his daughter had been particularly compliant. So it was because Xiangzi had returned! Look at her eyes, always following him around! Ruminating over this he felt even more lonely and gloomy. Just think, without a son, he couldn't by flaring up get together a family; and once his daughter left, what a waste of a lifetime of effort! Xiangzi wasn't bad, but he fell far short if considered as a son or son-in-law — a stinking rickshaw puller! Was it possible that he had struggled all his life, fought gang fights and undergone torture only to have his daughter and property snatched away by a country bumpkin before he died? Nothing doing! No one could take such advantage of Fourth Liu! Fourth Liu who ever since childhood had blasted a hole in the ground each time he farted!

At three or four in the afternoon, more visitors came to offer congratulations, but the old man was already fed up. The more his guests complimented him on his good health and fortune, the more meaningless it became.

By lamp-lighting time, most of the guests had gone, leaving some ten who lived closest or who had known him longest. They started to play mahjong. Gazing at the empty marquee, green in the light of the kerosene lamps, at the tables divested of their cloths, the old man felt desolate and depressed. At his death it would be just like this, he thought, only the marquee of felicity would be changed into one of mourning; but there would be no sons or grandsons to wear mourning clothes and kneel to keep vigil before his coffin, only some casual acquaintances who would play mahjong during the night watch. He really felt like sending his few remaining guests packing. While there was still breath in his body, he ought to show what he was made of! But it would be too uncivil to vent his temper on his friends. So his anger switched to his daughter, who grew more and more obnoxious in his eyes. Xiangzi was sitting in the marquee. What an ugly blighter he was, with that scar on his face jade-green in the lamplight! What a thoroughly repulsive pair they were!

Tigress had always been wilful and unrestrained. Today however, bedecked from top to toe, she had given herself airs as a hostess, not only to win the approval of the guests but also to impress Xiangzi. In the morning she thoroughly enjoyed herself, but by the afternoon she who growing tired — her nerves frayed and her temper wore thin. By the evening, every scrap of patience was gone and her eyebrows were fixed in a deep scowl.

Shortly after seven o'clock, Fourth Master Liu felt sleepy, but he wouldn't admit it and refused to go to bed. The players invited him to join them for a few games, but instead of saying that he hadn't the energy he declared that mahjong was too dull and that ordinary betting games were more to his taste. As none of them wanted to switch half way through a game, he had to sit at one side watching. To pep himself up he drank several more cups of wine, complaining over and over again that he hadn't eaten enough, and that the cook had squeezed him and stinted the food. From this he went on to find fault with all that had so satisfied him that morning: the marquee, the furnishings, the cook, everything was a dead loss. He had paid for a great swindle!

By this time, Mr. Feng the accountant had finished an inventory of the gifts: twenty-five birthday scrolls, three sets of longevity "peach" cakes and noodles, a jar of longevity wine, two pairs of longevity candles and twenty-odd dollars of gift-money. The list of contributors was quite long, but the majority had given only forty coppers or ten silver cents.

When he heard this, Fourth Master Liu's blood boiled. Had he known this in advance, he would have prepared fried noodles with vegetables! Eat a feast with three king-size bowls and give only ten cents? So they expected to cash in on him, did they? Well, from now on, no more celebrations, never again was he going to pay through the nose! Of course, everyone had come with family and friends in tow, all set on a free meal at his expense. A man of sixty-nine to let himself be taken in like this, after being so sharp all his life! A band of bastards and monkeys sponging off *him*! The more he brooded, the more enraged he became. Even what had gratified him earlier on now seemed sheer foolishness, and his feelings expressed themselves in out-moded curses.

As there were still some friends around and Tigress wanted to keep up appearances, she considered restraining her father. However, as all the players were concentrating on their mahjong counters as if they had not heard the old man's tirade, she decided to keep quiet rather than stir up trouble. Let him grumble. Since they all acted deaf, the incident would pass.

But, unexpectedly, he started venting his spleen on her. Now that was too much! His birthday preparations had kept her on the go for several days and this was the thanks she got! It was insufferable! Sixty-nine? Even at seventy-nine he had to be reasonable!

"You wanted to spend the money, what's it got to do with me?" she snapped back.

At this, the old man came wide awake. "What to do with you? Everything! You think I'm blind and don't see things?"

"What have you seen? I'm fagged out as it is without you venting your spleen on me! Go ahead. What did you see?" Tigress, quite revived too, spat her words out.

"You don't have to go green with envy at my party. See? Hah, I saw through it all long ago!"

"Why should I go green with envy?" Tigress wagged her head as she spoke. "Come on, what have you seen?"

"That!" Fourth Master Liu pointed to the marquee where Xiangzi was bent over sweeping the floor.

"Him?" Tigress' heart contracted. Who would have thought the old man's eyes were so sharp? "So, what about him?"

"Don't act dumb when you know very well!" The old man stood up. "Either him or me, take your choice and that's that. I'm your father, I have a right!"

Tigress had not thought the showdown would come so soon, with her plan still only half carried out. Now what? Under the greenish lamplight her face, flushed a dark red and streaked with powder, looked like an over-cooked pig's liver, mottled and repulsive. Tired and provoked, her dander was up but she could not think what to do and felt very confused. There was no pulling back now. However upset she was, she must think of something and quickly too. Even a bad idea was better than none, and besides she had never bowed down to anyone. Very well then, he might as well have it straight from the shoulder. For better for worse the die was cast.

"Well, we may as well have it out today. Suppose you are right, so what? Just tell me that. You've brought this on yourself, don't accuse me of needling you!"

The mahjong players vaguely heard father and daughter quarrelling, but didn't wish to be distracted; so to drown out the sound they plonked their pieces down more vigorously as they shouted "Red," "Strike. . . ."

Xiangzi heard what was happening, but continued to sweep with lowered head. His mind was made up, if it came to a bust-up he'd fight!

"Trying to make me mad, are you?" The old man was glaring, round-eyed. "Think if I popped off in a rage, you could buy yourself a man, eh? Don't count on it. I plan to live a few more years yet!"

"Keep to the point! So, what are you going to do?" Tigress' heart was thumping but her voice was metallic.

"Didn't I say, it's either him or me? I'm not going to let a stinking rickshaw puller have it all his own way!"

Xiangzi tossed his broom aside, straightened up and fixed his eyes on Fourth Master Liu. "Who's that you're talking about?"

Fourth Master Liu laughed wildly. "Ha, ha, thinking of rebelling, are you? Who am I talking about? Why, you of course! Now, scram! I thought you were decent and treated you well, but you forget who I am! Didn't stop to find out! Scram, I say. I never want to set eyes on you again, and don't think you're going to take any fucking advantage of me!"

The old man's voice had become really loud and several pullers came out to see what it was all about. The mahjong players did not pause or look up, as they imagined it was just Fourth Master Liu quarrelling again with some rickshaw puller or other.

Xiangzi didn't have a ready tongue. There was much he wanted to say, but not a word could he get out. He stood there dumbly, craning his neck and swallowing noisily.

"Get out, and look sharp about it! Hoping to get something on the cheap here, were you? I knew all the tricks before you were born!" By now, the old man was ranting for ranting's sake, for he resented his daughter far more bitterly than Xiangzi. Even in his fury, he still knew that Xiangzi was an honest, decent fellow.

"All right, I'll go!" Xiangzi had nothing more to say. Best to get out as quickly as possible, for he knew he was no match for them in a brawl.

The other pullers had come out to watch the fun. When they remembered what had happened that morning, they were very pleased to see Fourth Master Liu cursing Xiangzi. However, when they heard that the old man was chasing him out, their sympathy swung back to Xiangzi. Why, he had worn himself out these last few days for the old man and now Fourth Master Liu was ungrateful enough to turn his fury on him. Each felt the injustice of it. A couple of them hurried over and asked: "What's up, Xiangzi?" He only shook his head.

"Wait, Xiangzi! Don't go yet!" In a flash Tigress saw her way clearly. Her old plan was no use now. She must act fast to keep hold of Xiangzi, otherwise she'd lose the hen and the egg would be broken too. "We're like two grasshoppers tied to one cord: neither can get away! Wait until I've made it all clear!" She turned to her father and blurted out: "Let's get it straight once and for all! I'm going to have a baby and it's Xiangzi's! Wherever he goes, I go too! Will you marry me to him or chase us both out? It's up to you!"

She had not expected things to come to a head so fast, forcing her to play her last card so soon. Fourth Master Liu was even more flabbergasted. But as matters stood, he couldn't give in, especially in front of so many people.

"You have the face to say it? I blush for you!" He slapped himself on the mouth. "Pah! You shameless hussy!"

The mahjong players froze, aware that something was wrong. But not being clear about it they could say nothing. One stood up, while the others stared dumbly at their mahjong pieces.

Now that she had spoken out, Tigress warmed up. "Me, shameless? Who are you to talk? You wouldn't like me to crake out all *your* muck, would you? This is my first slip-up, and you're the one to blame! A full-grown man takes a wife and a full-grown girl wants a husband — that's only natural. Yet here you are, sixty-nine, and you don't know that! Well, I'm not saying this for them." She pointed to all the on-lookers. "It's just as well to get things clear, so that we know where we stand. You may as well make use of this birthday marquee to get my business settled."

"Me?" The old man's face changed from red to white. He was on his old bachelor mettle. "I'd burn it down first!"

"Have it your own way!" Tigress' lips were trembling, her voice was ugly. "I'm packing up and leaving. How much money do I get?"

"The money is mine and I'll give it to whom I please!" Actually the old man felt aggrieved that his daughter wanted to leave, but he couldn't back down now. He hardened his heart.

"*Your* money? So that's what you think after all these years I've helped you! Remember, if it hadn't been for me, you'd have spent it all on prostitutes. Let's be fair, after all!" Her eyes sought out Xiangzi. "Say something!"

Xiangzi stood there, straight as a ramrod. As usual, he could think of nothing to say.

CHAPTER 15

*I*T was impossible for Xiangzi to hit an old man or a woman, so there was nowhere for him to use his strength. Brazen it out? He wasn't the sort. He could easily ditch Tigress and make a run for it, but she had quarrelled with her father to follow him and, since no one knew the inside story, on the face of it she seemed to be sacrificing herself for him. So before all these people he had to put on a bold front. The least he could do to show that he was a man was to stand there, even though he had nothing to say, and wait for the situation to sort itself out.

Father and daughter were reduced to glaring at each other. Xiangzi was silent. As for the other pullers, no matter whom they sided with it was difficult to butt in. The mahjong players, embarrassed by the silence, felt constrained to break it. They were reduced to banalities, however, and could only urge both parties to talk things over calmly because no problem was insoluble. What more could they say? It solved nothing, and they knew it. When it became clear that neither side was prepared to give in, they took the opportunity to slip away for, as the saying goes, "an upright official never intervenes in family disputes".

Before they all left, Tigress button-holed Mr. Feng of Tianshun Coal Shop. "Mr. Feng, you have room in your shop, don't you? Let Xiangzi stay there for a couple of days. We shall soon be fixed up so he won't be on your hands long. Xiangzi, you go with Mr. Feng, we'll meet tomorrow to talk over our affairs. If I don't leave this house in a bridal sedan-chair, I won't go! Mr. Feng, you keep an eye on him, tomorrow I'm coming to pick him up!"

144

Mr. Feng was breathing heavily, not wanting to take the responsibility.

Xiangzi, in a hurry to leave, rapped out, "I won't run away!"

Tigress glared at her father, went into her room and broke into strident sobs. She locked her door from the inside.

Mr. Feng and the others tried to persuade Fourth Master Liu to go to his room too, but acting as a man of the world he insisted on their staying to drink some more wine. "Be assured, gentlemen, that from now on she goes her way and I go mine, we won't quarrel any more. Once she's gone, it'll be as if I never had a daughter. After making my way in the world all these years she's made me lose face completely. Twenty years ago I would have torn them to pieces. But now, let her have her way. Thinks she's going to get a copper out of me? Nothing doing! I won't give her a cent, not one! We'll see how she lives! Let her try and then she'll know who's best, her father or some good-for-nothing! Don't go yet, have another drink!"

The guests excused themselves and hurried away to avoid getting involved.

Xiangzi went to Tianshun Coal Shop.

Sure enough, everything was fixed up very quickly. Tigress rented two small rooms with a southern exposure in a large tenement yard in the Maojiawan district. She hired a paperhanger to paper them in white from floor to ceiling, then asked Mr. Feng to write some "happiness" characters and pasted these on the walls. After that, she went out to hire a sedan-chair decorated with silver stars and sixteen musicians, but no gold lanterns or escort. That settled, she made her red satin wedding clothes, hurriedly finishing them before the New Year so as to keep to the rule of no sewing between the first and fifth day of the New Year. The great day was set for the sixth, an auspicious day and one on which leaving home was not taboo. All these arrangements made, she told Xiangzi to get himself a complete new outfit. "One only gets married once in a life-time!"

Xiangzi had only five dollars in his pocket.

Tigress glared at him. "What? And those thirty dollars I gave you?"

The truth had to be told and out came the whole story of what had happened at the Cao house. She blinked, half believing and half doubting him.

"All right, I've no time to argue with you. Each of us must act according to our conscience! Here's fifteen dollars. If you're not dressed like a bridegroom on the day, just watch out!"

On the sixth day of the New Year, Tigress climbed into the bridal sedan-chair. She left without a word to her father, without any escort of brothers, without the good wishes of friends or relatives, accompanied only by cymbals and drums which made a festive din along the streets still lively after New Year. The procession made its way steadily past Xi'anmen Gate and the Xisi Arch, arousing the envy and stirring the emotions of the spectators in their new clothes, especially the shop-attendants.

Xiangzi was wearing the new clothes he had bought in the Tianqiao district. He was flushed and had on one of those little satin caps that cost thirty cents. He seemed to have forgotten who he was, though he stared stupidly at everything and listened to all that was going on around him. From a coal shop he had been plunged into a freshly papered bridal chamber as white as snow, and he was completely bewildered. The past was as dark as the heaps of coal in the shop. Now suddenly he was standing in a new dazzling white room with blood-red "happiness" characters on the walls. He felt it was a mockery, white, nebulous, oppressive.

The rooms were furnished with Tigress' old chairs, table and bed. The stove and chopping board were brand-new, and in one corner stood a multicoloured feather duster. He only recognized the old furniture, and this combination of new and old reminded him of the past and filled him with apprehension for the future. Manipulated in everything, he himself resembled an old yet new ornament, a strange, unrecognizable object. He could neither weep nor laugh, and moved about clumsily in the cosy little rooms like a big rabbit in a small wooden cage, gazing longingly outside, unable to escape though so swift of foot.

Tigress in a red jacket, her face powdered and rouged, followed him with her eyes. He dared not look her in the face. She seemed another strange object, old yet new, girl yet woman, female yet male, human yet beast-like. This beast in the red jacket had already caught him and was preparing to finish him off neatly. Anyone could make short work of him, but this beast was particularly vicious and watched him every instant, glaring at him, laughing at him, capable of holding him firmly and sucking out all his strength. There was no escape. He took off his little satin cap and stared fixedly at the red knot on the top, stared until his eyes blurred so that when he looked away the wall was covered with jumping, whirling red dots. In the middle was the largest of them all: Tigress, with a repulsive smile on her face.

Only on his wedding-night did Xiangzi finally catch on: Tigress wasn't pregnant after all. Like a magician explaining a trick, she told him, "If I hadn't deceived you like this, you'd never have caved in and agreed. I stuck a pillow inside my trousers! Ha ha, ha ha!" She laughed till the tears came to her eyes. "You dumb-bunny! Forget it! At any rate I haven't disgraced you! Who are you and who am I? I've quarrelled with my old man just to follow you. You should be thanking heaven and earth!"

The next day, Xiangzi went out very early. Most of the shops had opened again, though some were still boarded up. New Year mottoes showed bright red on the doors, but some of the strings of yellow paper ingots had been torn by the wind. The streets were very quiet, yet there were quite a few rickshaws around. The pullers seemed smarter than usual, nearly all of them wearing new shoes; and some of the rickshaws had a piece of red paper stuck on the back.

How Xiangzi envied these pullers who, he felt, had a festive air about them, whereas he had been bottled up in a gourd these last few days. They were going contentedly about their work, while he was idling about the streets. It irked him to be loafing, but any projects for the future had to be discussed

with Tigress, his wife. He had to beg for food from this wife —
and what a wife! His height and strength were useless. His
first job was to wait on that red-jacketed, tiger-toothed creature
of a wife. He wasn't human any more, he was a piece of meat.
He didn't exist any more, he was struggling in her jaws like a
mouse caught by a cat. He didn't feel like talking anything
over with her, he had to escape and once he had a plan of action, clear out without a word. Nothing shameful about that,
since she was a witch who had used a pillow to deceive him!
He felt wretched. He wanted to tear his new clothes to shreds,
to douse himself inside and out with clear water and wash off
that nauseating layer of filth stuck all over him. He never
wanted to see her face again.

Where should he go? He didn't know. Normally his legs
followed directions given by others, today they were free but
his mind was a blank. Walking south from the Xisi Arch
through Xuanwumen Gate, the road stretched straight before
him and he felt even more at a loss. He left the gate behind
and saw a bath-house. He decided to go in.

When he had stripped himself naked, he looked at his body
and felt thoroughly ashamed. In the pool, the water was so
hot it numbed him. He closed his eyes and all the collected
filth seemed to ooze out of his limp form. Not daring to rub
himself, he lay there in a daze, huge drops of sweat running
off his brow. Only when his breathing quickened did he crawl
lazily out, bright red all over like a new born child. He was
afraid to walk around like that and even wrapped in a large
towel still felt ugly. Sweat pattered off him, yet the unclean
feeling persisted, as if that black stain on his heart would never
wash off. To Fourth Master Liu, to all who knew him, he
would forever be a seducer of women.

Before he had stopped sweating, he hurried into his clothes
and rushed out. He was afraid to let others see his naked body.
Outside, the cold wind gave him a sensation of lightness. The
streets were far more busy now and the clear sky added an
extra shine to everyone's face. Still he could not decide where
to go. South, east and then south again, he headed for the
Tianqiao district. After the New Year, shop-attendants would

congregate there around nine o'clock after their breakfasts, for peddlers and showmen of every kind set up their stands very early. By the time Xiangzi arrived, the sound of cymbals and drums here and there had already attracted large crowds. Yet he wás in no mood to enjoy these amusements for he had forgotten how to laugh.

Usually, the comic dialogues, performing bears, conjuring, clapper ballads, acrobatics, folk-songs and stories told to the accompaniment of drums could all give him genuine pleasure and make him open his big mouth in a smile. The fact that he could not bear to leave Beiping was half due to this Tianqiao district. The sight of its mat sheds and throngs of people reminded him of many amusing and likable things. But today he didn't feel like pushing his way into the crowds nor could he share their laughter. He knew he ought to go to some quiet spot but could not tear himself away. No, impossible to leave this dear bustling place, impossible to leave Tianqiao, leave Beiping. Go away? There was nowhere to go. He still had to consult her — that woman! He couldn't escape yet neither could he remain idle. He must stop to think, just as everyone does when he feels he has reached the end of his tether. After all the wrongs he had suffered, why should he take this one more seriously than the others? The past couldn't be altered, the only thing was to carry on.

He stood still listening to the babel of voices and din of cymbals and drums, watching the stream of people and vehicles. Suddenly he thought of those two small rooms. The tumult faded from his ears, the crowds melted from his sight, and all he could see were those two white, cosy rooms with their red "happiness" characters squarely confronting him. He had spent only one night there, yet they were so familiar and intimate. It seemed that even that red-jacketed woman could not be lightly forsaken. Here in Tianqiao he had nothing, was nobody. In those little rooms, he had everything. He had to go back, it was the only way. All his future was there. Shame, timidity, grief were useless. If he wanted to survive he had to go where there was hope.

He walked back in one breath, and arrived at about eleven o'clock. Tigress had already prepared lunch: steamed bread, boiled cabbage with meat-balls, a plate of jellied pork skin and pickled turnips. Everything was on the table except the cabbage which was still simmering on the stove and giving off a delicious smell. She had taken off her red jacket and was wearing her ordinary cotton padded trousers and jacket, but in her hair was still a small red velvet flower with a tiny gold paper ingot stuck on it.

Xiangzi glanced at her. She didn't look like a bride. All her movements seemed to indicate that she had been married for years, so brisk, efficient and self-satisfied was she. Yet there was still something new about everything, her cooking, the way she had arranged the rooms, the faint fragrance in the air, the warmth — these were things he had never experienced before. No matter what she was, he felt he had a home here, and a home is always lovable. He didn't know what to do with himself.

"Where've you been?" she asked as she served the cabbage.

"Had a bath." He took off his long gown.

"Oh? Well, next time you go out, say something. Don't just walk out without a word!"

He said nothing.

"Can't you get at least one word out? If you can't, I'll show you how!"

He grunted, what else could he do? He knew he had married a she-devil who could cook and clean, could curse him and help him too, and this made him acutely uncomfortable. He started eating the steamed bread. The food was really tastier than what he usually had, piping hot too, but it didn't seem as good and while he chewed he didn't feel his customary ravenous enjoyment.

After the meal, he lay down on the brick bed, his head pillowed on his arms, his eyes on the ceiling.

"Hey, come and help wash up, I'm nobody's slave!" she callled from the outer room.

Lazily he stood up, glanced at her and went over to help. Normally so willing, he now worked with a feeling of resentment. At the rickshaw yard he had often helped her, now the more he looked at her the more she annoyed him. Never had he loathed anyone so much, though he couldn't say why. But as he couldn't express his feelings, they remained bottled up inside him. Since he could not break with her, there was no point in quarrelling. Turning round and round in the small rooms, life seemed just one big grievance.

When she had finished tidying up she looked around and sighed. Then she smiled. "How about it?"

"What?" Xiangzi was squatting by the stove warming his hands. They weren't really cold but he had nowhere else to put them. The rooms certainly looked like a home, but he didn't know where to place his hands and feet.

"Take me out for some fun, will you? How about White Cloud Monastery? No, it's a bit late for that. How about a stroll around the streets?" She wanted to make the most of being married. Although the wedding itself had been so shabby, this new freedom was fine and now was the time to enjoy herself with her husband for a few days. In her father's house she had never lacked food, clothes or spending-money, only a man with whom to be intimate. Now she was going to make up for this, she wanted to swagger around the streets and markets enjoying herself with Xiangzi.

Xiangzi didn't want to go out. In the first place he considered it shameful to go out strolling in public with his wife. In the second, he felt that a wife acquired in this way should be kept hidden at home. She was nothing to be proud of and the less people saw of her the better. Besides, they would be sure to run into acquaintances. All the rickshaw pullers of the West City knew about Xiangzi and Tigress. He didn't want to have them laughing behind his back.

"Let's talk things over, shall we?" He remained squatting.

"What's there to talk over?" She came to stand by the stove.

He stopped warming his hands and rested them on his knees, staring fixedly at the flames. After a while he managed to say, "I can't stay idle like this!"

"Ill-fated chap!" She laughed. "I suppose you feel itchy not pulling a rickshaw! Look at the old man. He amused himself all his life and opened a rickshaw yard in his old age. He doesn't pull a rickshaw or sell his muscle but lives by his wits. You'd better catch on a bit too. What's so good about pulling a rickshaw all the time? We'll amuse ourselves for a few days first, we don't have to decide anything right away, why hurry? I'm not going to quarrel with you now, so don't try and pick a fight!"

"Talk things over first!" Xiangzi wasn't going to give in. Seeing he couldn't walk out on her, he had to work. And the first thing was to take a firm stand, he couldn't keep wobbling.

"All right, shoot!" She moved a stool over and sat down by the stove.

"How much money have you got?" he asked.

"There you are! Didn't I know you'd ask just that? You married me for my money, didn't you?"

Xiangzi felt as if choked by a gust of wind and swallowed several times. Fourth Master Liu and the pullers at the yard had all thought he was after money when he took up with Tigress, and now here she was accusing him of the same thing! Without rhyme or reason he had lost his own rickshaw and his money. His wife's few dollars put him under her thumb — even to eat he had to rub her up the right way! If only he could put his hands around her neck and choke her! Choke her until she showed the whites of her eyes! After choking her to death he'd cut his own throat. They weren't human and deserved to die. Neither of them deserved to live!

He stood up to go out again, thinking he shouldn't have come back earlier on.

Tigress could see that something was wrong. She said more affably, "All right, I'll tell you. I had five hundred to start with. The sedan-chair, the rent — three months, the papering, the clothes, other expenses and what I gave you added up to just short of a hundred, so I've got about four hundred now. I tell you, no need to worry. Let's enjoy ourselves while we can. You've been pulling all these years and sweating your guts out, it's about time you dressed up smartly and had a good time. As for me, I've been an old maid all these years and should have some fun too. When our money starts running out we'll go and ask the old man to help. If I hadn't got mad that day, I would never have left home. I've calmed down now and, after all, a father is a father. I'm his only daughter and you're someone he's always liked, so if we knuckle under and apologize he'll probably let bygones be bygones. It's all there for the taking! He has the money and we inherit it, all straight and above-board and perfectly reasonable. That's much better than you slaving for other people like a beast of burden. In a few days you go and see him first. If he refuses to see you, you can go again. If we give him all that face, he's sure to change his mind. Then I'll go and butter him up. You never know, we might be able to move back again. Then we can really lift up our heads and no one will dare look down on us. If we stick on here, putting up with this, we shall always have a bad name — don't you agree?"

None of this had occurred to Xiangzi. Since she had looked him up at the Caos', he had thought that by marrying her he could use her money to buy a rickshaw which he would pull himself. Using his wife's money wasn't exactly honorable, but since their relationship was rather shady anyway what did it matter? It had never occurred to him that Tigress had this card up her sleeve. If one were thick-skinned enough it certainly was a way out. But Xiangzi wasn't that sort of person.

On thinking things over he began to see that if you had some money and someone grabbed it there was nowhere to go for justice. When someone gave you money, you were forced to accept, and from then on you were no longer your own master. Strength and ambition were useless, you were a servant, your own wife's plaything, your father-in-law's slave. People were like birds: If you tried to feed yourself you ended up in the net; if you ate other people's grain you had to stay contentedly in your cage, singing for them, expecting to be sold at any moment.

He didn't want to seek out Fourth Master Liu. His relationship with Tigress was of the most intimate kind, but he had no such connections with the old man. She had cheated him, how could he now beg from her father?

"I must have something to do!" was all he said, not wanting to waste his breath or quarrel.

"You're just fated to be a slave!" she said mockingly. "If you want something to do, go into business!"

"Don't know how! I couldn't make money! I can pull a rickshaw, I like pulling a rickshaw!" The veins stood out on his forehead.

"Well, I'm telling you, that's just what you won't do! I won't have you reeking with sweat on my bed! You have your ideas and I have mine, we'll see who'll win. You married me, but I paid for it, you didn't fork out one cent. Just think, will you, which of us should have the say?"

Once more, Xiangzi had no answer.

CHAPTER 16

X IANGZI remained idle until the fifteenth day of the first month of the lunar calendar, which was the Lantern Festival. By then he could stand it no longer.

Tigress was in high spirits. She bustled about boiling sugar-filled glutinous rice balls for the festival, as well as ravioli, visited the temple fair in the morning and admired the coloured lanterns on the streets at night. She allowed Xiangzi no say in anything but kept him busy tasting all sorts of tidbits, bought and home-made.

There were seven or eight families living in their tenement courtyard, most of them crowded seven to eight, old and young, into one room. Among them were rickshaw pullers, peddlers, policemen and servants. Each went about his or her job with never a moment to spare. Even the children went off with small baskets to fetch rice gruel in the morning and to scrounge for cinders in the afternoon. Only the very youngest remained in the courtyard, tussling and playing, their little bottoms frozen bright red in their split pants. Ashes, dust and slops were all tipped into the yard, which no one bothered to sweep. The middle of it was a sheet of ice which the older children used as a skating-rink when they came back from scrounging cinders, shouting loudly as they slipped and slid about. The worst off were the old folk and women. Hungry and threadbare, the old people lay on icy cold brick-beds, waiting anxiously for the pittance the able-bodied ones earned to buy them a bowl of gruel. Sometimes the younger people made some money, sometimes they came back empty-handed; and then they would lose their tempers and find some pretext to quarrel. The famished old folk could only swallow their tears. As for the women, they had to look after old and young alike besides catering for their money-earning menfolk. When pregnant they worked as usual though their food was only maize meal bread and sweet-potato porridge. In addition, they had to fetch gruel from the relief station and take on other odd jobs, and when finally old and young were fed and in bed, they had to wash, mend and sew what they had taken in beneath a dim oil-lamp. The small room was icy cold, for the freezing wind which whistled through the cracks in the walls carried off what little warmth there might have been. Dressed in rags, with a bowl or half of gruel in their bellies, maybe six or seven months pregnant, they must first let old and young eat their fill though they too had to toil. Riddled with disease, they were bald by thirty yet could never rest; and when illness carried them off their families had to beg "philanthropists" for a coffin. The girls of sixteen and seventeen had no trousers and, wrapped in rags, stayed in the room — their natural prison — helping their mothers out. To go to the latrine, they first made sure the yard was empty before slipping out. The whole winter they never saw the sun or the blue sky. The ugly ones would later take their mother's place, the better-looking ones knew very well that sooner or later they would be sold by their parents to "enjoy good fortune".

Tigress felt very smug in a tenement yard like this. She was the only one who need not worry about food or clothing, who had time to stroll about and amuse herself. She moved around, head high, conscious of her own superiority and ignoring her poor neighbours, afraid of being contaminated by them. The peddlers who frequented the place all sold the cheapest goods: meat parings from bones, frozen cabbage, unboiled bean juice, mule and horse meat. After Tigress moved in, others selling more expensive wares such as sheep's head, smoked fish, buns and fried beancurd in spiced sauce also came to call outside the gate. When she returned, her nose in the air, to her room with some goodies, the little children would stuff thin, grubby fingers into their mouths and stare at her as if she were a princess. She was out to enjoy herself and couldn't, wouldn't see the sufferings of others.

Xiangzi disapproved of her conduct. He had been poor all his life, he knew what misery was, and he didn't want to eat all those snacks — he thought it a waste of money. What's more, he had come to the painful conclusion that she didn't want him to pull a rickshaw at all and was just trying to feed him up with good food, as if fattening a milch cow in order to get more milk. He had become her plaything. He hated this life, and was worried about himself too. He knew that a man who sold his muscle had to look after his body, that health was everything. At this rate, he would one day become an empty hulk. The thought made him shudder. If he wanted to survive, he must start working right away. By running all day he could sleep soundly at night, and would not be around to eat her tidbits. That way, he would no longer be her plaything. He was determined to stick to his guns. If she was willing to pay for a rickshaw, so much the better; if not, he would rent one. And that is just what he did, without letting on.

On the seventeenth day of the month, he started pulling once more round the clock. After two longish fares, he felt a novel sensation: tenderness in his calves and an ache in the hips. He knew the reason, but to console himself ascribed it to his being rusty. After all, he had not been out for twenty days, and once he had run himself back into condition all should be well.

He got another fare as one of a group of four, who were hired to run together. By common accord, they let the tall forty-year-old puller take the lead. Smiling, he started off, knowing very well that the other three were all faster than he. Yet he was unwilling to make age an excuse for going slowly and put all his strength into running.

After one *li*, one of the young pullers praised him, "How're you feeling? Tired? You're pretty good!"

Breathlessly he replied, "How can I take my time running with you chaps?"

And really he wasn't slow at all, even Xiangzi had to exert seven to eight parts of his strength to keep up. The older man had an ugly stance. He was unable to bend at the waist, as if his whole back were one solid piece of wood, so that he had to incline his whole body forward, his arms stretched out behind.

This meant that he had to move his hips more rigorously, while his feet just cleared the ground, twisting rapidly forward. He was fast but obviously it was hard work. He took the corners so narrowly that the others held their breath, for he didn't seem to care whether the rickshaw could make it or not.

When they reached their destination, the sweat was dripping off his nose and the lobes of his ears. He put down the shafts, hurriedly straightened up and grimaced, his hands shaking so violently he could hardly hold his fee.

One trip together had made them cronies, and all four parked their rickshaws together. Xiangzi and the other young men dried themselves off and started joking as usual. The older man kept to himself for a while, racked by coughing. Only after he had spat out a lot of white phlegm did he rally sufficiently to join in the conversation.

"I'm finished! Heart, back and legs are all too weak! However much I try to straighten up, I just can't lift my legs. Really riles me!"

"Didn't do so badly just now, think that was slow?" a short twenty-year-old said. "I'm not kidding. We three are quite tough and which of us didn't sweat?"

The tall man seemed gratified but sheepish too. He sighed.

"With your way of running, you're sure to lose out," another young man said.

"At your age, it's no joke," put in another.

The tall man smiled and shook his head. "It's not altogether a matter of age, mates. I'm telling you, in our line, you mustn't start a family, and that's the truth!" When the others drew closer, their ears pricked up, he continued in a lower voice, "Once you have a family, there's never a moment's peace day or night, you're always on the go. Look at my hips, stiff as a board, not a bit of spring in them! If you strain to run fast, you start coughing and feel a constriction in the chest. There's only one way, stay single if you take up this trade! Even the fucking sparrows have mates, but we must stay single! What's more, once you get married, it's a kid every year. I have five now! All waiting to be fed too! Rickshaw rent is high, grain is dear, business is bad, what can you do? Better to be a bachelor for life and go to brothels when you're turned on. To hell with the pox! You only die once! This family business, old and young, so many mouths, you can't even die in peace for worrying about them! What do you say?" he asked Xiangzi.

Xiangzi nodded but said nothing.

At this point, a fare came along and the short young puller clinched the charge. But he told the tall older man, "Come on, mate, you take it. Five children in that old family waiting for you!"

The other smiled. "All right, I'll make another trip, though this is no way to do things! I'll be able to take a few more griddle cakes back. See you later, mates!"

As he watched the other leave, the short puller muttered to himself, "What a bloody life: we sweat out our guts and can't even bed a wife! Yet those mother-fuckers in big houses hog four or five women each!"

"Never mind about them," said the other young man. "He was right, in this line you have to be careful. Where does marriage get you? Is it a knick-knack to look at? No! That's the whole trouble! Gnawing maize-bread day in and day out, burning the candle at both ends, even the strongest chap would crack!"

At this point, Xiangzi picked up the shafts of his rickshaw and said casually, "I'm moving south, no fares here."

"See you later," the other two answered.

Xiangzi didn't seem to hear. He walked along, gently kicking; his loins really did ache! He had intended going home, but now he didn't dare. It wasn't a wife waiting there for him but a blood-sucking vampire!

The days were getting longer. He kept going for a while and yet it was only five o'clock. He turned in the rickshaw and spent some more time in a teahouse. After two pots of tea, he felt hungry and decided to eat outside before going home. He downed twelve ounces of meat-filled pancakes and a bowl of red-bean millet porridge, then made his way slowly back, belching noisily. He knew a storm was awaiting him but felt quite calm. He was not going to quarrel or fight but go straight to bed and sleep. Tomorrow he would take out the rickshaw again, whether she liked it or not.

He found Tigress sitting in the outer room. She glanced at him and her face lengthened. Xiangzi wished to smooth things over and greet her as usual, but found he really couldn't. With lowered head he walked into the inner room. Tigress was silent and the small rooms were as still as a cave deep in the mountains. The neighbours' coughs and conversation, the children's cries were distinct yet remote like sounds heard from a mountain-top.

Both remained silent and went to bed one after the other like a pair of big dumb tortoises. After a brief doze, Tigress asked half-crossly, half-jokingly, "Where've you been all day?"

"Pulling a rickshaw!" he mumbled half asleep, as if something were stuck in his throat.

"I knew it! If you don't sweat you feel itchy, you cheap beggar! You don't eat the food I cook for you but gad about all over town, eh? Don't provoke me too far. My father started out as a desperado, nothing scares me. If you go out tomorrow, I'll hang myself just to show you! I mean it!"

"I can't stay idle!"

"Can't you go and see the old man?"

"NO!"

"Hoity-toity!"

Xiangzi, really roused, had to say what he felt or bust. "I'll pull and save up to buy my own rickshaw. If anyone stands in the way, I'll clear out and never come back!"

"Heh! . . ." This snort reverberated in her nose. It expressed her pride and her contempt for him, but at the same time she was thinking things over. She knew that, though honest and simple, Xiangzi was strong-minded. People like that meant what they said. He hadn't been easy to catch, she couldn't let him slip through her fingers. After all, he was an ideal husband: honest, hard-working, strong. At her age and with her looks, it wouldn't be easy to find another such treasure. An iron fist in a velvet glove was needed. She tried soft-soaping him.

"I know you're ambitious, but I really am keen on you. If *you* don't want to see the old man, I'll go. I'm his daughter, after all, it doesn't matter if I lose face."

"Even if the old man takes us back I'm still going to pull!" Xiangzi wanted to get things clear.

Tigress was silent. She hadn't thought him that smart. Those few words had shown quite plainly he was no longer taken in by her and that he was no fool. She would have to use more finesse to rein in this big mulish creature who would buck if provoked. She mustn't push him too hard, for he certainly hadn't been so easy to nab! Tightening and loosening the reins by turn was the way to keep him.

"All right, if you want to pull, I can't stop you. But you must promise not to take a monthly job, and come home every evening. One day without you drives me frantic! Promise me you'll come back early every evening!"

Xiangzi remembered the tall man's advice. Staring into the darkness he seemed to see a host of pullers, peddlers, coolies, all with stiff backs and dragging feet. He would be that way one day. But there was no need to contradict her now, her agreement was already victory enough. So he said, "I'll pull odd fares!"

However, Tigress was not so very eager to hunt up her father. Though they had often quarrelled before, it was different now that she had married out of the Liu family, and this problem would be harder to sort out. A married daughter is never as close to her parents as before, so she didn't dare march straight in. If he really disowned her and refused to give her a cent, there was nothing she could do about it, no matter how much fuss she made. Even a mediator, if there was a deadlock, could only urge her to go home, now that she had a home of her own.

Xiangzi went on pulling a rickshaw while she, left alone in their rooms, paced to and fro. Several times she thought of dressing up to go and see the old man, but her hands were reluctant to move. She was really in a dilemma. For her own comfort and happiness she had to go, but if she did she would forfeit her self-respect. If the old man calmed down and she could drag Xiangzi back to Harmony Yard, some job could easily be found for him there. He needn't pull a rickshaw any more and they could be sure of taking over the business eventually. She brightened up.

But what if her father refused to budge? Not only would she lose face, she'd be condemned to being a rickshaw-puller's wife the rest of her life. Why, she, Tigress, would be no different from any other woman in this yard. The thought filled her with black despair. She almost regretted having married Xiangzi. No matter how hard he tried to get ahead, if her father didn't help he would remain a rickshaw puller forever. At this, she even considered returning alone to the paternal house and breaking with Xiangzi. She couldn't lose everything because of him. But then she thought of the indescribable happiness she had known with him. Sitting on the edge of the brick-bed, her thoughts wandering, she savoured her conjugal bliss and felt like a large red flower opening in the sun. No, she couldn't give up Xiangzi. Let him pull a rickshaw or become a beggar, she would stay with him forever. If the women in this yard could stand it, so could she. That was that, she wouldn't go to see her father.

As for Xiangzi, since leaving Harmony Yard he had avoided Xi'anmen Gate Street. Since he had started pulling two days before, he always headed for the East City to spare himself the embarrassment of running into his old mates in the West City. Today, however, after he'd turned in his rickshaw, he purposely walked past Harmony Yard just to have a look. Tigress' words still rang in his ears, and he wanted to see if he had the courage to return in case she really managed to patch things up with the old man. The best test was walking down the street first.

His hat pulled well down, he kept a wary eye on Harmony Yard from some distance away, fearful of running into an acquaintance. When he saw the light over the gate, he felt strangely unhappy. He recalled the first time he had come here, how Tigress had seduced him and the scene on the night of the birthday party.

Intermingled with these distinct mental pictures were others equally distinct but shorter: the Western Hills, camels, the Cao house, the detective. . . . Everything combined to form a clear frightening whole, so clear that he felt quite overwhelmed, as if he had forgotten his own part in all this and was really looking at pictures. When he realized his involvement his thoughts were thrown into confusion. Dazed, he wondered once more why he had been so wronged and tormented. These scenes seemed to occupy so much and yet so little time that he lost track of his own age. He just felt that he had aged tremendously since first coming to Harmony Yard. His heart had been full of hope then, but now he had a bellyful of worry. He couldn't grasp what had happened, but these pictures were real enough.

When he reached Harmony Yard, he stopped on the opposite side of the road and stared at the bright light over the gate. Suddenly he noticed something. The golden characters — Harmony Rickshaw Yard — had changed! Though illiterate, he remembered very well what the first character had looked like: two sticks joined together, neither cross nor triangle, the strange yet simple character 人 . Judging by the sound, that meant "man". Now it had changed into a stranger character 仁. Why was that? Those two rooms on either side — rooms he would never forget — were both in darkness.

When he was out of patience with standing there he walked home, head down, pondering. Could Harmony Yard have closed down? He must find out, but no need to say anything to his wife yet. When he arrived back, Tigress was cracking melon seeds to distract herself.

"Late again!" She looked cross. "I'm telling you, if this goes on I can't stand it. You're out all day, and I don't dare move with this yard full of paupers, in case we lose something. No one to speak to all day! It won't do, I'm not made of wood. Think of something else, I won't take it!"

Xiangzi said nothing.

"Speak up! Purposely making me mad, are you? Where's your mouth?" Her words tumbled out faster and faster, like a string of snapping fire-crackers.

Still Xiangzi said nothing.

"How about this?" She was really upset, yet didn't seem to know how to tackle him. An urgent, helpless expression, neither happy nor sad appeared on her face. "We'll buy two rickshaws and rent them out and you stay at home and live off the rent. Will that do?"

"Two rickshaws would only bring in thirty cents a day, not enough to live on. We'll rent one out and I'll pull the other. Should manage that way!" Xiangzi spoke very slowly but naturally. Talk of buying rickshaws made him forget everything else.

"But that's the same thing! You'd still be out all day!"

"How about this then." Xiangzi seemed full of ideas since rickshaws had come up. "Rent one out the whole day. The other I'll pull half a day and rent out the other half. If I take the morning shift, I'll go out early and be back by three in the afternoon. For the evening shift, I'll leave at three and come back in the night. Should do!"

Tigress nodded. "Let me think it over. If we can't find anything else, that's what we'll do."

Xiangzi was very happy. If this worked out, he would be pulling his own rickshaw once more. It might be bought by his wife, but by saving up gradually he would be able to buy another. Only now did he feel there was some good in Tigress, and he smiled at her. It was a simple heartfelt smile, as if all previous bitterness were forgotten, and in a trice the world had changed — as easily as changing into new clothes.

CHAPTER 17

X IANGZI gradually found out what had happened to Harmony Yard. Fourth Master Liu had sold some of the rickshaws, the rest he had turned over to another well-known rickshaw owner in the West City. Xiangzi guessed that at his age Old Liu had found the business too much for him without his daughter to help him, and decided to sell out. With the proceeds he had gone off to enjoy himself, but where, Xiangzi was unable to discover.

He didn't know whether to be glad or not at this news. Tigress' plans had fallen through now that her father had abandoned her, so he could keep his self-respect and make an honest living without relying on anyone else. On the other hand, it was a pity about Fourth Master Liu's property. No one knew how he was using the money, for Xiangzi and Tigress had not touched a copper of it.

However, that was that and he didn't give it much further thought or let it upset him. He felt that his muscles were his own and, as he was willing to work, food was no problem. He broke the news quite calmly and simply to Tigress.

She, however, was terribly upset for she saw at once what this meant — she was done for, finished! All her life she would just be a rickshaw-puller's wife! Never would she escape from this tenement courtyard! She had thought her father might marry again, but never had she dreamt he would throw her over like this. Had he married again, she would have fought for part of his property and might even have made a deal with her stepmother to gain some little advantage.... She'd have found some way, as long as the old man kept the rickshaw yard. It was unbelievable that he should have made such an irrevocable and spiteful decision to change the property into cash and then go into hiding! She had rowed with him thinking that a reconciliation was just round the corner, for she knew she was indispensable in the Yard. Who would have thought the old man would close down entirely?

Spring was in the air, the buds on the trees swelled pink. But in the tenement yard there wasn't a single tree or flower. First the ice in the yard was pocked by the spring wind, which blew stinking odours out of the dirty earth and swirled rubbish and scraps of paper against the walls. For the people here, each season brought its worries. Only now did the old folk venture out to sun themselves; only now did the young girls rub some of the soot from their noses, disclosing their old-gold skin; only now could the women herd the children to play in the yard with kites made of torn paper, without their grubby hands chapping from the cold. But the gruel station closed down, there was no more grain on credit, and philanthropists stopped giving handouts. All seemed to have abandoned the poor to the spring breeze and the sun!

The young wheat was still only like grass, grain was in short supply and as usual the prices soared. As the days lengthened, not even the old folk could turn in early to try to cheat their empty stomachs with dreams. The return of spring only increased the troubles of the yard. Lice that had survived the winter — most vicious, these — sometimes crawled out of the padded clothes of the children and old people to enjoy the spring sunshine too.

Tigress watched the ice melting in the yard, saw the tattered clothes, smelt the mixture of warm odours, heard the sighs of the old and the crying of the infants, and her heart contracted. In winter everyone stayed indoors, the filth was frozen; now, people emerged, things showed their original form. Earth was even flaking off the walls of broken bricks, as if they were just waiting to collapse on the first rainy day. The garish yard, filled with the flowers of poverty, was uglier by far than in winter. Ugh, only now did she realize that she would have to live here the rest of her life. Her bit of money would soon be spent and Xiangzi was nothing but a rickshaw puller.

She told him to mind the place while she went to see her aunt at Nanyuan to find out more about her father. The aunt told her the old man had indeed been to see her, around the twelfth day of the first month. He had come to thank her and tell her that he was thinking of going on a pleasure jaunt to Tianjin or Shanghai. If he never in his life left the capital, he said, he couldn't pride himself on being a man. While he still had breath in him he ought to have a look round. Anyway, he was ashamed to stay in town after his daughter had disgraced him completely. That was all the aunt had to tell; her conclusion was even more simple: maybe he really had left town, maybe it was just a blind and he was lying low somewhere — there was no knowing!

When Tigress got home, she threw herself on the brick-bed and had a good cry — this wasn't a put-on act. She wept till her eyes were swollen.

When she had cried herself out, she wiped her tears and told Xiangzi, "All right tough one! Have it your way! I made the wrong bet. Now I'm stuck with you, there's no more to be said. Here's one hundred dollars, go and buy a rickshaw!"

In fact, she still had something up her sleeve. Her original plan had been to buy two rickshaws, one for Xiangzi to pull, the other to rent out. But she had changed her mind. She'd buy only one for Xiangzi to pull and keep the rest of the money. This way, she still retained her authority. She was unwilling to fork out the whole sum in case Xiangzi ditched her after buying the rickshaws. One had to be prepared. Besides, the old man going off in this way made her feel that nobody could be relied on. Who knew what tomorrow would bring? The thing was to enjoy herself while she could and for that she needed money to buy anything she fancied, used as she was to nibbling between meals. They could live off Xiangzi's earnings — he was a first-class puller — and with her bit of cash as pocket-money they could get along quite well for the time being. Money didn't last forever but neither was one immortal! Marrying a rickshaw puller — though she'd had no alternative — had been marrying beneath her; she couldn't lower herself further by asking him for money every day. This decision cheered her a little, for though she knew the future was bleak, at least for the time being she could hold up her head. It was like walking at sunset: the distant sky was already dark, but there was light enough for her to take a few more steps.

Xiangzi didn't argue with her, satisfied to be getting his own rickshaw with which every day he could earn sixty to seventy cents — enough to keep them. He even felt rather pleased. All his previous sufferings had been to buy a rickshaw. Now that he was going to get one, what more did he want? Of course, one rickshaw to support two people would mean nothing left over, and when the rickshaw wore out they'd have nothing put by for a new one. It was risky. But why think so far ahead? Buying one now was difficult enough so he should be satisfied.

One of their neighbours, Er Qiangzi, happened just at this time to want to sell his rickshaw. The summer before, he had sold his nineteen-year-old daughter Joy to an army officer for two hundred silver dollars. For a while he had rolled in wealth, redeemed everything he had pawned and had new clothes made, so that the whole family had been spruced up. His wife was the shortest woman in the yard, the most repulsive too with her bulging forehead, high cheekbones, bald head, freckled face and protruding teeth. Though her eyes were red from weeping for her daughter, she still wore her new blue gown.

Er Qiangzi had always had a violent temper. After selling his daughter, he often went to have a drink; and after drinking, his eyes brimming with tears, he would be particularly cantankerous. So for his wife, new clothes and decent meals were no compensation at all, for she got beaten more than ever before. Er Qiangzi, in his forties, decided to stop pulling a rickshaw. He bought a pair of baskets and fixed himself up with a carrying-pole to peddle melons, fruit, peanuts and cigarettes. After two months, he made a rough calculation and found he was not only losing, but losing heavily. Accustomed to pulling a rickshaw, he didn't know how to do business. Pulling was a straightforward business of getting fares or not, whereas peddling was tricky and he didn't know the ropes. Rickshaw men all live on credit, and he couldn't demean himself by refusing things to his old cronies; but it wasn't easy to get his money back. He couldn't find good patrons, all his customers tried to avoid paying up, so inevitably he lost money. This upset him so much that he drank more heavily. Then he would get into drunken brawls with policemen or come home and vent his frustration on his wife and children. Alcohol was to blame. When he sobered down he bitterly regretted his action and felt very bad. The thought that he'd squandered the money he'd got from selling his daughter, and on top of that he had got drunk and beaten people, made him thoroughly ashamed. At such times, he'd stay in bed for a whole day, trying to drown his unhappiness in dreams.

He decided to give up peddling and go back to pulling. He couldn't let his money slip through his fingers like this. So he bought a rickshaw. When drunk he was absolutely unreasonable; when sober, he liked to keep up appearances to give himself airs and do things in style. With a new rickshaw and smart clothes, he considered himself a high-class puller who should drink good tea and pull stylish customers. At a stand, he would show off his rickshaw and white clothes and chat with the others but never compete for a fare. He would flick his new blue cloth dust-whisk over the rickshaw, stamp his new black cotton shoes with their white soles, look at the tip of his nose and stand there smiling, waiting for someone to come and praise his rickshaw and then start an interminable conversation. He could do this for several days running. Even when he did get a good fare, his legs would belie his appearance — he couldn't run fast! Then terribly depressed, he would think of his daughter, and there was nothing for it but to go and have a drink. In this way he spent all his money and all he had left was the rickshaw.

Round about the winter solstice he got drunk again. When he came home, his sons — one thirteen, the other eleven — tried to dodge out of his way. Infuriated, he gave them each a kick. When his wife said something, he charged her and kicked her in the stomach. For a long time she lay on the ground quite speechless. The two boys frantically grabbed the rolling pin and the coal shovel and set on their father. In the mêlée that followed they trampled their mother a couple of times. The neighbours rushed over and managed to pin Er Qiangzi down on the brick bed while the two boys wept over their mother.

She came to but never set foot on the ground again. On the third day of the first lunar month, she died, still wearing the blue gown bought with the money for her daughter. Her parents, infuriated, threatened to go to court and only after friends had intervened was a compromise reached. Er Qiangzi guaranteed to bury her decently and give her family fifteen dollars. So he pawned the rickshaw for sixty dollars. After New Year he wanted to get it off his hands as he had no hope of redeeming it. When drunk, he considered selling one of his sons, but no one would buy him. He even went to see his daughter Joy's husband, who refused to recognize this "father-in-law", thereby closing all further discussion.

Now Xiangzi knew the history of this rickshaw and wasn't too keen on buying it. There were plenty of rickshaws for sale, why choose this one which had a jinx on it, bought at the price of a daughter and sold because of the murder of a wife?

Tigress didn't see it this way. She thought she could get it for just over eighty dollars and that was a good bargain. It had only been used six months and the tyres hadn't even changed colour. What was more, it was a good make, a genuine product of Decheng Factory in the West City. Why, a half-new rickshaw cost fifty to sixty dollars! She really couldn't let such a bargain slip through her fingers. Besides, just after New Year money was short and Er Qiangzi wouldn't push up the price as he needed cash so badly. She went personally to inspect the rickshaw, bargained with Er Qiangzi and handed over the money. All Xiangzi could do was wait to pull it; he could hardly object since the money wasn't his own.

He examined the rickshaw closely and had to admit it was a good strong one. Still he felt a little uneasy. What he disliked most was the black paint of the chassis and the nickel metalwork. Er Qiangzi had thought the combination smart, but Xiangzi found it depressing, so funereal. He felt like changing the metalwork to something bronze or milky in colour, to liven it up a bit; but he didn't propose this to Tigress, not wanting to listen to her scathing comments.

This rickshaw attracted attention when he pulled it out and some people even called it the "little widow". This annoyed Xiangzi and he tried not to think about it, but the vehicle followed him around all day, keeping him on edge, as if expecting something to go wrong. At times, the sudden thought of Er Qiangzi's sad fate made him feel he was pulling not a rickshaw but a coffin. Often he seemed to see shadows of ghosts around it.

However, nothing happened though he continued to feel jittery. The weather was warming up. Off came padded clothes and there was almost no need for lined clothes — an unlined shirt and trousers were enough, as Beiping has so short a spring. The days were annoyingly and wearisomely long for everyone. Xiangzi would go out bright and early and by only four or five in the afternoon would feel he had done enough. Yet the sun would still be high in the sky. He didn't feel like pulling any more, neither did he want to knock off. He hung about undecided, yawning long and lazily.

If he was tired and bored by the long days, Tigress at home was even more lonesome. In winter, she could sit warming herself by the stove and listen to the wind whistling outside and, though bored, could comfort herself with the thought that it was better to stay indoors. Now, the stove had been moved out under the eaves, there was absolutely nothing to do inside. The yard was filthy and smelly, without so much as a blade of grass in it. She didn't trust her neighbours so when she went shopping she had to hurry straight back without any loitering. She was like a bee trapped in a room, seeing the sunlight outside but unable to fly out.

She had nothing in common with the other women there. Their gossip was all about the neighbours and that held no interest for her, used as she was to straight blunt talk. Their unhappiness stemmed from their bitter life, the smallest thing made them weep; hers came from dissatisfaction with her lot and, having no tears to shed, she would rather relieve herself by quarrelling with someone. Incapable of understanding each other, it was best that they minded their own business.

171

Not until the middle of April did she finally find a companion. Er Qiangzi's daughter Joy returned. Her "man" had been an army officer, who set up a simple home wherever he was stationed by spending one or two hundred dollars to buy a young girl, a large plank bed and a couple of chairs, which enabled him to live happily for a time. When his unit moved away he would just walk out, leaving girl and bed behind.

This outlay was well worth while for a year or two, as hiring a servant to do the washing, mending and other chores would anyway have cost him nearly ten dollars a month, including food. "Marrying" a girl meant he not only had a servant but someone to sleep with too, and he could be sure she had no venereal disease. If she pleased him, he would spend a dollar or so on a flowered print gown for her; if not, he would leave her at home stark naked and there was nothing she could do. When he decamped, he abandoned bed and chairs without a pang, because it was up to her to find some way of paying the last two months' rent, which the money raised from the furniture might not cover.

Joy had sold the bed, paid the rent and come home with nothing but a gown of imported print and a pair of silver earrings.

Having sold the rickshaw and paid back the sum for which he had pawned it, complete with interest, Er Qiangzi was left with about twenty dollars. At times he felt that a middle-aged man who lost his wife was really to be pitied; and as no one else commiserated, he would start drinking alone to console himself. At such times he seemed to bear money a grudge and spent it recklessly. At other times, he felt he should work hard at pulling a rickshaw in order to bring his sons up properly so that they might have some future. Then he would frantically buy great piles of food for them. With tears in his eyes, he would watch them wolf it down and mutter to himself, "Poor motherless children! Ill-fated children! Dad's sweating blood for you! I'm not kidding, I don't mind going hungry myself if you get enough to eat. Tuck in! Just don't forget me when you grow up, that's all!" At such times he spent freely too, and so all twenty dollars were slowly used up.

Penniless, drunk and in a foul mood, he neglected the boys then for a couple of days. They were forced to think up some way of earning a few coppers to fill their stomachs. They acted as attendants at weddings and funerals, sold scrap-iron and waste-paper scrounged from garbage carts and sometimes earned enough to buy a few griddle cakes, sometimes only a pound of small, late sweet-potatoes which they swallowed skins, roots and all. Sometimes, with only a copper between them, they had to make do with a handful of peanuts or roasted kidney-beans which, though not filling, could be chewed on longer.

When Joy came home, they hugged her legs and smiled up at her, speechless and in tears. Mother was gone, Big Sister would mother them now!

Er Qiangzi appeared indifferent to Joy's return. It would mean another mouth to feed. But when he saw his sons' delight he conceded that a family did need a woman to cook and do the washing. So he decided to let things take their course.

Joy was not bad-looking. She had been very thin and slight, but while living with the army officer she had put on weight and even grown a bit. There was nothing particularly striking about her, but her round face and shapely eyebrows and eyes gave her a wholesome appearance. She had a short upper lip which, whether she smiled or frowned, always lifted first to show her even white teeth. The officer had particularly liked these teeth. When they showed, her rather silly, helpless expression made her appear somewhat childish. As in the case of all girls from poor homes who are pretty, this look of hers made her like a flower which as soon as it has any colour or scent is picked to be put on the market.

As a rule, Tigress ignored her neighbours, but she took to Joy right away. In the first place, Joy was pretty; in the second, she had that gown of imported flowered print; in the third, having been married to an officer, she had seen something of the world and so was worth knowing. Women don't make friends readily, but once they start they soon become very thick: within a few days Tigress and Joy were close friends.

Tigress loved to nibble, and whenever she had some melon seeds or other snacks she would call Joy over to share them and they would chat and laugh together. Joy would show her white teeth in that simple way of hers and tell Tigress all sorts of things she had never heard of before. Joy hadn't lived in the lap of luxury, but when the officer was in a good mood he had taken her to restaurants or the theatre, so she had much to recount that roused Tigress' envy.

There were many other things she blushed to speak of, as to her they were degrading; but to Tigress hearing about them was a treat. And when Tigress begged her to tell them, for all her embarrassment Joy didn't like to refuse. Tigress considered her the most lovable and enviable of people. After hearing these tales she would think of herself — her looks, her age and her husband — and feel her whole life had been a raw deal. She'd had no youth to speak of and now she had no future, what with Xiangzi so stubborn and mulish. The more he vexed her, the fonder she grew of Joy. Though the girl was destitute and pitiable, Tigress felt that having enjoyed life and seen the world she could die on the spot with no regrets. For Tigress, Joy symbolized the best a woman could expect from life.

Tigress didn't seem to notice Joy's difficulties. The girl had returned empty-handed, yet she had to provide for her two brothers since her father made no effort to do so. Where could she get the money to feed them?

When Er Qiangzi was drunk he came up with an idea. "If you really feel for your brothers, you'll find a way to feed them! Me, if I'm a beast of burden all day, I have to eat first! Do you think I can run on an empty stomach? I suppose you'd think it funny if I dropped dead in the street! You're idling away your time when you've something ready-made to sell. What are you waiting for?"

Joy looked at her drink-sodden father, at her peaked, famished brothers and then at herself. She could only cry. But tears could not move her father nor feed her brothers, she had to do something more practical. To feed the boys she had to sell her own flesh. Hugging the youngest to her, her tears fell on his hair while he said, "Big Sister, I'm hungry!" Big Sister! Why, she was a piece of meat to be given to her brothers to eat!

174

Tigress, far from commiserating, offered her a loan (repayable later on) to make herself more presentable. Joy's own place being too dirty, Tigress also agreed to rent her one of her rooms which were more decent. She had two anyway so there was space for them both. As Xiangzi was out all day, Tigress was eager to help her friend and at the same time get to know more about what she'd missed out on and couldn't do herself, much as she longed to.

She made only one condition: Joy must pay her twenty cents each time she used the room. Friends are friends, business is business. For Joy's sake, she'd have to keep the place clean which meant not only work but also expenses. Didn't a broom and dustpan cost money? Twenty cents wasn't much, and it was only because they were friends that she was willing to do her this favour.

Joy's lips parted to show her teeth as she swallowed her tears.

Xiangzi knew nothing of this, but his nights were disturbed once more. Since Tigress had started "helping" Joy, she wanted to recapture her lost youth through him.

CHAPTER 18

BY June, the tenement courtyard was completely silent during the day. Very early, the children would go out scavenging with their broken baskets. By nine o'clock, the sun would be blistering their skinny backs and they would return with what they had scrounged and eat what their parents could provide. Then the older ones, if they could scrape together a few coppers' capital, would buy or filch some lumps of ice from the ice-carts and resell them. If they hadn't even this bit of capital, they would go in groups to the moat to bathe. On the way they might steal a few pieces of coal from the station or catch dragon-flies and cicadas to sell to rich families' children. The younger ones dared not wander far but stayed in the shade of the trees outside the courtyard, playing with the insects they found on the locust trees or digging up their larvae. With the children out and the men at work, the women stayed indoors bare-breasted. None stepped outside, not from shame, but because the yard was already like an oven.

Towards evening, men and children came trickling back. There would be some cool breeze in the yard shaded by the walls, while indoors, the heat of the day was trapped as if in a steamer. Everyone sat outside waiting for the women to cook supper. The yard would be as full of bustle and excitement as a market-place without wares. Tempers were short after the long, hot day and hunger didn't improve them. One word out of turn, and the men would hit their children or beat their wives, or take it out on them by a violent tongue-lashing. This din lasted till after supper. Some of the younger children would then go to sleep in the yard, others played in the street. Stomachs filled, the adults' tempers improved and the sociable ones would gather in threes and fours to talk over the day's hardships. With the coming of night, those who hadn't earned enough for the evening meal could neither pawn nor sell anything, even supposing they still had something left. The man would throw himself down on the brick-bed, regardless of the heat in the room. Sometimes he would be glumly silent, at others curse loudly. With tears in her eyes, the wife would make the round of the neighbours and only after many rebuffs would perhaps get a tattered twenty-cent note. Clutching this treasure, she would go and buy some middlings to make the family a pot of porridge.

Tigress and Joy did not fit into this pattern. Tigress was pregnant, this time truly so. Xiangzi went out very early every day, while she lay in bed until eight or nine, having the traditional mistaken notion that pregnant women should move about as little as possible. Apart from that, she wanted to show the neighbours her standing. While they had to get up early to work, she could laze about as long as she pleased. In the evenings, she would take a stool outside the yard to a breezy spot and stay there until everyone else had gone to bed, for she thought it beneath her to chat with them.

Joy also rose late, but for other reasons. She was afraid the men in the yard would eye her askance and so waited for them to leave before venturing out. During the day, she would drop in to see Tigress or stroll outside to advertize herself. In the evening, to escape the notice of the neighbours, she would roam the streets once more, only stealing back when she reckoned everyone was in bed.

Amongst the men, Xiangzi and Er Qiangzi were the odd ones. Xiangzi feared coming into this yard, and even more going into his own rooms. The incessant talking got on his nerves and he longed for a quiet place where he could sit by himself. At home, Tigress seemed more and more to live up to her name. The little rooms were hot and stifling, and with Tigress there he found them suffocating. Before, he had come back early to avoid rows. Now with Joy for company, she didn't pester him so much and he came home later.

As for Er Qiangzi, he had hardly shown up recently. Knowing his daughter's trade, he felt ashamed to face the neighbours. Yet he couldn't stop her, being unable himself to support his children. So he kept away, for "out of sight is out of mind". Sometimes he hated his daughter. Had she been a man she would not have sunk so low. Why did she have to be born into his family? At other times, he pitied her because she was selling her body to feed her brothers. Either way, he could do nothing. When drunk and broke, he neither hated nor pitied her but came back to demand money. At such times he saw her only as a money-earning object while he, as her father, had every right to ask for some of it. He still tried to keep up appearances: everyone looked down on Joy, well, he didn't let her off either. He would shout abuse at her as he pressed her for money, as if to tell everyone that he was blameless while she was naturally shameless.

Joy never said a word when he bawled her out. It was usually Tigress who scolded him and talked him into leaving. Of course, he always left with a few coppers which he continued to drink away, for if he were to come to his senses and see them he would either jump into the river or hang himself.

The fifteenth of June was a broiling hot day. As soon as the sun rose the ground was scorching. A grey miasma, neither cloud nor mist, hung low in the sky and the atmosphere was stifling. There was not a breath of wind. Xiangzi gazed up at the greyish-red sky and decided to pull the night shift, starting after four o'clock. If he earned too little, he could keep on until dawn for the night would surely be more bearable than the day.

Tigress urged him to go out, not wanting him around in case Joy brought back a customer. "You think it's better inside? By noon even the walls are hot!"

He said nothing, drank a ladle of cold water and left.

The willows lining the streets seemed sick, their dusty leaves curling, their branches hanging limp and motionless. The street was bone dry and glaring white. Dust rose from the foot-paths to meet the grey miasma, forming a vicious veil of sand that scorched the faces of the passers-by. Everywhere was parched and stifling as if the whole ancient city were one lighted brick-kiln. Dogs sprawled on the ground, pink tongues lolling out; the nostrils of mules and horses were distended; the peddlers dared not cry their wares; the roads were oozing tarmac; even the brass shop signs seemed about to melt.

The streets were strangely quiet, with only monotonous, aggravating clanging sounding from the blacksmiths' forges. The rickshaw pullers couldn't work up enough energy to call for fares though they knew their next meal depended on it. Some had parked their rickshaws in a shady spot, put up the hood and were napping on the seat; others were drinking tea in small teahouses; still others had come out without their rickshaws to see if there was any business to be had. Those who had fares, even the smartest youngsters among them, were content to lose face and walk slowly along, head down. Every water-well was a life-saver. Even after a few steps, they would rush over and if they had missed a fresh bucket would gulp thirstily from the trough along with the mules and horses. Others, overcome by the heat or an attack of colic, suddenly pitched headlong never to get up again.

Even Xiangzi was daunted. After a few steps with his empty rickshaw, he felt burning hot from top to toe, even the backs of his hands were sweating. Yet when he saw a fare he decided to take him, because he thought there might be a breath of wind once he got moving. But when he started off with his passenger, he realized that nobody could work in such lethal heat. As he ran, he felt he was suffocating and his lips became parched. He wasn't thirsty, yet the mere sight of water set him craving. Whenever he slowed down, he could feel the scorching sun blistering his back. By the time he managed to reach his destination, his clothes were sticking to his body, yet a palm-leaf fan was quite useless for the very wind was hot. Although he'd already had countless drinks of cold water, he made a bee-line for the nearest tea-shop and only after two pots of hot tea did he feel a bit better. With every sip, sweat poured off him as if his body were a void and could no longer retain a single drop of liquid. He dared not move.

After sitting there a long time he was fed up. Afraid to go out yet with nothing to do, he felt the weather was trying to spite him. No, he wouldn't be beaten. This was neither his first summer nor his first time out, he wasn't going to waste a whole day like this. But his legs were leaden and he felt as listless as if he had emerged sweating from a bath without having washed the weariness out of his bones. He sat on a while longer and then decided to leave. Even sitting there he was sweating, so why not try moving on?

But once outside, he knew he had made a mistake. The grey miasma had lifted and it was less stifling, but the sun was beating down more fiercely than ever. No one dared look up because all around was so dazzling, with the air, roofs, walls and ground a glaring white tinged with crimson. The whole world seemed one burning-glass on which the sun's rays had focussed to cause combustion. Under this white light, all colours hurt the eyes, all sounds grated on the ears, all odours reeked of baked earth. The streets seemed deserted and suddenly much wider, but in all that space there was not a breath of cool air — the glare was frightening.

Xiangzi didn't know what to do. He bent his head and plodded on aimlessly, leadenly, his body stinking with sticky sweat. The soles of his feet soon stuck to his socks and shoes, as if he were sloshing through mud. It was disgusting. Each time he saw a well he went over to have another drink, not so much to quench his thirst as to savour the coolness of the water. Trickling down his throat to his stomach it made him shiver, his pores suddenly contracting in a most refreshing way. Then he belched repeatedly as his stomach churned.

Walking and resting by turns, he wandered about until noon without the energy to solicit fares. He didn't feel hungry and though it was time to eat something the mere sight of food made him sick. His stomach chock-full of water was gurgling a little, like the belly of a horse or mule when it has drunk its fill.

He had always dreaded winter more than summer, not knowing how unbearable summer could be. He couldn't remember such heat in all his previous years in town. Was it really hotter, or was he weaker? All of a sudden he felt less muzzy and his heart missed a beat. That was it, he was cracking up! Fear gripped him, but what could he do? He couldn't get rid of Tigress, he was going to become like Er Qiangzi, like that tall puller he had met or Little Horse's grandfather. He was finished!

Shortly after mid-day he got another fare. It was the hottest time of the hottest day that summer, but he decided to take this passenger anyway. Never mind if the sun was broiling, if he made this trip without mishap it would prove he was still fit; if not, he might as well drop dead on the burning ground.

After a few steps he felt a breath of cool air, like a draught from a crack in a door. Hardly believing his senses he glanced at the willow branches — they really were quivering. Suddenly the streets filled with people as those in the shops rushed out clutching rush-leaf fans, jumping up and down as they shouted, "A breeze, a cool breeze! At last!" The willows had become angels bearing tidings from heaven. "The willow branches are swaying! Give us some cool, Old Man Heaven!"

It was still hot but everyone felt much better, for the breeze, though slight, brought them hope. A few more breaths and the sun seemed less scorching. It was bright and dim by turns now, as if a drift of sand were floating across it. Suddenly a wind sprang up and the petrified willows, galvanized by joy, tossed and waved their branches which seemed to have grown longer. A gust of wind and the sky darkened. The air was full of dust and, by the time it settled, the sky to the north was black with clouds. Xiangzi had stopped sweating. He looked northward, then stopped to put up the rain-hood and sheet. He knew the speed with which storms break in summer. There was no time to lose.

Barely had he done this when another gust rolled the dark clouds over half the sky. The heat from the ground mingled with the cool wind which swirled the dry, fetid dust into the air. It seemed both cold and hot. The southern half of the sky was still bright and sunny, the north was black as pitch. As if some catastrophe impended, confusion broke out. Rickshaw men hurriedly put up their rain-hoods, shopkeepers took down their shop-signs, peddlers frantically packed up their wares and passers-by rushed on their way. Another blast and the streets were empty: shop-signs, stalls, pedestrians, all seemed to have been swept away. Only the willow branches remained, dancing madly in the wind.

Even before the sky had become completely overcast, darkness settled over the earth. The bright scorching noon had suddenly become black night. Raindrops carried by the wind spattered now here now there, as if in search of something. A flash of red lightning far away in the north made a bloody gash in the clouds. The wind was dropping, but its soughing made men shiver. Then it passed, leaving everything in a state of suspense, even the willow branches waiting apprehensively. Another flash just overhead was followed by bright rain slashing down, raising dust which now smelt damp. Large raindrops beat on Xiangzi's back and he shivered. The rain stopped and the sky was completely overcast. Another, stronger gust blew the willow branches straight out; dust swirled and a downpour started. Wind, dust, rain, all mingled in one raging cold, murky vortex so that neither trees, earth nor clouds were distinguishable. When the wind died away again the downpour continued, pelting vertically down in a solid mass. Countless arrows shot up from the earth, thousands of waterfalls cascaded down from the roofs. Within a few minutes, earth and sky blended to form a watery world of greyish brown interspersed with flashes of white.

Xiangzi was long since soaked through, with not a dry spot on his body. His hair under his straw hat was sopping wet. The road was already ankle-deep in water, which made walking difficult. Rain slashed his head and back, swept into his face and whipped at his eyes. He couldn't lift his head or open his eyes, couldn't breathe or walk. Stalled in the water, he lost all sense of direction. Conscious only of bone-chilling rivulets running all over him, he was dazed. The only spot of warmth was deep in his heart, and his ears were full of the rushing sound of rain. He wanted to put the rickshaw down, but didn't know where. He wanted to run, but his feet were bogged down.

Laboriously, head bent, he trudged on step by step, pulling a passenger who seemed to have passed out, so silent was he as he let the puller struggle through the water.

The rain lessened and Xiangzi straightened his back slightly. Breathing out hard he asked, "What about taking shelter a while, mister?"

"Keep going! You can't leave me here!" the other shouted, stamping his feet.

Xiangzi really felt like dumping the rickshaw down and finding shelter. But he knew from the water running off him that he would start shivering if he stopped moving. Gritting his teeth, he broke into a run regardless of the depth of the water. Soon the sky darkened then brightened again, and once more rain blurred his eyes.

When they reached their destination, his passenger did not give him one copper extra. Xiangzi said nothing, he was already past caring.

The rain stopped a while, and then it started to drizzle. Xiangzi ran home without stopping for breath and huddled close to the stove. He was shivering like a leaf pelted by rain. Tigress brewed him a bowl of sugared ginger water and he downed it in one unthinking gulp. Then he crawled under his quilt and fell half asleep, the swishing of the rain sounding in his ears.

By four o'clock, the black clouds seemed to have worn themselves out and the flashes of lightning had become feebler. The clouds in the west split apart, their black crests edged with gold, while white mists swirled beneath them. The lightning moved south followed by a few claps of muted thunder. Shortly after, the sun shone through the western cloud gaps, turning the rain-soaked leaves a golden green. In the east, a double rainbow spanned the clouds, its arches holding up a patch of blue sky. Before long this disappeared from the now cloudless sky which, newly washed like everything on earth, seemed to have emerged from darkness into a cool, new world of beauty and brightness. A few colourful dragon-flies even came to flit over the puddles in the tenement yard.

However, apart from the barefooted children chasing the dragon-flies, no one in the yard had time to enjoy the clear skies. Part of the back wall of Joy's room had collapsed and she and her brothers were busily covering the gap with the mat from their brick-bed. The courtyard wall had caved in in several places, but no one had time to attend to that, being much too occupied with their own rooms. Some were flooded because the doorstep was too low and the occupants were making shift to bail them out with dustpans and broken bowls. Other people were rebuilding crumbling walls. Yet others, whose roofs had leaked, were hastily moving out their soaked belongings to dry them around the stove or to sun them on the windowsill. They had taken shelter from the storm in these rooms liable to collapse any minute and bury them alive; the rain over, they cleared up and assessed the damage. After such a downpour, the price of a catty of grain might drop half a copper, but that couldn't make up for their losses. Though they paid rent, no one came to repair the houses unless they became too derelict to live in, when a couple of masons would be sent to patch them up with mud and broken bricks, till they fell apart again. Yet if the rent wasn't paid, the whole family would be thrown out and their belongings impounded. No one cared if the houses were death-traps. What did the tenants expect if they could only afford to rent such wretched hovels?

The worst result of a storm was the illness it caused. Grown-ups and children who spent the whole day in the streets earning a living were the most likely to get caught in summer downpours. Selling their strength, they were constantly in a sweat; and chilling storms break without warning in North China, sometimes with hail-stones the size of walnuts. The cold rain pelting on their open sweat-pores was enough to bring them down with fever for at least a couple of days. When a child fell ill, there was no money for medicine; so though the rain made the corn and sorghum grow, it also killed many of the city's poor children. And if the grown-ups fell ill it was even worse. Poets might sing of lotus flowers pearled with rain or double rainbows; for the poor, when the man of the house fell ill, the whole family starved. Each storm added to the number of prostitutes, thieves and gaol-birds. When the breadwinner is ill, his children will do anything rather than starve. Though rain falls on rich and poor, on good and bad alike, in fact it is unjust because it falls on a world where there is no justice. Xiangzi was ill. Nor was he the only one in that tenement yard.

CHAPTER 19

*A*FTER Xiangzi had been dead to the world for two days and two nights, Tigress began to panic. She went to the Temple of the Goddess and asked for a magic prescription, which called for a little incense ash and two or three medicinal herbs. She poured this brew down Xiangzi's throat and he did indeed open his eyes, but soon he fell asleep again, mumbling incoherently. Only then did she call a doctor. Some acupuncture and a dose of medicine brought him round. As soon as he opened his eyes he asked, "Is it still raining?"

The second bitter brew of medicine he refused, partly because he begrudged the money it cost, partly from shame at having let a wetting lay him up. To prove that he needed no medicine, he decided to get up at once. However, barely had he sat up when his head seemed crushed by a heavy weight, his neck went limp, gold stars danced before his eyes and back he fell on the bed. There was no arguing about that, so he picked up the bowl and downed the brew.

For ten days he lay there, more frantic every day. Sometimes he buried his face in the pillow and wept soundlessly. As he wasn't earning anything, Tigress was paying all the expenses; and when her money gave out, they would be entirely dependent on his rickshaw. She was extravagant and loved to nibble, how could he support her with a child on the way too? The longer he was laid up, the more he brooded and worried, which only delayed his recovery.

As soon as he felt a bit better he asked, "What about the rickshaw?"

"Don't worry," said Tigress. "I've rented it to Ding Si."

"Oh." He felt anxious, for what if Ding Si or someone else damaged it? But as he couldn't get up yet, it obviously had to be rented out, it certainly mustn't stand idle. He started reckoning. If he pulled the rickshaw himself, he could usually bring in fifty to sixty cents a day, barely enough for rent, food, fuel, lamp-oil and tea, not counting clothing for two. Even then they had to skimp and not spend carelessly as Tigress was doing. Now only ten cents' rental was coming in every day, which meant they must stump up forty to fifty cents, not including the cost of medicine.

What if he didn't get better? No wonder Er Qiangzi drank, no wonder his down-and-out friends behaved so disgracefully — this trade was a dead alley! No matter how hard you tried to get on, you must never get married, fall ill or take one false step. Huh! He thought of his first rickshaw, and his savings. He had not offended or wronged a soul, yet though neither sick nor married at the time he had lost them both for no reason. Whatever you did, good or bad, this path led to death and there was no knowing when it would come either. At this thought, his worry gave way to despair. To hell with it, if he couldn't get up, he wouldn't — it was all the same anyway. He lay there quietly, his mind a blank. But soon he couldn't stand it any longer and wanted to get up at once and take up the struggle again.

It might be a dead end, but he wasn't yet in his coffin, and while there's life there's hope. However, he still wasn't strong enough to stand.

Out of sheer frustration he said miserably to Tigress, "I knew that rickshaw was unlucky!"

"Think of getting better. Always talking about the rickshaw, you're rickshaw-mad!"

He said no more. Yes, he was rickshaw-mad! Ever since he had started pulling, he had believed a rickshaw was everything, after all. . . .

As soon as he felt a bit stronger, he got up and looked in the mirror. He barely recognized himself. His face was covered with black stubble, his temples and cheeks had sunk in, his eyes were two pits and even his scar was wrinkled! It was stifling indoors yet he daren't go out, partly because his legs felt soft and boneless, partly because he was afraid to meet anyone. Why, everyone in this yard and at the rickshaw stands of the East and West City knew Xiangzi as one of the strongest young stalwarts. How could he be reduced to this miserable state? He didn't want to go out, but it was very hot in the room. He wished he could eat himself back to health in one mouthful and go and pull once more. But a wasting disease like his comes and goes at will.

He rested for one month, then not caring whether he was completely better or not he took out his rickshaw. With his hat pulled low over his face, he hoped to escape recognition and so be able to run a bit slower. As Xiangzi had always been synonymous with "speed", if he openly crawled along he'd make a laughing-stock of himself.

However, because his health was still undermined and he wanted to take more fares to make up the losses incurred during his illness, he soon had a relapse, this time with dysentery too. He slapped himself in impatience, but it was no use, his stomach seemed to be sticking to his spine and still his bowels were loose. By the time the dysentery finally stopped he could hardly get up from a squatting position. Pulling was out of the question. He rested another month, knowing that Tigress had probably spent nearly all her money.

On the fifteenth of August, he decided to start working. If he fell ill again, he swore, he would drown himself in the river.

Joy had often come to see him during his first illness, and since he could never beat Tigress in argument and had so much on his mind, he had sometimes unburdened himself to her. This had enraged Tigress. When Xiangzi was out, Joy was a good friend; with him back, she was what Tigress called a "shameless strumpet". She pressed Joy to repay what she owed and said, "From now on, you keep away!"

With nowhere to receive clients as her own room was so ramshackle — the mat from the bed still hung over the broken wall — Joy had no alternative but to go to the "Transport Company", to register her name. But the "Company" had no use for her as it specialized in "girl students" and "daughters of good families". It had high connections and charged high prices; it didn't want common prostitutes like Joy. She didn't know what to do. If she went to a brothel, she'd have to turn over all her earnings to it as she had no capital and couldn't work for herself. That would mean complete loss of freedom, so who would look after her brothers? Death was the simplest way out, life was already hell on earth. She was not afraid of death, but neither did she wish to die, for she had something braver and nobler to do. If she could live to see her brothers earning their keep, she could die with an easy mind. Death would come sooner or later anyway, but she would have saved two lives.

After much thought she could see only one way out: to sell herself cheaply. Anyone willing to come to her hovel would obviously not pay much. Very well, then, anyone would do, as long as he paid. This way at least she saved on clothes and make-up. The men who came to enjoy her couldn't expect anything fancy, not for the pittance they paid. She was so young anyway they were getting a bargain.

Now that Tigress was big with child, she was afraid even to go out shopping for fear of a miscarriage. With Xiangzi out the whole day and Joy keeping away, she was as lonely as a house-chained dog. This only increased her bitterness and she felt that Joy was selling herself cheaply just to spite her. To get her own back, she took to sitting in the outer room with the door open, waiting. When she saw anyone going to Joy's room, she would bawl out abuse, embarrassing both the visitor and Joy. When Joy's customers fell off, she gloated.

Joy knew that at this rate, the other tenants would soon join with Tigress to run her out of the place. She was afraid but couldn't afford to be angry, for people in her situation have to be realistic. She led her younger brother over and knelt down before Tigress. She said nothing, but her expression made it clear that if this humiliation were not enough she was prepared to die, but she would have it out with Tigress first. The acceptance of shame is the greatest sacrifice, and the deepest shame is the prelude to resistance.

It was Tigress' turn to be nonplussed. She felt she was being out-manoeuvred, but could not risk a fight with her swollen belly and so had to trump up an excuse. Why, she had only been teasing! Fancy Joy taking it so seriously! After these explanations, they made it up and Tigress helped Joy in everything as before.

Since the Moon Festival when he started pulling, Xiangzi had been taking extra care of himself. Two illnesses had proved to him that he was not made of iron. Though he still had hopes of making money, these setbacks had shown him the weakness of one man on his own. There are times when a real man must grit his teeth, but even then he may spit blood! Though the dysentery was over, he still had gripes from time to time. Sometimes, just as he had got into his stride and was thinking of putting on a bit of speed, his bowels would seem to twist and he would slow down. He might be forced to stop abruptly with his head down, to bear the pain in his stomach as best he could. Pulling alone was not so bad, but when he was with a group and stopped like that, the surprise of the others would make him most embarrassed. He was only in his early twenties yet already making such a fool of himself. What would happen when he was thirty or forty? The thought made him break out in a cold sweat.

A monthly job would have been better for his health, providing some chances to rest. Though you had to run fast, the breaks were long, so it was much easier than pulling odd fares. But he knew Tigress would never agree to it. Marriage had ended his freedom, and on top of that Tigress was such a termagant. It was just his rotten luck!

So for half a year he made do with half-way measures, neither going all out nor slacking, unhappy yet grimly determined. With this new circumspection, he still managed to earn more than an ordinary puller for, unless his stomach-ache was unbearable, he hauled all the fares he could. He had never acquired such tricks of the trade as demanding exorbitant prices, switching fares midway or waiting for one who paid well. This way he worked harder but earned a steady income. He never tried to cheat and so ran no risks.

Still he could not earn enough to put something by. Money came into his left hand and went out from his right, each day he was cleaned out. He gave up all hope of saving anything. He might know how to pinch, but Tigress certainly knew how to spend. Her confinement was due early in the second month after the lunar New Year, and since the beginning of winter she had really begun to swell up. What's more, she liked to stick her belly out to show off her importance. When she looked at herself, she didn't even feel like getting out of bed and let Joy do the cooking. Naturally the left-overs went to the girl's brothers and this meant more expense.

Aside from meals, Tigress had to eat between-whiles. As her belly got larger, she felt she couldn't deprive herself of tasty snacks. Not only did she buy tidbits herself, she ordered Xiangzi to bring some back each day too. So however much he earned, she spent it, her demands growing and lessening with his income. And he could say nothing. During his illness they had spent her money, he owed it to her now to buy what she fancied. If he tried to tighten the purse-strings a bit, she would get ill at once.

"Carrying a child is a nine months' sickness," she told him. "You know nothing about it." And that was the truth. As New Year approached, her demands increased. Unable to get about, she sent Joy on one errand after another. Though she disliked being housebound, she pampered herself too much to go out, so she was bored to death. Her sole distraction lay in more purchases. These, she insisted, were not for herself but for Xiangzi.

"You've slaved a whole year, why not have a bite?" she would say. "You've never completely recovered since that illness. It's the end of the year, eat something, or are you waiting to get as thin as a bed-bug?"

Xiangzi didn't like to argue, didn't know how to. When the food was ready, she would eat two or three large bowls and then, because she took no exercise, would feel so bloated that she clutched her belly and complained that pregnancy was causing her nausea.

After New Year, she refused to let Xiangzi go out in the evenings at all, for she didn't know when the baby might arrive and she was afraid. Only now did she remember her real age and, though she still would not admit it, she stopped saying, "I'm just a *wee* bit older than you."

Her fussing upset Xiangzi. The birth of children is what perpetuates life, and Xiangzi couldn't help feeling rather happy though he had no use for a child; for that simplest, most magic word "Dad", when applied to himself, must surely touch even the heart of a man of stone. Clumsy and awkward as he was, Xiangzi could see nothing about himself to be proud of; but at the thought of that magic word he suddenly became conscious of his own worth. That he had nothing didn't seem to matter; if he had a child his life would not be empty. And so he tried to do all he could for Tigress and wait on her, for she was no longer "one" person any more. True, she was thoroughly disagreeable, but in this matter she deserved full credit.

Yet for all that, the commotion she kicked up was becoming positively unbearable. She was constantly changing her mind and carried on as if possessed by the devil, while Xiangzi had to earn a living and needed rest. Even if the money was squandered, he still needed a good night's sleep to be able to begin another day's hard pulling. Tigress wouldn't let him work at night, neither would she let him sleep in peace, so he went about in a daze all day, heavy-headed. He felt pleased, anxious and annoyed by turns, with sometimes a sense of guilt over his pleasure or of consolation in his anxiety. And being such a simple soul, these conflicting emotions made him lose his balance. Once he even forgot the address his fare had given him and passed the destination!

Round about the Lantern Festival, Tigress sent Xiangzi for a midwife — she could stick it out no longer. The midwife told her it was still too early, and explained to her how to tell when her time had come. Tigress bore up another two days, then made such a commotion that the midwife was sent for again. However, it was still too early. Tigress wept and screamed that she wanted to die, she couldn't stand such torment. Xiangzi didn't know what to do, but to humour her he stopped taking out his rickshaw.

So it went till the end of the month when even Xiangzi could see that her time had really come. Tigress hardly looked human. The midwife returned and hinted to him that it was going to be a difficult birth on account of Tigress' age and the fact that this was her first child. Because she had taken no exercise and eaten too many fatty things, the foetus was very large, and they couldn't hope for an easy delivery. What's more, she had never seen a doctor and it was too late to alter the baby's position in the womb, which was wrong. The midwife had no such skill. All she could say was that it might come out cross-wise and be a difficult delivery.

In this tenement yard, having children and dying in childbirth were mentioned in the same breath. But for Tigress, the danger was greater. Other women worked right up till the time of delivery, and because they had little to eat their babies were never too large, which made for an easy birth. Their greatest risk came afterwards. Tigress was just the opposite. Her privileged position now proved her undoing.

Xiangzi, Joy and the midwife watched over her for three days and three nights. She called on spirits and Buddhas and made innumerable vows, all to no avail. Finally, she became so hoarse she could only moan, "Ma! Oh, Ma!" The midwife was at her wits' end and so was everyone else. It was Tigress herself who told Xiangzi to fetch Grandmother Chen from outside Deshengmen Gate. The old woman, a medium through whom the Toad Spirit spoke, wouldn't come unless paid five dollars; so Tigress brought out her last seven or eight dollars.

"Good Xiangzi, go quickly! Never mind the money. When I'm better, I'll obey you for the rest of my life. Hurry!"

It was nearly lamp-lighting time when the old woman finally arrived with her "acolyte" — a great strapping sallow-faced fellow of about forty. Grandmother Chen herself was around fifty. She wore a blue silk jacket and red pomegranate flowers in her hair, in addition to a complete set of gold-plated jewellery. Her eyes were as sharp as gimlets. First she washed her hands and lit some incense sticks, then kowtowed and sat down behind the table with the incense and stared fixedly at their burning tips. Suddenly her whole body shook in a violent spasm. Her head drooped, her eyes closed and she remained motionless for what seemed a long time. The room was so still you could have heard a pin drop, for even Tigress had bitten back her moans.

Slowly, Grandmother Chen raised her head and looked around, whereupon the "acolyte" tugged at Xiangzi to make him kowtow. Xiangzi wasn't sure that he believed in spirits but felt kowtowing couldn't do any harm, so in a daze he knocked his head on the ground a number of times. When he stood up once more, he looked at those sharp "spirit" eyes, those glowing red incense tips, and sniffed the fragrant smoke, vaguely hoping that something good would come of all this. As he waited blankly, his palms began to sweat.

The Toad Spirit now broke into hoarse and halting speech. "No, no, no matter! Write a charm to hasten, hasten birth!"

The "acolyte" promptly handed her a piece of thick yellow paper. The medium grabbed an incense stick and, wetting it with spittle, began to write. Then she babbled out a few words to the effect that, in a previous life, Tigress had incurred a debt to this child which was why she now had to suffer. Xiangzi, his head humming, didn't understand but began to feel afraid.

Grandmother Chen yawned mightily and, after sitting a while with her eyes closed, opened them as if awaking from a dream. The "acolyte" immediately told her what the Toad Spirit had said, at which she seemed very pleased. "The Spirit is in a good mood today and has spoken!" Then she showed Xiangzi how to get Tigress to swallow the magic charm along with a pill which she gave her.

As the old woman was eager to wait and see the effect of the charm, Xiangzi had to give her a meal. He entrusted this to Joy, who bought some hot sesame paste griddle cakes and a jellied pig's leg. Even then the old woman complained because there was no wine.

After Tigress had taken the charm and Grandmother Chen and the "acolyte" had finished eating, Tigress kept on writhing and moaning for an hour and her eye-balls were beginning to roll upwards. Grandmother Chen had another idea and calmly told Xiangzi to kneel in front of a tall incense stick. By this time, Xiangzi had lost most of his faith in Grandmother Chen, but since he had paid her five dollars he thought he might as well give all her methods a try. As he couldn't beat her up, he might as well comply — there was just a chance they might work.

Kneeling erect before the incense stick, he didn't know which spirit to pray to, but he felt he should be sincere. Gazing at the flickering incense, he seemed to see shadowy forms on its glowing tip and it was to these that he prayed. The incense burned low, its red tip began to turn grey; he lowered his head, put his hands on the floor and dozed off, for it was three days since he had had a good sleep. When his head jerked forward and he woke with a start, the incense had nearly burnt out. Without caring whether it was time to get up, he rose slowly, his legs numb.

Grandmother Chen and the "acolyte" had already stolen away.

Xiangzi had no time to hate her but hurried over to Tigress, aware that there was no help for her now. She was at her last gasp, unable even to moan. The midwife, not knowing what else to do, advised him to take her to the hospital.

Xiangzi's heart seemed to split in two, he burst out sobbing. Joy was weeping too, but as a bystander she kept her wits about her. "Brother Xiangzi, don't cry! Let me go to the hospital and ask!"

Without caring whether he had heard or not, she ran out wiping her tears.

An hour passed before she came running back, almost too breathless to speak. Leaning against the table, racked by a hacking cough, she finally gasped out that the doctor charged ten dollars for one visit, just to examine the patient. A delivery cost twenty. For a difficult birth, they would have to go to the hospital, which would cost several dozen dollars. "Brother Xiangzi, what shall we do?"

There was nothing that Xiangzi could do except wait. Those who were doomed must die!

Ignorance and cruelty are part of the natural order of things, for which there are different reasons.

At midnight, Tigress breathed her last with a dead child in her belly.

CHAPTER 20

XIANGZI sold his rickshaw!

Money slipped through his fingers like water. The dead have to be buried, and even a death certificate to paste on the coffin cost money.

He watched woodenly as everyone bustled about, while all he did was fork out money. His eyes were frighteningly red, with a yellowish rheum at the corners; and like a deaf man, not knowing what he did, he stumbled round after the others.

Only when he had followed Tigress' coffin outside the city did his mind clear a little; still he was unable to collect his thoughts. Joy and her two brothers were the only other mourners, each holding a thin sheaf of paper money to throw to the spirits who might bar the way.

In a daze, dry-eyed, he watched the bearers lower the coffin into the grave. There seemed to be a ball of fire in his chest which had dried all his tears so that he could not weep. He stared blankly, as if unaware of what they were doing. Only when the head-bearer told him they had finished did he think of going home.

Joy had tidied up the rooms. He threw himself on the brick-bed as soon as he got back, bone-tired. His eyes were too dry to close, so he stared fixedly at the patches on the ceiling where the roof had leaked. Sleep evading him, he sat up, glanced around and then lowered his eyes. Not knowing what to do, he went out and bought a packet of cigarettes, then sat on the edge of the bed to light one, not that he ever liked smoking.

As he stared at the wisp of blue smoke at the tip of the cigarette, tears suddenly started to stream down his cheeks as he thought not only of Tigress but his whole life. A few years in town and all his efforts had ended in this! Even his weeping was silent. Why, a rickshaw was his rice-bowl. He had bought one and lost it, bought another and sold it. Twice he had attained his ideal only to lose it again, putting up with all those hardships and wrongs for nothing. He had nothing, nothing, even his wife was gone! Tigress might have been a termagant, but without her what home could he have? All the things in the room were hers, yet she was buried outside the city gates! Bitterness flooded his soul, blazing anger dried his tears and he puffed furiously at his cigarette. The more he disliked smoking, the harder he smoked. When the packet was empty, he rested his head in his hands, the same acrid bitterness in his soul as his mouth. He felt like screaming or spitting out his heart's blood.

At some point Joy had come in. She was standing by the chopping-board in the outer room, watching him fixedly.

When suddenly he raised his head and saw her, the tears rushed out once more. In his present state, he would have wept at the sight of a dog, for the presence of any living thing tempted him to pour out all his grievances. He wanted to speak to her, to get some sympathy; but there was too much to say and so he remained silent.

"Brother Xiangzi!" She edged nearer. "I've straightened things up."

He nodded without thanking her; for in grief conventional politeness rings false.

"What are you going to do?"

"Eh?" He didn't seem to understand. Then the words registered and he shook his head — he hadn't thought that far yet.

She moved nearer and blushed suddenly, showing her white teeth, but said nothing. Life had forced her to forget modesty, but when it came to something really important she was still a decent woman who tried hard to act properly.

"I was thinking . . ." was all she said. She had much in her heart to say, but as she flushed it vanished and she could not remember a word.

People seldom tell each other the whole truth, but a woman's blush is more expressive than words. Even Xiangzi knew what she meant. In his eyes she was a most beautiful woman, lovely to her very bones. Were she to become covered in sores, her flesh rotting away, he would still find her beautiful. She was pretty, young, anxious to better herself and thrifty. If he wanted to remarry, she would be an ideal wife. However, he was in no hurry to remarry — it was too early to make any plans. But since she was willing and driven by harsh reality to propose it so soon, he could not very well refuse. She was so decent and had helped him so much, he could only nod, longing to take her in his arms and have a good cry, cry all his grievances away and start life anew with her. To him, she personified all the comfort a man could and should receive from a woman. Normally taciturn, with her he felt like saying all sorts of things. With her to listen, he wouldn't speak to no purpose. A nod or smile from her would be the best of replies and would really make him feel he had a home.

At that moment, Joy's second brother came in. "Elder Sister! Dad's come!"

She frowned and opened the door just as Er Qiangzi lurched across the yard.

"What are you doing in Xiangzi's place?" Er Qiangzi was glaring and swaying on his feet. "It's bad enough selling yourself, do you have to give yourself free of charge to Xiangzi? You shameless slut!"

Hearing his name, Xiangzi came out and stood behind Joy.

"I say, Xiangzi!" Er Qiangzi tried to throw out his chest, though he couldn't even stand straight. "I say, call yourself a man? Why try to get something for nothing from her of all people? Swine!"

Xiangzi didn't feel like brawling with a drunk, but all his pent-up misery made him unable to control his anger. He took a step forward. The glare from their blood-shot eyes seemed to clash in the air and throw out sparks. Xiangzi grabbed the other man's shoulders, lifted him like a child and hurled him across the yard.

Er Qiangzi felt a pang and, being in his cups, put on a show of fury, acting drunker than he really was. The fall had so-bered him in part. He wanted to fight back, but knew he was no match for Xiangzi. On the other hand, beating a quiet retreat would be far too humiliating. So he sat on the ground, unwilling to get up yet embarrassed to remain there. In his confusion, all he could do was growl disjointedly, "What business is it of yours if I scold my daughter? Beat me, would you? Fuck your grandmother! You'll have to pay for it!"

Xiangzi did not reply but waited quietly for him to fight back.

Joy, with tears in her eyes, didn't know what to do. It was no use trying to reason with her father and she didn't want to see him beaten by Xiangzi. Rummaging in all her pockets she scraped together a dozen coppers which she handed to her brother. Normally, the boy dared not approach his father, but today after seeing him thrown he plucked up his courage. "Here you are. You'd better go!"

Er Qiangzi squinted at the money, then pocketed it and stood up muttering, "I'll let you bastards off this time! If you go too far, I'll kill the lot of you!" Just before stepping out of the yard he shouted, "Xiangzi, we're not finished yet! We'll meet outside!"

Once he had gone, Xiangzi and Joy went back into the room.

"What can I do?" Joy muttered to herself, this sentence expressing all her desperation and her hope that Xiangzi would have her, to give her some way out.

However, this incident had shown Xiangzi many drawbacks to Joy. He still loved her, but didn't feel he could take on the responsibility of keeping her brothers and drunken father. He still couldn't believe that Tigress' death had freed him. Even she had had her strong points and had at least helped him a lot with her money. He didn't think Joy would live off him, but it was a fact that her family was unable to earn anything. Love or no love, the poor have their minds made up for them by money. The "shoots of love" grow only amongst the rich.

He began to pack his things.

"You moving out?" She was white to the lips.

"Yes!" He hardened his heart. In this unjust world, the poor have to be hard-hearted to retain their modicum of freedom.

After glancing at him she lowered her head and went out. She felt no hatred or resentment, only despair.

Tigress had been buried in her jewellery and smarter clothing, leaving behind only some old clothes, a few sticks of furniture and her pots and pans. Xiangzi picked out some of the slightly better clothes and sold everything else without bargaining to a scrap-vendor for a dozen odd dollars. He was in such a hurry to move out, to get rid of everything, that he couldn't be bothered to hunt around for someone to give him a better price. When the peddler had left, all that remained were his bedding-roll and the old clothes on the bare brick-bed. With the room so empty he felt easier, as if he had thrown off his bonds and was free now to fly far away.

After a while, though, he recalled all those objects. The table was gone, but it had left marks in the form of small squares of dust round where the four legs had rested on the ground. Such traces reminded him of the furniture; of Tigress, all vanished like a dream. Good or bad, without them his heart had no resting place. He sat on the edge of the bed and pulled out a cigarette.

With the cigarette came a tattered note and without thinking he fished all his money out. These last few days he had not got around to counting it. There was quite a pile: silver dollars, ten cent notes, cent notes and coppers. All told, not quite twenty dollars. Plus the dozen or so from the stuff he had sold, his entire capital only came to just over thirty dollars.

He stared at the money on the brick-bed, not knowing whether to laugh or cry. There was nothing else in the room apart from himself and this pile of tattered dirty money. It didn't make sense.

He gave a long sigh and stuffed the money back into his pocket. Then he picked up his bedding-roll and the few clothes and went to find Joy.

"These clothes are for you. I'll leave my roll here while I find a rickshaw yard. Be back later to pick it up." He dared not look at her as, head lowered, he rattled this off.

Her only answer was a murmured assent.

By the time Xiangzi had found a rickshaw yard and come back for his bedding, Joy's eyes were swollen from weeping. Not knowing what else to say he blurted out, "Wait for me. When I've made good, I'll come back, I really will!"

She nodded, still silent.

After only one day's rest, Xiangzi started pulling again. No longer was he so eager, nor was he lazy, but let the days drift by. After a month or so, he felt quite placid and his face had filled out a bit, though it was not as ruddy as before. He looked neither robust nor weak. His eyes were very bright but devoid of expression, as if he were on the alert all the time yet saw nothing. He was like a tree after a storm, standing quietly in the sunshine, afraid to move again. Never talkative, he was even more taciturn now. The weather was already quite warm and the willows were bright with tender green leaves. Sometimes he pulled his rickshaw into the sun and sat with lowered head, his lips moving slightly, or turned his face up to the sunlight and dozed for a while. Unless obliged to, he hardly spoke to a soul.

Smoking had become an addiction. Whenever he sat in the rickshaw waiting for a fare, his big hands would grope under the footrest where he kept his cigarettes. He would puff slowly, his eyes intent on the spirals of smoke drifting upwards. Then he would nod, as if he had reached some kind of conclusion.

He still ran faster than most other pullers, but he no longer tried so hard. Especially at corners and on slopes he was almost excessively careful. No matter how hard anyone tried to provoke him into racing, he would lower his head and keep on at his own steady pace. It was as if, completely disillusioned, he no longer cared about winning praise or fame.

However, in the rickshaw yard he made friends in spite of his taciturnity, for even a silent wild goose likes to fly with the flock. Without cronies, his loneliness would have been unbearable. As soon as he produced a packet of cigarettes he would pass it around. If there was only one left which no one would take, he would say briefly "I'll buy more!" When the rest were gambling, he no longer stayed away but came over to have a look and sometimes even added a stake without caring whether he lost or won, as if to show that he was one of them and knew that they all needed some amusement after the day's hard work. When they drank he did too, though not much, and he would stand everyone drinks and snacks. Everything he had formerly disapproved of now seemed quite reasonable. Since he had failed, why not admit that others might be right?

When one of his friends had a wedding or funeral, he would also contribute forty cents or chip in to buy a present, a thing he would never have dreamed of doing before. Not only that, he would go to mourn or offer congratulations, because he realized now that gestures like these were not just a waste of money but an essential part of human fellowship. The grief or joy on such occasions were genuine — people weren't putting on an act.

However, he did not touch those thirty-odd dollars. He got a piece of white cloth and with a big needle clumsily sewed the money up in it and kept it next to his skin. He didn't want to spend it, didn't want to buy a rickshaw any more. Keeping it on him was a kind of precaution — you never knew when some calamity might strike. He might fall ill or meet with some other disaster, and it was always better to be prepared. He knew now that men were not made of iron.

Just before the autumn set in, he got a monthly job. It was lighter than all his previous ones; otherwise, he wouldn't have accepted it. He knew now how to pick and choose. If there was something suitable he accepted, if not, he was quite willing to pull odd fares. No longer did he go all out, aware that he needed to look after his health and that if a puller drove himself too hard, as he had before, he would kill himself quite pointlessly. Experience teaches men craftiness — after all, you only live once!

His new job was near the Yonghe Lamasery. His employer Mr. Xia was in his fifties. An educated man who understood the proprieties, he had a wife and twelve children. However, he had recently taken a concubine and, not daring to tell his family, he had chosen this quiet spot in which to set up another little household. Apart from himself and the concubine, it comprised a maid and a rickshaw puller — Xiangzi.

Xiangzi liked this job very much. The house was small with only six rooms of which Mr. Xia occupied three, the kitchen one and the servants the other two. The yard was very small. By the southern wall grew a young date tree with a dozen fat red dates on its top branches. Two or three sweeps of the broom took him from one end to the other, and that was extremely easy. With no flowers to water he was tempted to prune the date tree; but knowing the stubborn propensity of date trees to grow gnarled and crooked, he refrained.

There was little else to do. Mr. Xia went to his yamen to work in the morning and didn't come back till five in the afternoon. All Xiangzi had to do was take him and fetch him back; for once home, Mr. Xia never went out, just as if he were in hiding. Though Mrs. Xia often went out, she always returned by four to let Xiangzi go and fetch her husband, and that done he was free for the rest of the day. What's more, Mrs. Xia only went to the Dong'an Market or Zhongshan Park, so there was plenty of time to rest there too. It was child's play to Xiangzi.

Mr. Xia was very tight-fisted and never parted lightly with a cent. Wherever he went, he looked straight ahead as if there were no one and nothing around. But the concubine was free-handed and went shopping every few days. If she bought food and didn't like it, she gave it to the servants. She'd hand over other articles to them too when she wanted to ask for money to buy new ones. Mr. Xia's mission in life seemed to be to lavish all his energy and money on his concubine — he had no other interests or enjoyments. All his money passed through his concubine's hands; he himself never spent any, much less gave any away. His original wife and twelve children lived in Baoding and, it was said, sometimes went four or five months without receiving a cent from him.

Xiangzi disliked the way this Mr. Xia crept about like a thief, hunched up, his neck pulled in, his eyes on his toes, silent and stingy and joyless. Even seated in the rickshaw, he looked like a skinny monkey. On the rare occasions when he did say something, it was bound to be offensive, as if everyone else were a rascal and he the only upright learned gentleman around. Such a man was impossible to like. But business was business, and as long as Xiangzi got paid every month what did he care about the rest? What's more, the concubine was easy-going and kept giving him food and other perks. Why quibble? It just amounted to pulling an inconsiderate monkey.

Xiangzi didn't particularly like the concubine, simply considering her as a provider of tips. She was far lovelier than Joy, who could never compare with someone so scented and powdered, dressed in silks and satins. But though she was beautiful and smartly dressed, she reminded him in some strange way of Tigress. It was neither her clothes nor her face, but something which he couldn't quite pin down in her attitude and behaviour. In his words, she was the same line of goods.

Though only twenty-two or three, she seemed very mature with nothing of the new bride about her, as if like Tigress she had never shown girlish gentleness and shyness. Her hair was waved, she wore high-heeled shoes and her clothes were made to show off her curves as she swayed along. Even Xiangzi could see that, stylish as she was, she hadn't the tone of normal married ladies. Yet she didn't look like a prostitute. Unable to place her he found her as intimidating as Tigress. More so, in fact, as she was younger and more beautiful. She seemed the personification of all the female cruelty and viciousness which he had experienced. He really dared not look her in the face.

Some days later, he grew even more scared of her. Xiangzi had never seen Mr. Xia spend much money, but now and then even he would go and buy medicine in a large pharmacy. What kind, Xiangzi didn't know, but after each such purchase, Mr. and Mrs. Xia would seem particularly affectionate and Mr. Xia, usually such a feeble creature, would display extraordinary energy. Within a few days, however, he would be deflated again, more stooped than ever, just like a fish bought live in the street and put in a bucket of water, where after thrashing about for a while it presently quiets down. Whenever Mr. Xia looked like a shrivelled-up ghost crouched in the rickshaw, Xiangzi knew it was time to make another trip to the pharmacy. He disliked the man, but each time they went to buy medicine he couldn't help pitying this skinny old monkey. Then he would think of Tigress and feel quite miserable. He didn't wish to hate the dead, but when he looked at himself and Mr. Xia he couldn't help blaming her. He wasn't as strong as he had been, no doubt about it, and Tigress was largely responsible for that.

He considered quitting the job, but it seemed a ridiculous thing to do for reasons that didn't concern him. As he puffed at a cigarette he muttered to himself, "What's it got to do with me anyway?"

CHAPTER 21

*W*HEN the chrysanthemums came on the market, Mrs. Xia bought four pots and the maid, Yang Ma, broke one of them, for which she was roundly abused. Yang Ma came from the country and, to her, there was nothing special about flowers and plants. Still, as she had been careless enough to damage someone else's property, no matter how insignificant, she said nothing. But when Mrs. Xia went on and on about it, calling her a country bumpkin and a vandal, Yang Ma couldn't keep her temper and answered back. When country folk get worked up they don't watch their tongues, so Yang Ma came out with the crudest curses. At that, Mrs. Xia hopped with rage and ordered her to roll up her bedding and clear out.

Xiangzi had not intervened because he was slow of tongue and two quarrelling women were quite beyond him. When he heard Yang Ma call Mrs. Xia a tart, he knew that her job was gone and guessed that he too would be fired, for Mrs. Xia wouldn't want to keep any servant who knew of her shady past. After Yang Ma had left, he waited for his dismissal which he reckoned would come when the new maid arrived. He didn't care, for experience had taught him to take and lose jobs with equanimity. There was no need to get worked up about anything.

However, after Yang Ma had gone, Mrs. Xia became quite surprisingly polite to Xiangzi. With no maid, she had to cook herself and she gave him money to go marketing. When he returned, she told him what to wash and what to peel, while she chopped up the meat and boiled the rice, talking away all the time.

She was wearing a pink bodice, black trousers and white satin embroidered slippers. Xiangzi did his chores clumsily and dared not look at her, much as he wanted to, for her perfume tickled his nose tantalizingly, impelling him to look, just as the scent of flowers attracts the bees. Against his will he glanced at her.

He did not despise this beautiful concubine who was also a tart, for though she was both these things she was also nothing. To justify this attitude, he thought it was that skinny old monkey Mr. Xia who was disgusting and reprehensible. With a husband like that, nothing she did could count as wrong and with such an employer he, Xiangzi, could do as he pleased. His courage returned.

Yet she didn't notice his glances, and when the meal was ready she ate alone in the kitchen then called to him, "Come and eat! Then wash up. When you go to fetch the master this evening, you can pick up the evening groceries and so save yourself a trip. Tomorrow is Sunday, the master will be at home. I must go and find a maid. Know of anyone you could recommend? So difficult to find! Never mind, eat first before the food gets cold!"

She spoke quite naturally and easily. Suddenly that pink bodice seemed to Xiangzi much less vivid. He felt disappointed and then ashamed. Clearly, he was no longer a man with a goal in life, but actually a bad lot! He swallowed two bowls of rice feeling quite fed up. After washing up, he went to his room and chain-smoked for a while.

In the afternoon when he went to fetch Mr. Xia he suddenly found himself loathing this skinny old monkey. He really felt like putting on a spurt and then dumping the rickshaw to knock the old fellow silly. He deliberately jerked the shafts to rock him a bit. When Mr. Xia said nothing, Xiangzi felt rather put out. Never had he ever done anything like this before and, though he might have good reason for it now, that was no excuse.

When he had calmed down, he forgot this futile incident; and when he happened to remember it, it seemed quite ridiculous.

The next day, Mrs. Xia went out to find a maid and presently returned with one on probation. Xiangzi foresaw that he would have to go, but the whole business left a bad taste in his mouth.

After lunch on Monday, Mrs. Xia dismissed the maid, saying that she was too dirty. She then sent Xiangzi to buy a pound of chestnuts.

When he had brought the hot chestnuts back, he called to her from outside the door of her room.

"Bring them in!" she replied from inside.

He went in to find her powdering her face before the mirror. She was still wearing the pink bodice but had changed into a pair of pale green trousers. Seeing him in the mirror, she quickly turned round and smiled. In this smile, Xiangzi saw Tigress, a young and beautiful Tigress. He stood there woodenly. His boldness and hopes, his fears and caution vanished, leaving only a hot breath of air to buoy him up. This breath was his motive force — he had no will of his own.

Three or four days later, in the evening, he returned to the rickshaw yard with his bedding.

What he had previously dreaded and would have died of shame to admit, he now spoke of jokingly to everyone: he could not urinate!

Everyone was only too eager to tell him what medicine to buy, which doctor to go to. No one felt it was anything to be ashamed of but sympathetically offered him advice and, a little red in the face, proudly told of similar experiences. Some young pullers had paid to get this disease; several middle-aged ones had got it free of charge; quite a few who had held monthly jobs had been in much the same kind of situation; yet others, who hadn't experienced this themselves, had different tales of employers well worth telling. Xiangzi's illness loosened their tongues and made them speak freely. Though he forgot his shame he felt no pride, but took it all in his stride as one would a cold or a mild attack of sunstroke.

The medicine and prescriptions cost over a dozen dollars yet didn't cure him completely, because as soon as he was slightly better he stopped taking medicine. On cloudy days or at a change of season when his joints ached, he would dose himself again or just stick it out grimly. He didn't care any more. When life was already so bitter, what did health matter?

When he did recover at last, he was a changed man. Still tall, but no longer so vigorous, he purposely let his shoulders sag and kept a cigarette dangling from his lips. Sometimes he would stick a butt behind his ear, not because that was a convenient place but to make himself look tough. Still taciturn, he could, when he wanted, engage in repartee which though neither fluent nor smart had the right twang to it. His will was sapped and his whole attitude was lackadaisical.

However, compared to his mates, he still was not so bad. When he was alone, he would recall what he had been and still long to make good. He didn't want to go downhill like this. Though ambition got you nowhere, destroying yourself was not very clever either. At such times, he would think of buying a rickshaw. Over a dozen dollars of his original thirty had been spent on his illness. What a waste! But with twenty, he was still better off than those without a cent. He really felt like throwing his half-smoked packet of cigarettes away, cutting tobacco and liquor and grimly saving money. Then he would think of Joy and feel really guilty. Ever since he had left the yard he had never gone back to see her. Now, not only had he not made good, but he had even got a shameful disease.

Yet when he was with friends he went on smoking and drinking a little whenever he had the chance, and then he forgot her completely. He never took the lead but couldn't refuse to go along with his mates. A hard day's work and a bellyful of grievances could only be forgotten for a while when he talked and joked with them. Present enjoyment banished high ideals; he wanted to have some fun and then fall into a deep heavy sleep. Who wouldn't have preferred this with life so pointless, bitter and hopeless? The cankers of life could only be alleviated with tobacco, drink and women. Let poison fight poison. Everyone knew that one day it would corrode the heart, but who had any better way out?

His self-pity grew with his lack of will-power. Whereas nothing had daunted him before, he was now mindful of his comfort: on windy, rainy days he did not go out; if he felt any aches or pains he would rest for a few days. Self-pity made him selfish, unwilling to lend anyone a single cent of his money which he kept for those rainy, windy days. Standing others fags and drinks was all right, but not lending. He was more deserving of pity and care than anyone else. The more he took things easy the lazier he became and, feeling bored with nothing to do, he would find some amusement or buy something good to eat. Even when it occurred to him that he shouldn't waste time or money in this way, he had an argument culled from much experience, "I tried to make good before, and where did it get me?" This was irrefutable and unanswerable. So what was to stop Xiangzi from destroying himself?

Laziness makes people irascible, and Xiangzi now grew pugnacious. No longer did he humour fares, policemen or anyone else. No justice had been shown him when he worked hard. Now he fully appreciated the value of his sweat, and if he could shed one drop less, he did. No taking advantage of him any more! He would park his rickshaw where and whenever he felt like it, rules or not. When a policeman came over to move him on, he would argue and stay put as long as he could. When it was clear he would have to move, he became even more vociferous and started cursing. Should the policeman answer back, then a fight was nothing to get excited about, for Xiangzi knew he was strong. After beating up the policeman, he didn't care if he went to jail for a few days. Fights made him feel his strength and ability. Bashing into someone with all his might so exhilarated him that the sun seemed particularly bright. Before, he would never have dreamed of getting into a fight, yet now he actually got pleasure out of it. it was really laughable!

Unarmed policemen did not daunt him, neither did the cars in the streets. When they hurtled towards him, blowing up the dust, he refused to make way no matter how loudly they honked or the passengers ranted. Only when the vehicle was forced to slow down would he move aside so as not to choke on the dust. It was the same when the car came from behind. Knowing perfectly well no driver dared run into him, he didn't see why he should move away and let the car raise all the dust in

211

the street. Policemen cleared the way only for motorized vehicles, just so that they could go fast and swirl up dust. Xiangzi, not being a policeman, wouldn't let them career about. To the police he was a "prickly pear" of the first water and none of them dared provoke him. Among the poor, sloth is the natural result of hard work that goes unrewarded and they have some reason for their irascibility.

He also refused to be obliging to his fares. He would take them where directed, not one step further. If they told him the "mouth" of some alley and then expected him to pull them "into" it, nothing doing! If his fare glared, Xiangzi outglared him. He knew how afraid these gentlemen were of getting their foreign suits dirty, and how unreasonable and tight-fisted most of them were. So if they flared up, he was ready to grab one sleeve of their sixty-dollar suits and leave a great black handprint on it. After this they still had to pay up, knowing the strength of his grip which had left their skinny arms aching.

He still ran fairly fast, but would not speed up for nothing. If his fares hurried him, he would scrape his big feet along the ground and ask, "How much for going faster?" Why be obliging? He was selling his sweat and blood. He no longer hoped for a generous tip. Everything had its price which must be settled in advance before he exerted himself.

Neither did he look after the rickshaw as before. Since giving up the idea of buying his own, he didn't care about other people's either. It was only a rickshaw. By pulling it he could earn food and clothing and the cost of the rent. If he didn't pull, he needn't pay rent, so as long as he had enough money for a day's food why take it out? That was all there was to the relationship between man and rickshaw. Of course, he would never deliberately damage anyone else's vehicle, but there was no need to take extra care either. If some other puller knocked into it by accident, instead of flying into a rage he calmly pulled it back to the yard. If told to pay fifty cents for the damage, he would fork out twenty and no more. Should the owner protest, and be ready to come to blows to settle things, Xiangzi was quite willing to oblige.

Life feeds on experience, which shapes men's character — impossible to grow peonies in the desert. Xiangzi was now in a rut, neither better nor worse than other rickshaw pullers but cast in the same mould. This way he actually felt more comfortable and the others accepted him too. All crows are black, and he didn't want to be the solitary white one.

Winter came once more. In one night, the dust-laden wind from the desert froze many people to death. Listening to it howling outside, Xiangzi buried his head in his quilt and decided to stay put. Only when its fiendish whistling had stopped did he reluctantly get up, undecided whether to go out or not. He didn't feel like holding those icy cold shafts and was afraid of that choking, sickening blast. By four in the afternoon the sun went down and the wind dropped completely, while some evening pink appeared in the dusky sky. He forced himself to go out, walking slowly and listlessly. Hands tucked in his sleeves, he used his chest to push the crossbar, a half-smoked cigarette dangling from his lips.

Darkness fell. He hoped to get a fare quickly the sooner to knock off. He was too lazy to light his lamps and only did so after policemen along the way had reminded him four or five times.

Under the street lamps in front of the Drum Tower he managed to get a fare and started off towards the East City. Without taking off his thick padded gown, he trotted along. He knew it looked disgraceful but couldn't care less. Did anyone pay more for a presentable-looking puller? He wasn't pulling a rickshaw, just messing around. Even when sweat beaded his forehead he didn't take off his gown but decided to make do. In a small alley, a dog, unaccustomed to a long-gowned puller, nipped at his heels. He stopped, grabbed his dust-whisk by the whisk-end and raced after the cur. Having chased it away and waited to make sure that it wasn't coming back, he cursed with gusto, "Fucking thing! Think I'm afraid of you?"

"What sort of rickshaw puller are you anyway?" his passenger asked irately.

Xiangzi pricked up his ears: the voice was familiar. The alley was very dark, and though his lamps were bright the beams were directed downwards so that he couldn't see his passenger's face. The man was wearing a hood and his mouth and nose were muffled in a large scarf, leaving only his eyes showing. Xiangzi was still wondering who he was when the man asked:

"Aren't you Xiangzi?"

Xiangzi realized it was Fourth Master Liu! He was stunned and went hot all over. For a moment he didn't know what to do.

"Where's my daughter?"

"Dead!" Xiangzi stood his ground, scarcely able to recognize his own voice.

"What? Dead?"

"Dead!"

"What else, in your fucking hands!"

Xiangzi suddenly recovered himself. "You get out, go on, get out! You're too old for me to beat up, so get out!"

Fourth Master Liu climbed down, trembling. "Tell me, where is she buried?"

"None of your business!" Xiangzi picked up the shafts and walked off.

When he had gone quite a distance, he turned his head and saw the old man, a big black shadow, still standing in the alley.

CHAPTER 22

*W*ITHOUT thinking where he was going, Xiangzi strode along, head up, eyes shining, grasping the rickshaw shafts tightly, oblivious of direction or destination. He felt carefree and happy, as if he had heaped all the bitterness tasted since marrying Tigress on to Fourth Master Liu. Cold and fares forgotten, he wanted to walk on and on as if somewhere he would rediscover his old self, that unfettered, unburdened, decent, ambitious and hard-working Xiangzi.

The vision of that black shadow, that old man, in the middle of the alley called for no comment. By triumphing over Fourth Master Liu he had triumphed over everything. He had not struck or kicked the old man, yet Fourth Master Liu had lost his only close relative while he, Xiangzi, remained free as air. If that wasn't retribution, what was? Even if the old fellow didn't pop off with rage, this would hasten him to the grave! Old Liu had everything, Xiangzi nothing, yet Xiangzi was happily pulling a rickshaw while the other didn't even know where his daughter was buried. Old Liu might have pots of money and a redoubtable temper but he was no match for a penniless puller who just managed to fill his stomach.

The more he thought about it, the more his spirits soared, until he felt like singing a song of triumph to let the whole world know that he, Xiangzi, had come to life again, had won!

Though the icy night air seared his face, he didn't feel cold but invigorated. The street lamps shone frostily, but his heart was glowing with warmth, and there was brightness everywhere lighting up his future. He hadn't smoked for some time but felt no urge to. From now on, no more tobacco or alcohol;

Xiangzi was going to turn over a new leaf, to work and better himself as he had before. Today he had beaten Fourth Liu, beaten him for good. The old man's curses only filled Xiangzi with more hope of success.

His disgust, like a breath of foul air had found a vent: from now on he would always breathe fresh air. He was still young, wasn't he? Just look at him! Well, he would always be young. Let Fourth Liu die, he, Xiangzi would live on, happy and ambitious. All wicked people got their deserts and would die: those soldiers who had stolen his rickshaw, Mrs. Yang who starved her servants, Fourth Liu who bullied and despised him, Detective Sun who had blackmailed him, Grandmother Chen who had deceived him and that temptress Mrs. Xia . . . all of them would die. Only honest Xiangzi would live on for ever!

"But Xiangzi," he told himself, "from now on you must work really hard! Why shouldn't I? I have the will, the strength, I'm young!" And he assured himself, "Once I'm happy, who can stop me from making good? With all I've put up with, who wouldn't be depressed and go downhill? But that's all over. As from tomorrow, I'll be a new Xiangzi, an even better, much better one than before!"

Muttering to himself, he put on a spurt, as if to prove that he really meant what he said and was quite determined. So what if he had been sick, had contracted a shameful disease? This change of heart would surely make him strong again in no time.

Sweating and thirsty now he realized that he had reached Houmen Gate. Without bothering to go to a teahouse, he parked his rickshaw at the stand to the west of the Gate, called over a child selling tea from a large earthen pot, and swallowed two yellow bowls of wishy-washy liquid. It tasted bad but he told himself that from now on he would drink nothing else: no more wasting money on good tea and good food. This decision reached, he decided to eat something hard to get down as a start to his new, thrifty, hard-working life. So he bought ten gritty, underdone fried rolls stuffed with thick cabbage leaves. They tasted horrible, but he gulped them down and wiped his mouth with the back of his hand. What should he do next?

There were only two people he could count on and must look up if he wanted to make good, Joy and Mr. Cao. Mr. Cao was a "sage" who would understand him, help him and give him advice. If he did as Mr. Cao said and had Joy as a helpmate, with him working outside and her in charge at home he was sure to succeed, absolutely sure, there was no doubt about it.

But had Mr. Cao returned yet? Never mind, tomorrow he would go and inquire at Beichang Street. If he couldn't find out there, he would try the Zuo house. Everything would be all right once he found Mr. Cao. Very well, he would pull all night and look Mr. Cao up in the morning, then go to see Joy and tell her the good news: Xiangzi had not made good yet, but he was working hard and he wanted her with him.

These plans pleased him and his eyes, shining like an eagle's, darted this way and that. He saw a fare and rushed over, throwing off his padded coat before even settling the fee. Though his legs were not as strong as before, buoyed up by elation he put his whole heart into running. After all, he was still Xiangzi and no one could hold a candle to him when he went all out. He overtook other rickshaws like one possessed. Sweat poured off him. After one trip, he felt much lighter, his legs had regained their spring: he was game for more, like a champion horse that hasn't run enough and paws the ground after a race. It was one in the morning when he returned to the yard with ninety cents in his pocket, not counting rent.

He slept until daybreak, turned over and didn't open his eyes again till the sun was high in the sky. No enjoyment is sweeter than rest after exhaustion. He stretched and heard his joints cracking. His stomach was empty and he was ravenous.

After a bite of food, he cheerfully told the yard-owner, "I'm resting for a day, business to settle."

He had it all worked out: once everything was arranged today, he would start a new life tomorrow.

He headed straight for Beichang Street to see whether Mr. Cao had returned or not. As he walked he prayed: Let Mr. Cao be back, don't let me draw a blank! If things got off to a bad start then everything might go wrong. Now that Xiangzi had turned over a new leaf, surely Heaven would watch over him!

He stopped outside the Cao house and pressed the bell with a trembling hand. As he waited, his heart in his mouth, the past was forgotten; all he hoped was that this familiar door would open to show a familiar face. He waited. Perhaps there was no one there, otherwise why was it so quiet, so frighteningly quiet? Suddenly he heard a sound inside and he started nervously. The door creaked open and forthwith the dearest, most friendly voice cried out, "Well!" It was Gao Ma.

"Xiangzi? Long time no see! Why, you've got thinner!" Gao Ma was actually plumper than before.

"Is the master at home?" was all Xiangzi could say.

"He's in. You're a fine one, thinking only of the master as if the two of us didn't know each other! Not even a how d'you do! Quite a fellow!"

As she led the way she said, "Come on in. Have you made out all right?"

"Huh, not so well!" Xiangzi smiled.

"Eh, Master," Gao Ma called outside the study. "Xiangzi is here!"

Mr. Cao was moving some narcissuses into the sunlight. "Come on in!"

"All right, you go in, we'll chat later. I'll go and tell the mistress; we often talk of you. Fools have their fools' luck, I'll say!" Gao Ma went off muttering.

Xiangzi went in. "Master, here I am!" He felt he should say a word of greeting, but couldn't get it out.

"Ah, Xiangzi!" Mr. Cao, standing in the study wearing a short jacket, had a kindly smile on his face. "Sit down! Eh. . . ." He thought a moment, "We've been back some time. Old Cheng told us, eh . . . that's it, he said you were at Harmony Yard. Gao Ma went to look you up but couldn't find you. Sit down! How are you? How's business?"

Xiangzi was on the verge of tears. His most intimate thoughts were written in blood and buried in the inmost depths of his heart. He didn't know how to express them to anyone. It took him some time to calm down enough to try to turn some of that heart's blood into simple words. Everything was fresh in his mind, he only had to arrange it all bit by bit. He had a live history to tell and, though he didn't know its significance, his wrongs were very real and definite.

Mr. Cao saw that he was thinking and sat down quietly waiting for him to speak.

For some time Xiangzi remained quite still with head bowed. Suddenly he looked up at Mr. Cao as if to say he might as well keep quiet since no one would listen to him anyway.

"Go ahead!" Mr. Cao nodded at him.

So he began to talk of the past, beginning with when he came to the city from the countryside. He had not meant to mention these useless things, but unless he did he would feel no relief and his story would be incomplete. His memories, made up of blood, sweat and pain, couldn't be lightly voiced, and he didn't want to leave out anything either. Every drop of blood and sweat had come from his life, so everything that had happened was worth telling.

He described how he had come to town, worked as a coolie, then changed to pulling a rickshaw; how he had saved money and bought a rickshaw, then lost it ... and so on right up till the present. The length of his narrative and his fluency surprised him. One episode after another leaped out of his heart, seeming of their own accord to find the right words. The sentences followed each other, down to earth, endearing and tragic. He couldn't hold these memories back and so the words poured out, with no faltering or fumbling, as if he were eager to open his whole heart. His relief increased as he spoke, forgetting himself, because he had put himself into every sentence. Each embodied him — ambitious, wronged, hard-working, demoralized Xiangzi. Sweat stood out on his brow by the time he finished, and his heart felt empty and at ease like that of a man who has fainted and recovers in a cold sweat.

"You want me to advise you what to do?" Mr. Cao asked.

Xiangzi nodded. Having had his say he seemed reluctant to open his mouth again.

"Still want to pull a rickshaw?"

Again he nodded. What else could he do?

"In that case," said Mr. Cao slowly, "there are only two alternatives for you. One is to save up to buy a rickshaw, the other is to rent one for the time being, right? You have no savings and if you borrow money you'll have to pay interest, so what's the difference? Better to rent one and pull by the month. The job is steady and food and lodging are sure. You'd better come to me here. I sold my rickshaw to Mr. Zuo so you'll have to rent one, how's that?"

"That would be fine!" Xiangzi stood up. "Have you forgotten that business, sir?"

"What business?"

"When you and the mistress took refuge at Mr. Zuo's."

"Oh!" Mr. Cao laughed. "That affair! I was a bit too nervous then. The mistress and I stayed in Shanghai a few months. Actually there was no need to because Mr. Zuo had smoothed matters over. Forget it, I have. Let's talk about our own business. You mentioned that Joy, what about her?"

"I don't know!"

"Here's my idea. You can't afford to marry her and rent a room outside, because rent, coal and lamp-oil all cost money and you wouldn't have enough. If she worked in the same place as you . . . but things are never that ideal: it's not easy to find a post where you pull the rickshaw and she works as a maid. Certainly difficult!" He shook his head. "Now don't be touchy, but is she reliable?"

Xiangzi flushed and swallowed several times before replying, "She only did that because she was desperate. I'll stake my head she's a good girl! She. . . ." All his mixed emotions trying to find a vent left him at a loss for words.

"If that's the case," Mr. Cao continued slowly, "perhaps I can fix you up here. Whether you're single or married you'll have one room, no problem there. Can she wash and mend? If so she can help Gao Ma. The mistress is going to have another baby soon, Gao Ma can't cope alone. If I feed her, I won't pay her, what do you say?"

"That would be fine!" Xiangzi beamed ingenuously.

"But I can't decide all by myself. I'll have to talk it over with the mistress."

"Of course. If the mistress isn't sure, I'll bring Joy over so that she can see her."

"That's a good idea." Mr. Cao smiled. He had not credited Xiangzi with so much insight. "Look, I'll talk to the mistress and you bring her over another day. If the mistress agrees then it's a deal."

"Can I go now, Master?" Xiangzi was in a hurry to find Joy and tell her this undreamed of good news.

When he left the Cao house, it was around eleven, the best time of day in winter. The weather was particularly fine with not a cloud in the blue sky, and the sun shining down through the crisp air imparted a bright warmth. The crowing of cocks, the barking of dogs and the calls of vendors carried a long way so that they could be heard, clearly in the next street, rather like the cries of cranes coming down from the sky.

All the rickshaws had their hoods folded and their brasswork gleamed like gold. By the roadsides, camels plodded sedately along while cars and trams sped through the streets. The people and horses passing on the ground, the white pigeons flying in the sky, all gave the ancient city an air of tranquil activity. Bustle and happiness mingled. The clear blue sky formed a canopy for all the sounds and wealth of life, while everywhere stood silent trees.

Xiangzi's heart seemed about to take flight to circle in the sky with the white pigeons. He had everything — a job, wages and Joy. He had never thought it could all be settled so wonderfully with just a few words. Look at that clear crisp sky, just like the straightforward, easy-going people of the North. When one is happy, even the weather seems extra fine. He couldn't remember ever having seen such a lovely clear winter's day. In order to vent his high spirits, he bought a frozen persimmon. The first bite filled his mouth with icicles. The cold froze his teeth, then spread slowly down his chest, making him shiver. He finished it in a few mouthfuls, his tongue numb, his heart buoyant.

Off he strode then to find Joy. In his mind was a picture of that crowded courtyard, the little room and his sweetheart. He wished he had wings to fly there! With her, the past could be forgotten and a new life started. He was in more of a rush now than when he had gone to find Mr. Cao, for Mr. Cao was his friend and master — each of them helped the other. Joy was not only a friend, she was going to give her whole life to him. They were two people in a common hell who would now wipe away their tears and walk forward hand in hand, smiling.

Mr. Cao's words had moved him, but Joy could touch him without saying anything. He had confided in Mr. Cao but with Joy he could really bare his heart and say what could never be said to anyone else. She had become his life, without her nothing had any meaning. He could not work just to satisfy his own needs, he must rescue her from that hovel and bring her to live with him in a clean warm room, happy, decent and loving as two little birds.

She could stop taking care of her father and two brothers and must come and help him instead. Er Qiangzi could support himself anyway and the two boys could make shift somehow, maybe by pulling a rickshaw, but Xiangzi couldn't live without her. Body and soul he needed her, needed her for his work too. And she for her part needed a man like him.

His happiness increased with his impatience. Of all the women in the world none was such a good match for him as Joy. True, she was not the pure and spotless maiden of his dreams, but it was precisely this that made her more pitiful and able to help him. A simple country girl might be white as a lily, but she wouldn't have Joy's ability or character. Anyway, what about himself? He too was sullied. So they were a fitting pair, neither could look down on the other. They were like two cracked but still serviceable water-jars, just right to stand side by side.

However he looked at it as an ideal set-up. After savouring it, he finally came down to earth. First he must get a month's pay in advance from Mr. Cao and buy Joy a cotton-padded gown and some decent shoes, then take her to see Mrs. Cao. Once she was dressed in new clothes, spruced up from head to foot, with her youth, manner and looks, she would be thoroughly presentable and sure to please Mrs. Cao. No doubt about it!

He reached his destination soaked with sweat. The sight of that battered gateway was like a long-awaited home-coming: the rickety gate, the crumbling wall, the yellow grass on the gate-way roof, all seemed very dear.

He went in and made straight for Joy's room. Without knocking or calling out, he pushed open the door and instinctively recoiled. A middle-aged woman was sitting on the brick-bed. Because there was no stove in the room she had wrapped herself up in a ragged quilt. Xiangzi stood stock-still outside the door.

"What's the matter?" she called from inside. "You bringing bad news or something, walking into someone's room without a word? Who are you looking for?"

Xiangzi didn't feel like saying anything. Suddenly he wasn't sweating any more. Leaning against the battered door he dared not give up hope. "I'm looking for Joy."

"Don't know her! And next time you come looking for someone, call out before walking in, Joy or no Joy!"

He sat outside the courtyard gate for a long time, his mind a blank, his errand forgotten. Slowly a part of it came back to him, and Joy seemed to be walking back and forth in his heart, like a paper figure on a revolving lantern going pointlessly round and round. He seemed to have forgotten what was between them. Then slowly her figure shrank, feeling returned to him and his heart ached.

When the significance of anything is uncertain, people always hope for the best. Xiangzi guessed that Joy had probably moved, that was all. It was his fault. Why hadn't he come to see her more often? Shame goaded him into action to make amends. Better make some inquiries first. Back he went and asked an old neighbour, but without getting any definite news. Still hopeful, not stopping for a meal, he decided to look for Er Qiangzi or her two brothers. The three of them must be somewhere on the streets and shouldn't be hard to find.

He made inquiries wherever he went: at rickshaw stands, in teahouses, in tenement yards. As long as his legs would move he walked on, asking, but by the end of the day he still had no news.

At nightfall, he returned to the rickshaw yard dead-beat and preoccupied. After a day's disappointment he dared hope no longer. The poor die easily and are easily forgotten. Could Joy be dead already? If not, supposing her father had sold her again to someone far away? It was quite possible and much worse than death!

Wine and tobacco became his friends once more. If he didn't smoke, how could he think? And if he didn't get drunk, how could he stop thinking?

CHAPTER 23

*A*S he was walking dejectedly down the street, he ran into Little Horse's grandfather. The old man was no longer pulling a rickshaw and his clothes were more threadbare and tattered than ever. On one shoulder he carried a pole of acacia wood with a large earthen teapot suspended from one end and from the other a round broken basket containing some griddle cakes, fritters and a large brick. He still recognized Xiangzi.

After some conversation, the old man told Xiangzi that Little Horse had died over six months ago and he had sold his dilapidated rickshaw. Now he sold tea, griddle cakes and fritters at the rickshaw stands every day. Though still as gentle and kindly as before, his back was more stooped, his eyes watered in the wind and his eyelids were red as if from crying.

Xiangzi bought a cup of tea from him and briefly recounted his woes.

"You think you can make good alone?" the old man commented. "Who doesn't? Yet who has? In my time I was husky and decent, yet look at me now! Strong? Even a man made of iron can't escape from this huge trap we live in. Honest? What's the use? They say those who do good are rewarded and those who do wrong are punished. Don't you believe it! When I was young I was really warm-hearted and put myself out for others. Any use? None at all! I've saved people from drowning and hanging. What reward did I get? Nothing! I tell you, I could freeze to death any day now.

"I know that for us coolies it's the hardest thing in the world to make good alone. What future does a lone man have? Ever seen a grasshopper? It hops mighty far alone, but just let a kid catch it and tie it up and it can't even fly. But a swarm of them, ha! They polish off acres of crops in seconds and no one can do a thing! Isn't that so? For all my good heart, I couldn't even keep one little grandson. He fell ill and I had no money for good medicine. I watched him die in my arms. Forget it, what's the use? . . . Tea over here! Who wants a bowl piping hot?"

Xiangzi really understood now. All his cursing would not bring retribution down on Fourth Liu, Mrs. Yang or Detective Sun. As for him, he could do his level best and get nowhere. Alone without any support, he was like a grasshopper caught and tied by a child, just as the old man said. How could wings help him now?

He no longer felt like going to the Cao household. If he did, he would have to do his best and what good was that? Why not just muddle along? When there was nothing to eat, take out the rickshaw; when there was enough for the day, rest and think about tomorrow when it came round. Not only was this a way out, it was the only way. Saving to buy a rickshaw was just asking to have it snatched away, why bother? Why not enjoy oneself while one could?

If he found Joy, he would still do his best, if not for himself then at least for her. But he couldn't find her, so for whom was he trying? He was just like this old man who had lost his grandson. He told the old fellow about Joy, for he felt this was a real friend.

"Who wants hot tea?" the old man called. Then he said, "As I see it, she had only two ways out. Either she's been sold by Er Qiangzi to be a concubine or she's been sold to White Cottage. Most likely the latter. Why? Because if, as you say, she's been married before, it's not easy to find anyone else who'll want her. Men want virgins as concubines. So most likely she's at White Cottage. I'm nearly sixty, seen a lot in my time. If some sturdy young puller is missing from the rickshaw stands for a couple of days, either he's got a monthly job or he's flat out at White Cottage. And if the wives or daughters of rickshaw pullers disappear all of a sudden, like as not that's where they've gone. We sell our sweat, our women sell their bodies. I know, I know it all! You go there and look. I hope she's not there, but.... Tea here! Hot tea!"

In one breath Xiangzi ran all the way out of Xizhimen Gate. Once past Guanxiang he was struck by the desolation of the countryside. Trees stood starkly by the road without even a bird in their branches. Grey trees, grey earth, grey houses stretched silently beneath the leaden sky. In the distance loomed the cold bare Western Hills. To the north of the railway was a wood and at its edge stood a few low houses. Xiangzi guessed these must be White Cottage. All was still amongst the trees. Further north were the marshes outside Wanshengyuan, dotted with clumps of withered reeds and grasses.

There was no one outside the houses, no sound anywhere. The utter stillness set him wondering if this was really the notorious White Cottage. Plucking up courage, he walked towards it. Shiny new yellow mats hung over each door. He had heard that in the summer the women here sat outside, bare-breasted, soliciting passers-by. Their "guests" would sing bawdy songs as they approached, to show they were no green-horns. Why was it so quiet now? Could they stop business in the winter?

Just as he was wondering, the mat over the door nearest him moved and a woman's head appeared. He was startled by her close resemblance to Tigress. "I've come to find Joy," he thought. "What the devil if I were to find a Tigress instead!"

"Come on in, you big silly!" she said. Her voice unlike that of Tigress was hoarse and urgent, reminding him of the old man he had often seen selling wild herbs at Tianqiao.

The room was empty except for the woman and a small brick-bed. There was no mat on it, but the small fire heating it filled the room with an acrid smell. There was an old quilt on the bed, it's edges as shiny and greasy as the bricks on which it lay. The woman looked about forty, dishevelled and unwashed. She was wearing lined trousers and a black padded jacket that she had left unbuttoned. Xiangzi had to duck his head to get in, and the moment he entered she threw her arms around him. Her unbuttoned jacket opened to show two huge, pendulous breasts.

227

Xiangzi sat down on the edge of the brick-bed as the room was too low for him to stand up straight. He was pleased by this encounter, for he had often heard tell of a woman nicknamed "White Flour Sacks". This must be her. The name came from those two outsized breasts. Without any preliminaries, he asked her whether she had seen Joy. She didn't know. But when he described Joy she remembered her.

"Why yes, there was such a person. Young, and given to showing those white teeth of hers. That's right, we called her 'Juicy Tidbit'."

"Which room is she in?" Xiangzi's eyes gleamed wildly.

"She? She did herself in long ago!" White Flour Sacks pointed outside. "Hanged herself in the wood."

"What!"

"When Juicy Tidbit came, she was very nice. But she hadn't the stamina to stand it here. One day, at lamplighting time — I remember it clearly because I was sitting with two sisters at the door — well, at that moment, a client arrives and makes straight for her door. She didn't like sitting outside with us and even got beaten for this when she first came. But later on, when she made a bit of a name, we all let her sit alone in her room, as her customers never wanted anyone else. After about the time it takes for a meal, her client leaves and makes straight for that wood over there. None of us thought anything of it and no one went into her room to see her. When the madam came around to collect the money, she found a man in the room, stripped naked and sound asleep. He was dead drunk. Juicy Tidbit had taken his clothes and run away. Smart she was. If it hadn't been dark she'd never have got away, but at night she fooled us all, dressed as a man. The madam immediately sent people out to look for her. The moment they entered the wood, well, they saw her hanging there. When they cut her down she was already dead, but her tongue wasn't sticking out too much and she didn't look terrible. Even in death she was lovable! All these months, the wood has been very quiet at night and her spirit doesn't come out to frighten people. She really was a good sort. . . ."

Xiangzi didn't wait for her to finish but staggered out. He made his way to a burial ground planted neatly around with pines. There were a dozen grave mounds. The sunlight was pale and in amongst the trees it was even dimmer. He sat on the ground which was littered with dry grass and pine cones. All was still, apart from a few crows calling mournfully from the branches. He knew very well that this was not where Joy was buried, but his tears fell thick and fast. Everything was gone, even Joy was dead and buried! He had tried his best, so had she, yet all that remained to him were useless tears and she had hanged herself. A straw mat and a grave in this wasteland, that was where a life of toil led!

Back at the rickshaw yard, he slept numbly for two days. He would never go to the Cao house now, nor did he even send them word, for Mr. Cao could not save him. After two days he took the rickshaw out, his mind and soul a blank. Thought and hope were gone, he slaved only to fill his stomach then sleep. Why hope any more? Watching a skinny stray dog waiting by the sweet-potato vendor's carrying-pole for some peel and rootlets, he knew that he was just like this dog, struggling for some scraps to eat. As long as he managed to keep alive, why think of anything else?

AFTERWORD

*T*HE Chinese edition of this book has already been reprinted several times. In this present edition, I have taken out some of the coarser language and some unnecessary descriptions.

I wrote this story nineteen years ago. In it I expressed my sympathy for the labouring people and my admiration of their sterling qualities, but I gave them no future, no way out. They lived miserably and died wronged. This was because, at the time, I could only see the misery of society and not the hope of revolution, I did not know any revolutionary truths. The strict censorship of the period also made me careful not to say the poor should revolt. Shortly after the book came out I heard some working people comment, "Judging by this book we are really too wretched and hopeless!" I feel deeply ashamed about this.

Today, nineteen years later, the working people have become masters of their own destiny. Even I now understand something about revolution and am very grateful to the Communist Party and Chairman Mao. The present reprint of my book should surely have only one aim and that is to remind people of the frightful darkness of the old society and how we must treasure today's happiness and light. Never must the reactionaries be allowed to make a come-back. We must safeguard with all our might the victories of the revolution.

Lao She

September 1954
Beijing

HOW I CAME TO WRITE THE NOVEL "CAMEL XIANGZI"

I can't quite remember the exact day and month when I started writing *Camel Xiangzi*. Together with all my books, all my diaries of the pre-war days were lost with the fall of Ji'nan. So there's no way now of checking up to find out.

This book was a turning-point in my life as a writer. Before I started it, teaching was my profession and writing was only something I did in my spare time. That is to say, ordinarily, I spent all my time teaching and only wrote when school was closed during the winter or summer vacations. I was far from satisfied with such an arrangement, for I could neither concentrate on writing nor enjoy a proper holiday from one year to another. My health suffered. The idea of becoming a full-time writer had already been in my mind when I returned to Beiping from abroad. Only the persuasion of several good friends made me accept a teaching position at Qilu University in Shandong. When I resigned from Qilu University, I went to Shanghai with the main purpose of finding out whether or not it was possible to become a professional writer. In those days, books were not selling well, and there weren't many literary periodicals. Friends in Shanghai cautioned me against taking such a risk, so I accepted the offer of a post at Shandong University. I do not like teaching. For one thing, I'm not a very learned person and so I sometimes felt uneasy. Even if I had been really able to teach well, it did not afford me the same pleasure as writing. To provide for my family, I dared not impulsively throw away a reliable monthly income just like that. But in my heart of hearts, I never for one moment relinquished my desire to taste the delights of becoming a professional writer.

It just happened that after two years of teaching at Shandong University, there were some disturbances and, together with many colleagues, I resigned. This time, instead of going to Shanghai to assess the situation and without consulting anyone, I made up my mind to stay on in Qingdao and earn my living by writing. This was the year before the July 7 Incident in 1937, when the War of Resistance Against Japan began. *Camel Xiangzi* was my first attempt as a full-time writer. I had decided that if it succeeded I could continue to produce two novels a year free of care. However, should it turn out to be a flop, I would have to return to teaching, perhaps feeling so depressed that I might give up writing altogether. That is why I remember the writing of this book as being a crucial period in my development as a writer.

As I remember, it was in the spring of 1936 when I was chatting with a friend at Shandong University that he told me about a rickshaw man who had worked for him in Beiping. The man had bought his own rickshaw but was forced to sell it. This occurred three times and he remained wretchedly poor. I said at the time: "One could write a story about that." My friend went on to say: "Another rickshaw man was once nabbed by some soldiers. Who would have thought that good luck could come out of such a calamity. While the soldiers were marching, he slipped off with three camels."

I never bothered to ask the names of the two rickshaw men or where they came from. I only remembered what he'd said about them and the camels. That provided the inspiration for the story *Camel Xiangzi*. Spring changed into summer, as I thought about expanding this simple story and turning it into a novel of roughly a hundred thousand words.

Uncertain what use it would be, I started by inquiring about the life and habits of camels from Mr. Qi Tiehen, who grew up in the Western Hills outside Beijing where many families in the foothills kept camels. His reply made me realize that I should concentrate on the rickshaw men, using the camels merely as a literary device. To concentrate on camels might entail a special trip to Zhangjiakou in order to know more about the grassland and camels. But I wouldn't need to budge an inch if my main theme was the rickshaw men whom I could observe any day of the week. In this way I linked the camels with Xiangzi, but the camels were there merely to introduce my hero.

How should I depict Xiangzi? First, I considered the various kinds of rickshaw men so as to find a place for him among them. That done, I could describe the other types of rickshaw pullers in passing, Xiangzi remaining as the central figure, the others as secondary ones. Thus I not only had my hero but also his social environment. This made him seem more real. My eyes were focussed on Xiangzi all the time even when I wrote about others. This was done in order to elicit his character.

Besides his fellow rickshaw men, I thought of the type of rickshaw owners from whom Xiangzi might rent his rickshaw, and of the people who might ride in it. Thus I could expand his world of rickshaw men, introducing people of a higher social status. However, these people were only in the story because of Xiangzi. I was determined not to let anyone encroach on Xiangzi's place as the hero.

Once I had my characters, it was comparatively easy to work out the plot. Since Xiangzi is the main character, everything in the story must revolve around rickshaw pulling. As long as all the people were linked in some way with the rickshaw, I had Xiangzi pinned down exactly where I wanted him.

However, though my characters and events were all closely related to rickshaw men, I still felt there was something lacking in my description of their way of life. I thought to myself: How does a rickshaw puller feel when there's a sand storm? Or when it rains? If I could express this in detail, my hero would become more real. His life must be one endless torment, not only regarding his meagre diet but also regarding a gust of wind or a sudden shower of rain, grating on his nerves.

Then I began to consider that a rickshaw puller like everyone else would have problems other than simply his daily bread. He would have ideals and desires, a family and children. How would he solve these problems? How could he? In this way, the simple story I had heard developed into a story of dimensions huge enough to encompass a whole society. I needed to

233

know not just the little details to be gleaned from his clothing, speech and gestures, but the inner life of the man based on deep observation. It forced me to peer into hell itself. Everything in his outward appearance could be traced to his history and circumstances. I needed to return to his roots before I could depict the bitterness of the society for these poor workers.

From the spring of 1936 and on into that summer, I worked, like one possessed, gathering materials. Many times I changed Xiangzi's life and even his appearance, for when the materials I'd gathered changed, accordingly so did he.

That summer, when I resigned from Shandong University, I started to put Xiangzi down on paper. I had spent a fairly long time pondering over the plot and had collected a large quantity of material, so when it came to putting pen to paper I had no problems. The first installment of the serial *Camel Xiangzi* appeared in the magazine *Yuzhoufeng*, in January 1937. At that time, the novel was not yet complete, although I had an outline of the whole story and how long it was going to be. It was an outline detailed enough for me to know the end, otherwise I would never have dared publish it in installments while I was still in the process of writing. By early summer, I had finished it, twenty-four chapters to be exact. With the magazine publishing two chapters a month, it was just the right number for one year.

As soon as it was finished, I told the editor of the magazine that I was more pleased with this novel than any other of my previous works. Later when it was published in book form, the publisher printed these words in the blurb. Why was I so very pleased with it? First, the story had been sitting in my mind for a long time and I had collected a fair amount of material, so that when I started writing, the words came with precision, my pen never straying from the subject or branching off at a tangent. There was no padding. Secondly, I had just started writing full-time and that was constantly on my mind. Though I wrote more than one or two thousand words a day, when I put my pen down I did not stop but carried on working out the story in my head. Intensive thinking enables the pen to sweat blood and tears. Thirdly, I resolved, right from the beginning, to renounce witticisms and concentrate on writing seriously. Ordinarily, whenever an opportunity for humour arose, I would promptly seize it. Sometimes even when there was nothing really funny about a subject, I would use witty language to give it a humorous touch. Perhaps this helped to make the language more lively and interesting, but equally, at times, it could be quite tiresome. There wasn't that problem with *Camel Xiangzi*. While not completely devoid of humour, the humour was derived from the story itself and was not squeezed in artificially. This decision of mine altered my style slightly. I learned that as long as I had good material and plenty to say, I could succeed without having to resort to humour. Fourthly, once I had decided not to rely on humour, it followed that the language must be very simple and straightforward, limpid, like a calm lake. To achieve this, I paid great attention to avoiding dullness in my quest for simplicity. It happened that at this point my good friend Gu Shijun supplied me with many words and expressions in the colloquial Beiping dialect, which before I had thought impossible to write down. I had previously reluctantly avoided using them in my writing, because I'd thought they couldn't be put down on paper. Now with Mr. Gu's help, my pen became richer as it easily mastered the colloquialisms, adding a freshness and liveliness to the simple language, and making it more authentic to the reader. This is why *Camel Xiangzi* can be read aloud; the language is alive.

There are of course many faults in the book. I, personally, am most dissatisfied with the abrupt ending. Because it was coming out in installments, I had to write exactly twenty-four chapters. In fact, I should have written two or three additional chapters to round off the story. However, nothing can be done about this now, for I never care to revise anything once it has been published.

Camel Xiangzi's luck wasn't all that good at first. When only half of it was published in the *Yuzhoufeng*, the War of Resistance Against Japan started on July 7. As I do not know when the magazine ceased publication in Shanghai, I never knew whether *Camel Xiangzi* was ever serialized from beginning to end. Later, when the Yuzhoufeng Publishing House moved to Guangzhou, the first thing they did was to publish it as a book. But I was told the book was barely printed, when Guangzhou fell to the enemy, *Camel Xiangzi* with it. The publishing house moved again, this time to Guilin, and the book received a second chance of publication, but due to poor postal conditions, there was little evidence of it in either Chongqing or Chengdu. Only later, when the Cultural Life Publishing House bought the copyright, did more copies of the book appear in Chongqing and Chengdu.

Now, there seems to be a turn in *Camel Xiangzi*'s fortunes. According to friends' reports, the book has been translated into Russian, Japanese and English.

1945

DATE DUE

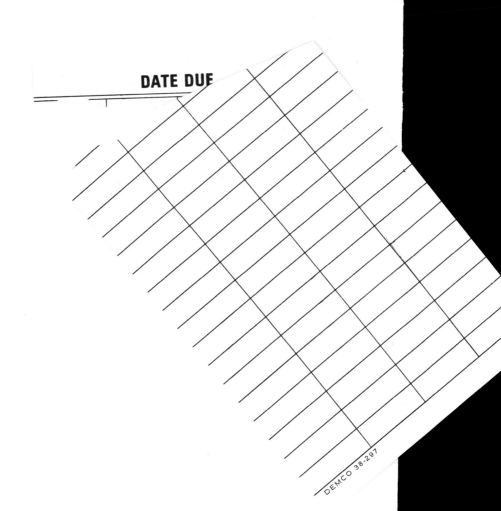

DEMCO 38-297

JAN 07 1982